A SCARLET
MOUNTAIN

Publishing Company: Fleur Hermitage Press

Cover Design by Daniel Eyenegho
Book Formatting by Brady Moller

ISBN: 979-8-9992155-0-5 (Paperback)
ISBN: 979-8-9992155-1-2 (Hardcover)
ISBN: 979-8-9992155-2-9 (Ebook)

A SCARLET MOUNTAIN

a novel

ANVIKA J. BLACKBURN

In loving memory of my cousin, Bhavya — whose inspiration continues to guide me, even in heaven.

To my mother, Kalpna — who recognized the writer within me long before I did.

To my husband, Jeremiah — whose unconditional support has carried me through every dream I've dared to chase.

Chapter 1

Eva

I turned onto the gravel driveway of my temporary dwelling.

The house was painted mustard yellow, with a homemade shed splitting the property in two. A kayak was holstered on top of a parked Subaru, while a Mercedes-Benz glimmered silently in the dark, protective crevices of the shed. The house stood among towering sugar maple trees and vibrant eastern hemlocks. The entire property was cocooned by the forest, leaving only a narrow slit of an opening through which I bumped my way along.

I tapped my index finger on the steering wheel, filled with the permeating self-doubt of this trip, alone in a place I'd never been before.

As the rental Corolla whined and moaned over the rocks, I realized I'd never received check-in instructions.

Odd for a "one-of-a-kind gem with a superb host" rating.

The thought quickly vanished as a man skipped down the double steps of a side door.

I couldn't take my eyes off him. He was stunning—some relative of Zeus—with glistening brown hair, long enough to be tied into a small bun, the body of a professional athlete, and green eyes that somehow dimmed the trees around us. Everything seemed to slow down as he waved to the spot he wanted me to park in. Did I just feel drool on the side of my mouth?

He's a human, not a Greek god. Get your shit together.

My knees buckled as I got out of the car after a three-hour drive from Boston. The brisk, sharp air sent goosebumps down my thighs.

"Eva, I presume." He caught my elbow as I stumbled, the touch involuntary. A second, more powerful jolt shot through me.

"I'm Aaron."

"Yes, hello" I scrambled to find something to say. "You have a beautiful home."

"Ah, thank you." He shrugged, with a hint of pride. "I refurbished the whole place when I decided to move out here."

He dropped his hand abruptly, surprised he was still holding on to me. "So, first time in Vermont?" he asked.

"Yes. I'm looking forward to a restorative weekend. Well, for me Sunday is my Saturday."

He lifted the right corner of his lip in a sly grin, like a poster child for the most popular boy in school.

"I get that. I work odd days too and Vermont is definitely the place to reset." He gestured toward the trunk. "Please, allow me."

He followed me as I got the trunk open.

"So, your profile says you're from New York?" he asked as he pulled out my duffel bag.

I nodded and he led me to a door on the opposite end from where he had come out. We squeezed through a tight entry hallway, bringing us into a perfectly nostalgic kitchen.

The walls were covered in sunflower wallpaper, and a small stovetop held a burgundy tea kettle. On the opposite end sat a pristine square oak table with two matching chairs, each accented with hunter green pillows. I took a deep breath of relief at finally arriving. The smell wrapped around me, pulling me back to when I was six years old, running around with my imaginary friend Atkin at my grandmother, Grams's, aged home. The musty scent of wood and the acrid warmth of the furnace blended with the dust in the deep corners of the structure. I could identify the wood and even the settled dust, but where was the infamous furnace?

Aaron turned through a narrow roundabout and revealed a spacious living room; a loveseat and futon angled toward a freestanding furnace. There it was, an exquisite, heavy piece of luxury. The pictures on the StayHere app hadn't deceived.

"It's a beautiful furnace," I said, eyeing the intricate lining and glass window that revealed the firewood inside.

"It's the best heating apparatus there is. That reminds me, it does get very hot upstairs, but feel free to play around with the thermostat connected to the furnace."

I took a slow 360-degree glance and noticed the high ceilings and a curved, man-made stairway. The white paint at the rail's edges had bled into the green wall. It held a sense of artistic integrity, and a tenderness for human error.

"Thank you, Aaron. I look forward to my stay," I said, my head still tilted upward.

"Absolutely! Feel free to reference the binder on the coffee table for recommendations around town."

I had just finished my self-guided tour when I turned and fixed my gaze on him.

"Or," he added, "you can also message me." His words lingered in the air as our eyes locked.

I want to climb him like a tree.

"I'm starving," I blurted.

He shot me a side glance, almost mischievous, like a door had just been unlocked and he fully intended to walk through it.

"Funny enough, I've been working on a lamb stew all day. I was just about to make myself a bowl." He cleared his throat and whispered, "Would you like to join me?"

"I would love to," I said.

Although only a single wall separated my space from his, Aaron's makeshift home felt completely different. Pristine white walls, white cabinets, and white tiles gave it the air of a millionaire's retreat—centered around a black quartzite island, with hanging light fixtures casting a golden mood over the living room and making his brown leather couch glisten. The open floor plan made his side feel expansive. While my side smelled like my Grams, his smelled of mahogany teakwood and warm spices.

"Shoes off or on?" I asked.

I hoped for off. I didn't want to tarnish his spotless home with the questionable inhabitants hiding under my overworn Air Max 270s.

"You can keep them—"

I was already kneeling to untie a shoelace.

"Sure," he added with a grin. I noticed how his dark brown facial hair traced the contours of his face, meeting the edges of those impossible green eyes.

He's intoxicating.

"The food smells delicious," I said, standing in the foyer, my feet chilled from the tile.

"Please, come in." He gestured toward the couch as he took a sharp right turn into the kitchen.

"So, what really brings you to Vermont?" he asked, maneuvering easily around the counters.

"I needed a break from all the chaos," I said.

"I get that."

He didn't press further and returned with two wine glasses and a bottle of Merlot.

"Wine okay?"

"Yes, please."

I needed an anti-anxiety, self-inducing aid.

"Cheers."

"Cheers," I echoed.

As our glasses clinked, our eyes met again.

"You have beautiful eyes," he said, almost like a song.

I'd always been complimented on my Caribbean blue eyes. Parents usually prophesize their child's destiny as a doctor, a lawyer, a chef, or an artist. I, on the other hand, was told I'd be a heartbreaker with my baby blues. Maybe it was parental conditioning or something wired into my genes, but I did manage to break many hearts. I preferred being non-committal rather than fight to make a relationship work. For the most part, I enjoyed my lifestyle, but the lonely nights were palpable. Thankfully, I had my best friend, Aubree. I don't know what I'd do without her. Maybe I'd force myself to settle down with a boring man with a receding hairline, just to avoid coming home to an empty house. Or better yet, I'd adopt a litter of kittens.

"Back at ya," I winked.

I downed the first glass like water. I was trained in the art of drinking, capable of tossing back four full glasses of wine before feeling a thing. But my head took a surprising spin. The elevation must be disturbing my tolerance.

As though time had lost all meaning, I looked down to find empty glasses, and an empty bottle. Aaron had left my side and returned with two handcrafted clay bowls, each steaming with stew. As he sat next to me, he watched me with intrigue and whispered, "you are one of the most beautiful women I've ever …"

His voice faded as my vision blurred. My feet were hot from ethanol and my libido was at an all time high. Next thing I knew, I was dipping my index finger into the stew, ignoring the scalding heat, and slowly licked it clean. His pupils dilated with raw hunger like a lion spotting a gazelle. Then, without a word, I wrapped my legs around his waist and pressed my lips to his neck. He moaned, one hand tangling in my hair, the other steadying me. His eyes locked onto mine with a wicked gleam just before his tongue found my mouth.

I straddled him, slow and deliberate, watching the tension build in his thighs and shoulders. His hands gripped my butt like it was something familiar, something he'd missed. He took over the rhythm, guiding my hips with impatience, his restraint beginning to fray. His tongue slipped from my mouth to my neck, where his lips grew rough, nibbling, searching. His fingers dug deeper as I rocked against the growing heat between us. He let out a low, guttural and unfiltered grunt of desire. I wanted him at my mercy, to yearn and beg for me.

I swayed, as I snaked my hand under his belt…

FIRST, I FELT MY FOREHEAD—SLICK WITH SWEAT. THEN MY STOMach chimed in like an ill-timed musical cue, forcing my eyes open. Sunlight poured through the skylight, sending my pupils back into its sockets. One thing familiar clung to me like a lifebuoy: the smell. That warm, comforting scent of Grams managed to push through the damp weight of a brutal hangover, lifting my spirits just enough to get me out of bed. Somehow, I was back on my side of the house. And it was excruciatingly hot.

I noticed the constricting wire beneath my breasts of my bra and even my undershirt, but what covered my tank top wasn't mine. It wasn't my white sweater.

It was a suit jacket.

Aaron's.

The shoulder pads swallowed my arms like a child playing dress-up in her father's clothes.

What happened last night?

Each slow, painful step toward the kitchen brought flickers of memory.

I remembered his kiss. It was harsh. Assertive. Even aggressive.

His ferocity for me made me smile with a keen sense of accomplishment as I let cold water run over my clammy hands. I leaned in for a glass and caught my reflection in a small round mirror mounted above the counter. My eyes were red and heavy-lidded, making the blue of my irises look almost silver—wolf-like. Most of my makeup had vanished, except for a faint streak of mascara. My head looked oddly small above the popped collar of his suit jacket.

I have to return his jacket.

I drank most of the water, before stumbling into my shoes, which were somehow neatly placed by the front door on my side of the house.

On my way out, I paused and glanced back at the mirror, wondering if I should clean myself up. But the memory hit me like a flash. His hands heavy, rough, gripping my breast with just enough force to make me scream. He liked it rough.

So rough is how I'm going to look.

Aubree always hated the bruises I showed up with after a date night. She'd say they were a direct correlation to my abusive mother. I was the apple of my mother's eye, until I turned eight. As a narcissist, my mother craved attention like air. When men, *grown ass men*, began paying more attention to me than to her, instead of chasing those predators away, my mother would see me as a threat. She'd beat me with her rolling pin, trying to make me look less *symmetrical*. But she did it "with love," so I didn't protest when, after a bitter divorce battle with my father, I was asked if I wanted my mother to have full custody.

I was left to survive, caught between a crazed mother and an estranged father, until I was fifteen.

As a young teenager, I did everything I could to hide my beauty—just to stay in Mom's good graces. That meant being a strict tomboy, even though I secretly flipped through her *Cosmopolitan* magazines like they were *Playboy*. One boring night, just after solving the cosine of some trigonometry problem, the phone rang. A woman's voice calmly informed me that my mother had been admitted to the hospital. She and one of her boyfriends, from a rolodex of many, had crashed into a tree just five minutes from our home. I remember my heart dropping, my eyes freezing open. In a daze, I vaguely recall dialing for a taxi.

Moments after I booked it, the landline rang again.

"I'm so sorry, your mother was just pronounced deceased." Her voice was sharp; hardly empathetic and completely rehearsed.

A fucking tree killed my psychotic mother.

I stepped outside Aaron's StayHere home, my right heel still stubbornly halfway into my shoe, when the myriad of trees swallowed my view. *Vermont really was a green ass state.* Trees held nature's contradictions: towering and imposing, yet somehow gentle, earnest and trustworthy. They stood like sentinels, holding onto the world's dirty secrets. I've always been grateful for trees, especially the one on Backerland Road, five minutes from my childhood home.

After my mom died, I was forced to move in with my father. He lived in a small house by the water on Long Island's coast and had opened an oyster restaurant. Everything changed—my guardianship, my home, my school, my clothes, even my demeanor. But the best thing my mother's death gave me... was Aubree. She lived just two minutes from my dad.

I inhaled deeply, letting the Vermont air move through me like an immunity shot.

Climbing the double steps to Aaron's door, I knocked.

"Hello?" I asked, as the door cracked slightly open on its own.

Silence.

Should I come back?

I knocked again, louder this time. My knuckles ached from the impact, and the echo reverberated through the quiet. I never understood the power of an echo until I was deep in a forest, knocking on a stucco door with only the mountains for neighbors.

Still nothing.

I nudged the door open, wincing at the obnoxious *creeeeek*. I slipped inside and beelined to the couch, gently placing his jacket on the cushion. Just as I turned to leave, something flickered in my peripheral vision. I paused, heart stuttering. I had to make sure what snagged out of the corner of my eye was not what I thought it was.

I slowly turned toward the kitchen, eyes narrowing to confirm the flash of red. A thick trail of scarlet streaked across the white tiles. Bile surged in my throat. I tilted my head for a better view, dread anchoring in my stomach like bricks. There he was, Aaron sprawled across the kitchen floor, a heavy stream of blood gushing from his head.

Chapter 2

Aleena

"**G**et up!"
I couldn't keep yelling at Shaan from the kitchen. My throat was already sore, and the day hadn't even started yet.

"Good morning." Rahul planted a kiss on my cheek as he grabbed the coffee pot.

Rahul and I had an arranged marriage, one of those *let's get our parents together to decide who our life partner will be because we clearly failed to do so ourselves.* Rahul was great, though. He moved all the way from California to settle here because of my job.

"Any new cases today?" He asked.

His voice was tired, worn by the same question with the same answer I gave him every Monday, with great lackluster.

But today was finally different.

"Yes, I do!" I spun around to face him, and he did the same, nearly spilling his coffee.

"It's a big one too," I said, taking a hearty bite of my almond butter toast.

Shaan came strolling down the stairs, rubbing the overnight crusts from his large hazel eyes, completely carefree.

"It's a murder case," I managed to whisper through a mouthful of gooey butter.

"What? Murder in Vermont?" Rahul exclaimed.

"Someone died!" Shaan said, with concerning excitement. I took a mental note to put away those violent video games.

"Go brush your teeth, and I want to see you dressed in less than five minutes, young man." I commanded.

He looked at his father for relief from my command.

"Do as your mother says, son."

We both waited attentively as Shaan dragged his feet up the stairs.

"I was called in because a man was found dead in his home by his StayHere guest."

Rahul's jaw dropped. "That's awful."

I took another bite of my toast, mentally working through protocol. It's been a while since I was called in on a murder case. Although I was promoted as detective, which paid for this newly renovated, farmhouse-inspired home overlooking the mountaintops, since then, I've mostly been babysitting officers on misdemeanor cases.

"It's been nine years, Aleena. How do you feel?" Rahul asked.

He placed his hands around my waist and kissed my neck. He always found the pressure points in my body, the ones that worked like truth serum.

"I'm a bit nervous," I admitted.

"You were promoted for a reason, babe. You're a superstar at catching criminals."

"But it's been nearly a decade. I had just gotten pregnant with Shaan when we solved Hunter's cold case."

"You solved." He corrected.

I remember the smell most of all. Musky, with a hint of mildew. It was the oldest precinct in New England. I had been called in to facilitate a potential confession. The perp, Santhi Folk, looked like your run-of-the-mill sociopath, thin, with immaculate posture and small rabbit teeth beneath a single-lined mustache. If it weren't for the facial hair, he could've passed for an adolescent. And honestly, anyone with a name like *Santhi Folk* felt doomed to be some sort of criminal. He had broken into a home, kidnapped Kevin Hunter, an eight-year-old boy, and later killed him. The case remained unsolved for years due to insufficient evidence. Until, nearly half a decade later, Santhi was spotted lingering near Kevin's younger brother Jordan at his eighth birthday party in the park.

Santhi was used to interrogations. I arrived after eleven grueling hours of him being pressed with questions, but he still looked sharp, unbothered, renewed. It sent shivers down my spine. He was a man of great patience and greater tolerance. But I had been called in to change tactics. I wasn't the intimidating detective, not at five feet tall, and I wasn't the bargainer either. I was the emotional intelligence specialist, as our Captain liked to boast after every successful confession.

I remember looking into Santhi's eyes. He worked hard to appear unassuming, but I could see the pain. There was something in the sporadic shifts, the subtle twitch in his right eye, like he was holding back tears.

I had my in.

Our training had an entire course on pedophiles, enough to make you go home, shield your child, and hiss at any adult who looked at them for a beat too long. But that's exactly what held us back. We were blinded by the sheer despicableness of the act, we failed to understand the motive. And motive transcends, from the creepiest of creeps to the holiest of the holy. Santhi wasn't just a pedophile. He was a romantic. He was in love with a young boy, and if he couldn't have him, then no one else could.

So I started with general questions, just enough to wear him down; lower his guard, raise his frustration. I knew he had answered these before, they were word-for-word copies of what I'd watched on the tape. And just when I saw it, that small slump in his shoulders, the subtle surrender from the repetition, I came in from left field with the truth. I told him he loved Kevin. I described how Kevin made him feel, like Aladdin after an adventurous night with Princess Jasmine. They were flying on a magic carpet, untethered from any of life's obstacles. I channeled the spellbound magic of a fairytale, sweeping him up in the illusion of a happily-ever-after. He leaned forward, eyes bulging, a glint of saliva forming at the corner of his mouth. He was enamored by the picture I painted. He felt understood and seen by my empathy.

I rode that wave all the way to a crisp, clean, and fully recorded confession.

"Rot in jail, you disgusting pedophile."

I caught myself muttering the last part of the memory out loud.

"That Santhi guy?" Rahul asked, grabbing his jacket.

"I guess my mind was replaying the most recent confession I landed."

He glanced at his watch, grabbed the two lunch boxes I'd just finished packing and scurried toward me as he called for Shaan to meet him in the car.

"We are running late, sweetie, but you're going to do great. You got a confession no one else could for years."

As soon as he planted a kiss on my cheek, Shaan came bounding downstairs. I pulled them both into quick hugs before they rushed out to the car.

CAPTAIN WARSHBURG HAD TOLD ME TO GO STRAIGHT TO THE crime scene. His voice carried an exhilarating edge, like he was reliving the job he committed to two decades ago. I matched his rush. Sometimes I think the reason I'm good at my job, and disturbingly excited by death, is the anguish I've endured. I walk a thin line between sanity and insanity, and more often than not, I resonate with both sides.

The sudden jolt of the car snapped me out of my thoughts. *Where was I?* I had followed the GPS blindly, lost in my own head, until the car lurched over jagged rocks, rattling me side to side. As the dust cleared, a mustard yellow house came into view.

No, no, no!

I never looked up a case ahead of time. My intuition was my best weapon—and the moment I opened a file, bias would creep in, clouding my gut instincts. The last thing I expected, after years away from homicides, was to be back at my ex-boyfriend's house.

My hands began shaking as I reached for the car door handle. I had to get my shit together, fast. I was the lead detective on this case, with all eyes on me. It was already hard enough being the token Indian in the precinct, and even harder being the only female lead among cock-thinking, ego-oozing men. The last thing I needed was to look weak, shaken, unsuited.

I inhaled deeply, held it for three rhythmic beats, and repeated until my exhale came out even. I used to make Shaan do this whenever his temper flared, as it often did. I'd watch my son's rage dissolve, slowly and steadily, after a few rounds of synchronized breathing. This band-aid solution was the only thing keeping him from being expelled. One day, it'll stop working, and he'll get into trouble again. But that was tomorrow's problem.

I shook my head to dispense the jitters. I had to stop the tornado spirling in my mind, dragging in other areas of anxiety, distracting me from what I was about to step into. I had to refocus and hone in on a role I've assiduously trained for. I closed my eyes and opened the door with vigor—ready to fully embody the tough, unphased, borderline ruthless Detective Gupta.

"Gupta?"

Officer Sanchez appeared from my left, catching me off guard.

Behind him, a stream of officers and forensic crew floated in and out of a house I used to call home.

"Sanchez. How are you doing?"

He looked at me, slightly bewildered.

"Considering," I punctuated.

"Definitely an unexpected Monday morning," he replied, handing me a manila folder.

This was the kind of exchange that made me want to be a detective when I was ten years old. The crisp handoff of information about an unspeakable act, shared only among those built to be the unsung heroes of justice.

But I wasn't ready to see the report yet.

"I'd like to see the crime scene for myself," I said, doing my best to keep my voice steady.

"Ah yes, the infamous Gupta Method," he smirked.

"Sure." I said it flat, reminding him who was boss.

He cleared his throat and extended his arm toward the door. "After you."

The crunch of dead leaves beneath my block-heeled ankle boots and the bite of cool wind as I walked forward only heightened my nerves. I felt like throwing up. I hoped Sanchez didn't notice as I went through two full cycles of deep breaths, trying to steady myself before stepping inside.

The decadent smell of his home hit me first, a familiar warmth. But mid-sniff, it was overtaken by the pungent, rotting stench of decay and coagulated blood.

"The victim was found dead in the kitchen," Sanchez said.

I held back a rising sob as I rounded the corner, past the couch where we'd spent countless hours together, and set my eyes on the fiasco. He was being examined by a full forensic team clustered around his body, flanked by jittery, over-caffein-ated cops jostling about, trying to piece together the night's events.

Aaron, my first love, was now dead.

"No signs of attack," Sanchez said, casually leaning over my shoulder.

"Time of death?" I asked.

"Between 1 and 3 a.m."

I swallowed the sour burn of my breakfast rising in my throat and stepped closer. The room seemed to peel open around me, officers quietly shifting aside as I moved toward Aaron's blood-ied corpse. Each step felt heavier than the last as I mentally braced myself.

I'm a goddamn detective. I was trained for this. I will not let my past compromise my career.

"Inform his family," I said firmly. "And I want a cause of death from the autopsy. STAT."

Chapter 3

Margo

I fucking hate this. I'd rather scrub motel toilets than be here every fucking Monday morning.

"More mimosa, Margo?" Tara asked, smiling with her brand-new veneers. Her brunette hair and curtain bangs only amplified the blinding gleam of her vicious smile.

They were all vicious—bored, rich, and petty housewives with a splash of glorified alcoholism.

"Yes, please," I said, smiling as genuinely as I could. I had to keep up appearances for these vultures.

"Happy ten-year anniversary." I raised my glass and the four other youth-hungry women mirrored.

As I sipped the mimosa, I strategized the best way to pivot the conversation. I needed the money and I needed it fast.

Cue the somber wife.

"I can't believe it's been ten years since Richard died." I squeezed my dry eyes shut, just enough to force out a tear or two.

"I know, sweetie. You've been so strong," Barbara whispered, brushing her newly manicured blonde extensions.

"I've actually been thinking."

Here goes nothing.

"I want to honor Richard—and what better time than on the ten-year anniversary of his death?"

I could only assume eyebrows were raised beneath the layers of Botox, because plump smiles began to form on each face.

"How exciting, Margo. Great idea!" exclaimed Sally, the alpha of the group.

Sally had been my shoo-in.

It all started at good ol' Urban Roast, an affordable yet addictive coffee chain scattered across the East Coast. I began working there in Roxden when I was sixteen. That location was the smallest of them all—run-down, with a manager who was rarely around. It was just me and one other barista, and since we alternated shifts, I was on my own most of the time. Still, that job was how I supported my mom and myself. Although my mother tried to hold down jobs, it was barely enough to cover rent for our apartment in a run-down complex known more for its prostitution rings than its plumbing.

My mom had a portfolio of minimum wage jobs throughout my childhood. She was often let go because of "mommy time." Whenever it was mommy time, I knew she'd be locked in her room for eighteen hours a day, isolated and unwilling to leave her tiny space. I got used to it, because when it ended, she was fresh and brand new again, happy and joyful about everything around her, especially me. It was worth the wait to have my mother at her best. During those times, I handled food in the form of canned goods, frozen meals, and junk. So when I started working at Urban Roast, it didn't feel like a downgrade because my paycheck bought us the same kind of meals I'd grown up eating.

Even though Roxden was less than twenty minutes from the posh and privileged streets of Boston, it felt like a discarded city. Boston's landfill. I used to wonder if Sam Adams unofficially decided to send all the trash—and all the trashy people, to Roxden when he developed the city.

I've seen a gun pulled out on three separate occasions while on shift. Two shootings in the parking lot and one robbery. One sunny and unassuming afternoon, a short, stubby man with a neck tattoo large enough to blanket most of his skin ordered an iced coffee with three pumps of caramel and an extra shot of espresso. All was going as expected until I punched in his order. He looked me over and said the coffee was on me as he slid a gun onto the counter. Then he forced me to empty the register and waltzed out with a cold drink and a bag of money, leaving me silent, stunned, and absolutely terrified.

I was nineteen when my life changed forever. I had landed a gig as a receptionist at a boutique gallery in Beacon Hill. Sally had come into Urban Roast two months earlier for a coffee, clutching her Saint Laurent purse and glancing back at her parked silver Audi GT every thirty seconds. She said, with unnerving amusement, that her navigation system should include crime rates at different pit stop locations. I wanted to punch her in the face for her blunt ignorance and entitlement. This pit stop was my salvation. This location was my home.

Instead, I batted my amber eyes, the same ones Mom used to call a gift from God, and smiled at her like she was my favorite celebrity. After all, she was carrying a Le 5 À 7 Bea in-grained leather bag that retailed for $4,500, and driving a $200,000 car.

"I absolutely love your Le 5 À 7 Bea purse," I said with a gentle smile.

"Good eye. Many confuse it with the Supple line."

"I can see the resemblance," I said.

"Sally."

"Margaret, but people call me Margo. Pleased to meet you."

I was about to extend my hand for a shake but held back. She likely wouldn't want to touch me—afraid I might rub my poverty off on her.

As I took her order, two Lexon Street Boys walked in and headed straight to the bathroom. I grabbed a cup and poured drip coffee into it. I handed it to her without taking her order.

"I would recommend leaving. Now," I whispered.

Her eyes flicked toward the sound of quick footsteps behind her as she carefully took the coffee and rushed out to her car.

She reversed so hard, the squeal of rubber against the cold pavement startled the two men out of the bathroom. High on cocaine, switchblades in hand, they burst out of the coffee shop and after her as she sped off. I hit the panic button and within seconds, the doors locked, the lights cut out, and the cops were on their way.

One cloudy Tuesday afternoon, six hours into my shift, I watched for Sally, like I did everyday since I met her. I hoped to see her again, even though it had nearly been a month. Even though I didn't expect her to ever step foot back into Roxden, my heart fluttered at the possibility. She was the wealthiest person I had ever spoken to, and I was enchanted by the peephole into another world. But Mom's voice kept ringing in my head: *"those people are ignorant bastards!"* She wasn't entirely wrong about the elite, even when she ranted to Larry, her imaginary best friend.

Mom was diagnosed with schizophrenia on my seventeenth birthday, after an incident with Larry. I came home to knives scattered across the kitchen floor, and her smiling victorious, as she sat awkwardly on her right side to support a self-inflicted stab wound to her left thigh. The doctor at the ER called in a psychiatrist and next thing I knew, my mother had moved out and I was alone in our dingy apartment, despite lying about having an uncle live with me. Most of my paycheck went toward Mom's mental asylum. She'd been court-mandated to stay for three months at a subsidized cost.

It had been two years.

In those two years, Mom became Karen. She refused to be called anything else. The last time I spoke to her, she was delighted to announce her rekindled friendship with Larry.

Finally, 8PM—time to clock out. I shut down the machinery, my feet moaning from the grueling pain of standing all day, when two men appeared. They wore matching black shirts and pants, standing like towers with folded arms, staring at me with hawk eyes. One had a Luigi-from-Mario-Kart mustache, the other was bald. Their biceps were bigger than my head, and my heart began racing at the thought of what those arms could do. Nestled between them, just barely visible, I caught the tail end of a pink dress. A whisper later, the men stepped aside, and Sally emerged with a wide smile.

"Margo, nice to see you again."

Luigi Mustache Man and Mr. Bald swept the store, scanning for hidden figures. I smiled as gently as I could, though I couldn't help raising a conspiratorial eyebrow.

"Sorry about them," she waved dismissively. "I had to bring reinforcements to come see you."

I couldn't blame her.

"It's nice to see you again, Sally," I said, keeping an eye on the wandering behemoths.

"I wanted to personally thank you for your kindness the other day. I'm opening an art gallery in Beacon Hill next month, and if I remember correctly, you have a pretty sharp eye for beautiful things."

She lingered on beautiful things, lips pouting almost involuntarily.

"Congratulations." I beamed, offering a faint smile.

I hope she didn't come all this way just to rub it in.

"Thank you," she said with a slight bow. "Well, Margo, I'm looking for a receptionist. A *loyal* receptionist."

I stared at her like a deer in headlights.

"After what you did the other day," she continued, "saving me without reason. I wouldn't want anyone else for the position."

Yessssssssss.

It was clear she needed a loyal receptionist to cover up shady business—but I couldn't care less. I was about to be granted access to a world so close I could smell the Armani perfume, yet so far I wouldn't dare enter it. Until now.

I tried to contain the excitement rising in my chest and flushing my cheeks. One thing street smarts had taught me was to keep an even keel at all times and never accept anything at face value.

"That's very generous, Sally, but I work overtime here to help pay for my sick mother."

"That's awful," she said, her tone flat and unperturbed. "How does a $200,000 starting base salary with a $40,000 sign-on bonus sound?" She looked around the store as she remarked, "I'm sure it's a competitive offer."

NOW SITTING AT OUR WEEKLY ROUND TABLE OVER A DECADE later—center stage in a members-only restaurant—I watched as Sally sipped her bubbly, pinky up. She had always supported my endeavors, especially after Richard's passing. Sally and Richard were investment partners and longtime friends. She was the one who brought Richard on my first day at the gallery. The one whispering in his ear, convincing him to take me out on a date. She argued that age was just a number: fifty-three was the new forty, and twenty was the new thirty. Richard gushed over me until I fell in love with him. She was also the one who officiated our wedding, while Aaron yelled at the bartender for refusing to serve him, even though he was underage.

Most importantly, Sally continuously gave me the only thing that ever made me feel close to home again. Closer to the best moments of my life, when my mother showered me with love, before the cloud of schizophrenia cursed our lives. On lonely nights, in my lavender silk robe, hair in a bun, a jasmine candle burning on Richard's hardwood desk, high on Sally's supply, I'd log onto LaVida Online Casino and gamble my late husband's life insurance away. The hands I'd win would slingshot me back into my mother's arms, twirling me in sheer glee after she won a hand at the same online casino, back when I was a child. Like any addiction, those seconds held a magnitude of bliss worth sacrificing everything for and doing absolutely anything to return to.

Although Richard and I had transferred Karen to the best mental hospital in New England, she lost visitor privileges after her third strike. Left to rot, constricted and sedated.

While Karen couldn't mother me, Sally became my fairy godmother, granting every wish.

New job? Check.

Rich husband? Check.

Socialite? Check.

More drugs? Absolutely, check.

I returned the favor by holding all her offshore accounts under my name. Any funds under the table went to Margaret Vessel. It's been more than ten years since I went into business with Sally, without a single repercussion. She gave me a new life. No more crippling fear of being shot or gang-raped during a shift. No more starving through three dinners in a row just to afford another form of risperidone for my mother. No more living in survival mode.

Karen now receives top-of-the-line care. And I drive a Range Rover.

"Let's host a gala to commemorate Richard!" Tara exclaimed after sipping the last of her mimosa.

A gala was exactly what I was fishing for. The last one earned me half a million dollars. But could I pull in a million this time?

"Don't forget. Not one penny less, bitch."

Sergio Marino's gritty voice still echoed in my ears from when I woke up to him strangling me last week.

"A gala is a wonderful idea," I said as tenderly as I could, taking her hand in mine.

Then my phone rang, cutting through the air like a blade.

"Pardon," I said, rising. I walked toward the dim back corner of the restaurant, away from earshot.

"Hello?"

"Ms. Vessel?" came the soft voice of a man I didn't recognize.

"It's actually Mrs. Moore."

Legally I was still Vessel. Which meant the voice belonged to either a government official or someone from my past.

"Yes, my name is Officer Eric Sanchez." A throat cleared. "Your stepson, Aaron Moore, was found dead early this morning."

Found dead?

My heart lodged in my throat. I couldn't speak.

"Ms. Ves—sorry, I mean Mrs. Moore— can you please make your way to Vermont as soon as possible?"

Fuck, the gala will have to wait.

Chapter 4

Eva

I was trembling. The tall, slender officer, sporting an obnoxious tan like he'd just returned from vacationing in Tahiti, placed a blanket over my shoulders. He sat across from me on Aaron's StayHere coffee table, waiting patiently as I collected myself. He mentioned his name—Officer Benfall or something—but I preferred to think of him as Mr. Tahiti.

It had been two hours since I called the police and was ordered to remain on the premises. In that time, I'd tried to unscramble the tangled network of broken memories, shaping only faint silhouettes of last night. I closed my eyes and inhaled deeply, transforming into the Eva of yesterday, the one who breathed in the mahogany teakwood air, laced with the scent of lamb stew. His stew. I ran my fingers through my tangled hair and winced as my index finger throbbed, swollen from the scorching hot meal.

My last memory, though blurry, was of his strong arms wrapped around my waist as I straddled him on the leathery couch.

"Were you with Aaron last night, Ms. Armstrong?" The officer's voice was deep, compensating for his disarmingly lanky frame.

"I was." A raspy chain smoker escaped my mouth.

I began to shift my weight from left to right, suddenly jittery. Mr. Tahiti extended his hand to help me steady myself.

"I'm sorry, I feel like complete shit. Could I please freshen up?" I looked straight into his light brown eyes. "And please, call me Eva." I smiled coyly.

I was relentless. I couldn't remember the late hours of yesterday with a man I found dead, yet I had the audacity to flirt with a police officer.

There's a reason I'm like this.

Mr. Tahiti smiled back playfully and cleared his throat. His hand was still outstretched.

"Not a problem, Eva. Detective Gupta will be questioning you further."

Was it the woman I'd seen in a navy-blue pantsuit, with supple bronze skin and luscious black hair? She was radiant, gliding toward Aaron's door with an unmistakable air of authority. I swallowed the bitter anxiety that had bubbled up my throat and replied as submissively as I could.

"Thank you, Officer. You're very kind."

I pressed my feet into the thin carpet and used all my strength to push myself up. My spine cracked like I'd turned geriatric overnight.

"Before you freshen up, we'll need to get a sample," he said.

"A sample of what?"

He nodded toward a short, wiry middle-aged woman holding a labeled hospital bag of equipment. She weaved past her colleagues with surprising speed and joined the officer.

She extended her hand to shake mine, then quickly pulled it back when she noticed her gloves.

"Hello, my name is Sue. I'll be collecting a sample of your skin, saliva and genital fluids."

I winced at the words *genital fluids*, and so did the officer.

"I'm sorry?" I looked down at the bag she was holding and caught a clearer view of the label: a rape kit.

"You must be mistaken." I let out two short pumps of breath. "Aaron didn't rape me."

"It's protocol," Mr. Tahiti said flatly. "That is, if you had sexual relations with the victim." He side-eyed me with a low frown.

I bat my lashes once, and men think they own me.

I straightened and met his gaze. "Yes. I was intimate with Aaron last night."

He rolled his eyes—it was fleeting, but I caught it. Offended, he turned to Sue and said, "Please proceed."

In one brief exchange, a flood of unspoken emotions passed between me and Mr. Tahiti. Despite behaving like every low-grade man I'd encountered, he was still a police officer—in a town where I knew no one, in a house where my host was found dead. I couldn't afford to let feminism, or whatever you'd call it, get in the way of potential allies. I had to regroup and work my way back into Mr. Tahiti's good—and flirtatious—graces.

I bit my lip, just briefly and gave Mr. Tahiti a delicate touch on his upper arm. "I'm sorry—this has all just been incredibly overwhelming. Thank you, Officer, for making this whole situation a bit more palatable." I let a soft smile curl across my lips, though I was acutely aware of how frayed I looked.

His eyebrows furrowed, a tense line forming across his forehead, but it smoothed out when he offered me a warm smile. "Not a problem, Eva. Please go ahead with Sue, and I'll check in on you in a bit."

I was directed upstairs, where birds chirped and sang. Fresh sunlight streamed through the skylight, casting a golden hue over the treetops. After what felt like a creepy slumber party— Sue combing through my hair, scraping under my fingernails, swabbing my mouth—she finally moved in for the more intimate part. As she collected the specimens she needed down there, I stared up through the roof windows, dissociating. Her exam felt more intrusive than the countless strangers I'd let inside me.

She was chatty. While swabbing, she launched into a monologue about how uncomfortable it is when your teenager starts dating. She spoke of her precious son and his new girlfriend, how she created a Facebook account just to keep tabs on them. She laughed as she worked, assuring me it wasn't like her to snoop—"just curious."

I lay there in silence, focusing instead on the way the bed eased the pain in my back and relieved the tension in my head.

"All done!" she said cheerfully, gathering her things as I dressed. "It was nice meeting you, Eva!" she called before skipping down the stairs.

Definitely not the meet-and-greet I wanted from you, Sue.

I was left alone for the first time in what felt like an eternity. I rushed to the bathroom and locked the door behind me. I couldn't afford to interact with anyone else until I got a grip. I looked at myself in the mirror. A face I barely recognized stared back. The woman in the reflection had aged, been stomped on, and had lost control of her own story. She looked translucent—almost ghostlike—and frozen in a frenzy.

It didn't matter that Aaron liked it rough. It didn't matter that I spent the first night of my weekend getaway sleeping with him. It didn't matter that I had been looking forward to relaxing in this serene town in the mountains. None of that mattered now. I was stuck in limbo, caught between what I could remember and what I couldn't, with prison looming as the consequence.

Think, Eva. Think. What happened last night?

I splashed cold water on my face, dampened my hair, and brushed my teeth. When I felt a little more refreshed, I took a deep breath and closed my eyes. I could feel Aaron's arms around me—his smell, his weight. I could hear his moans, his grunts. I tilted my head back, remembering doing the same while I was on top of him... and then—nothing. I slapped the edge of the sink in frustration. How could I have forgotten a whole chunk of the night?

A knock sounded on the door just as the pain from my hand started to radiate. "Eva, are you doing okay?" It was Mr. Tahiti.

I took one last look at the mirror, disappointed in the woman I saw, then opened the door.

"Yes. I accidentally dropped my toothbrush."

He didn't question it. "Detective Gupta will be interviewing you at a later time. Please remain on the premises until we can find you somewhere else to stay."

I nodded, my eyes drifting to the bed behind him.

Maybe some sleep would bring my memory back.

Chapter 5

Aleena

"We have to assume the worst until we know for sure," I told Officer Sanchez as we settled into the conference room. "Until the autopsy comes in, we need to treat this as a potential homicide. So, give me a rundown of Aaron's primary circle."

He pulled out a crisp folder of printed photos and stood beside me as we looked up at the blank investigation board. He then placed Aaron's crime scene photo at the center. I swallowed back the rancid taste of bile.

"We have Eva Armstrong. She's the one who found him."

He taped her youthful license photo in the upper right corner of the whiteboard.

"Do we know anything about her?"

"She was visiting from New York, came to Vermont for a short gateway. There's no prior relationship between her and the victim." He flipped through the folder again. "Based on her DMV records, it appears this was her first time in Vermont."

Her light blue eyes caught my attention. She was pretty. Definitely Aaron's type.

"One hell of a vacation," Sanchez said sorrowfully, shaking his head.

"Make sure she stays in Vermont," I ordered, still focused on her unblemished face. "Who's next—family?"

"Both of the victim's parents are deceased. His mother died of breast cancer when he was four, and his father in a car crash when he was…" Sanchez flipped through the paperwork. "Twenty."

Our late-night cuddles rarely led to anything beyond physical intimacy. He had told me both of his parents had died and sometimes said he felt like an adult orphan. But that was as far as he would open up. Through my own research, I discovered that Richard, Aaron's father, had died in a gruesome car crash caused by brake failure. The case was closed when Richard's autopsy revealed elevated blood alcohol levels. Late at night, when my mind drifted to the dark corners of my cerebral universe, I would wonder how a luxury car—one that prided itself on its quality—could have a faulty brake.

"Did the father remarry?" I asked.

"Yes. Margaret Vessel. They married one year before Richard's fatal accident. She lives in Boston, on the Moore estate."

He took her picture and placed it on the whiteboard, across from Eva's.

"She's young," I said. Her alabaster skin was dusted with freckles, and her copper hair framed her face like a mane of fire.

"Only about two years older than Aaron," he said.

"Interesting. Did you get in touch with her?"

"Yes. She's on the next flight here." His eyes squinted as he scanned an official statement, fingers grazing his thick black beard. "She received five hundred million dollars through Richard's life insurance."

"*Pheeeew*," I whistled. "That's a lot of money."

"I know," Sanchez said, drifting into a tropical daydream. "The things I'd do with five hundred million dollars."

"Not be an officer in a small town?"

"This small town just packed a punch. I might miss the adrenaline," he grinned.

"A double-edged sword, it is, being in law enforcement. We need crimes to feed our days."

Sanchez glanced over at me with a slightly raised eyebrow. "Gupta, I didn't peg you as the morbid type."

We both stared at the photo pinned to the center of the board, Aaron's bloodied body sprawled across his kitchen floor.

"It's hard not to be," I said.

My heart ached, and my eyes stung. But I couldn't allow myself to cry, so I quickly shifted gears. "Anyone else in his primary circle?"

"That's pretty much it. No significant other. Margaret is the only direct family, and Eva's the one who found him. Everyone else falls into his secondary circle."

"Well, we know where to start. Let's get Margaret to the station and begin gathering and slating everyone in Aaron's primary and secondary circles for interviews. Also, have a cadet call Eva's family to inform them we've requested she remain in Vermont."

He nodded, flicking his thick lashes as he mentally filed away the next steps.

"Oh, and Sanchez—make sure everyone stays at the Montpelier Inn."

"Great. Thanks, boss."

He hugged his files to his chest and walked out of the conference room.

I turned and stared at the investigation board, zeroing in on his graying body, his soulless corpse. I couldn't believe it. Even though I hadn't spoken to him in years, I often replayed our time together like a sepia-toned flashback set to romantic music. He was stored away in my heart as a memory of what could be, a potential to an alternate reality where we stayed together. What if we had? Would he still have ended up dead?

Chapter 6

Margo

"*Y*ou *filthy gold digger!*"

Aaron's shrill voice kept spinning in my head like a cursed merry-go-round.

"Excuse me, miss."

I remember seeing his face transform. It started with the same annoyed expression he'd reserved for me ever since Richard died. He was convinced I'd somehow killed his father. But this time—this time was different. His eyes contorted into a watery rage of red, his teeth clanked together, and his fists clenched so tightly I felt the panic ripple straight through my spine.

I had been desperate. Outstandingly desperate.

Sergio was following me. Everywhere. He'd given me a month to get my affairs in order, because I'd promised him interest for his grace. A clean one million dollars; I pitched it to him with the polish of a salesman. The end of the month was closing in, and I didn't have one million dollars. I didn't even have a hundred thousand. I was broke. And as desperation always does, it clouded my judgment, made the impossible seem just plausible enough. Maybe Aaron would pity me and give me money. Maybe he'd even call me "mom" and watch the sunset with me.

Fuck me.

I can't tell when I lost the millions I inherited from my late husband. Was it the silky whiskey soaring through my bloodstream, dulling my thoughts? Or the drugs I took, and the gambling I did, whenever I missed my mother? High and loopy, I'd dream I was back to being a child, sitting beside her on our rusty old balcony, waiting for butterflies. They had a fondness for the hollyhocks that grew around the edge of the building. When one fluttered past, we'd yelp with joy and wrap our arms around each other. I would relive, in slow motion, the way Karen jumped, wide-eyed and full of life at the world's extravagance. In those intoxicated moments, I'd feel a flicker of what I felt back then: deeply loved by my mother, the luckiest girl in the world.

"Excuse me!"

A Filipino woman, striking enough to be a model, raised her voice, snapping me back to earth.

"Yes, I'm sorry."

"No problem, madam. May I please see your ticket and passport?"

"Sure." I stood with a plastered smile as she glanced over my documents.

Aaron is dead, and our last conversation was him calling me a filthy gold digger.

Asshole.

I managed to hop on the next flight to Vermont that morning, right after a boozy brunch with the ladies. I'd decided not to tell them what happened to Aaron until I knew more. The flight was barely an hour, but I'd grown so used to first class that I couldn't bring myself to book economy. On Richard's points, I sat in the first row next to a teenage boy in brown khakis and a neon green rain jacket. If Silicon Valley needed marketing material for future tech prodigies, he'd be it. I glanced over, attempting a soft smile, but he was hunched over, completely absorbed in his tablet, headphones cocooning him in whatever world he was lost in. I felt a flicker of jealousy. This fetus didn't have to kiss ass to maintain his status, while I *wiped* ass for the tiniest speck of validation.

VERMONT ALWAYS MADE ME UNEASY. I WASN'T ACCUSTOMED TO being one with nature. I had way too much shit built up in my soul, to surrender to the mountains. On the bright side, Vermont was a composting-heavy state; maybe I'd find a spot to wither away in the soil of worms, apple skins and coffee grounds.

The desire to disappear compounded in my chest, as I made my way to the Montpelier police station. I was directed to come straight from the airport and the last thing I needed was to rack up points against me. So I ventured to the station with my red bottom Louboutins stiletto heels, along with my Louis Vuitton carrier.

These were the last few items I hadn't sold from Richard's curated wardrobe for me. I didn't have the heart to sell the limited edition Louboutins he gifted me in return for mind-blowing sex. Richard was not the type to make me get on my knees right after he gave me an expensive gift. He reserved that for his escorts. I held a special place as his wife—a place of patience and care. A place of methodical manipulation. "*Wifely duties,*" he'd whisper in my ear when he caught me feeling a sense of purpose, often while working on some kind of charity project. I was obligated to drop what I was doing and submit to whatever he wanted. It turned him on to undermine my value. I was tasked to look like a model, submit to him like a virgin, all the while tolerating him as he yelled his ex-wife's name while completing.

But these Louboutins.

I watched as my heels clanked and numbed on the gravel while the morning green air filled my lungs. I had decided— after my fourth glass of champagne on the plane—to upkeep the image of a rich widow. The best way to remain incognito was to remain in character. I flipped my hair, readjusted my shirt to show more cleavage, and sashayed into the station. As soon as I walked inside, all eyes began trailing me from head to toe. I was being frisked by the entire police department without a single touch.

I stood right at the entrance, with an air of importance— one hip propped to the side and my carrier on the other.

"Margaret Moore?"

"About time." I rolled my eyes.

"Hello. I'm Officer Sanchez." He stretched his calloused hand to shake mine. "We spoke on the phone."

"Yes." I stretched my hand like I was Cinderella, expecting an enchanté.

He looked down at my hand and decided to skip the non-verbal part of our introduction. "I'm sorry for your loss, Mrs. Moore."

Oh shit.

With all the preparation to be in character, I completely forgot how a stepmom should react if her stepson suddenly died.

"I ran out of tears," I tried to quiver, not meeting his eyes.-

"I understand."

For an officer, he had a tender voice and kind eyes.

He left me in an interrogation room without saying another word. I sat on the cold, hardened steel chair and felt a prickle of sweat form on my forehead. I'd always been a sucker for sweet men. It was my kryptonite, my fairytale, my vulnerability. For a pathetic second, I thought I found that in Richard. But as soon as we got married, his true colors seeped through and I was trapped in an abusive relationship.

The room was dark except for a lit ceiling bulb, illuminating the very blemishes I tried to conceal.

Could I have gained anything from Aaron's death?

My face felt dewy from the heart palpitations. I should have phoned Mr. Lebewisk before coming down here. I should phone him now. Okay, it's settled. I will ask for my lawyer before answering any questions.

Except—how will I afford Richard's old chum and absurdly expensive lawyer?

My stomach lurched from the incessant dead ends spiraling around my head that I almost didn't realize when the door opened. A short, brown woman with beautiful almond eyes strolled in. Her pantsuit was tailored to fit her in all the right places. I envied melanin more and more as I aged. She managed to rock the effortless no-makeup, makeup look as her blushy lips moved.

"Hello Mrs. Moore, I'm Detective Gupta. Is it okay if I record our conversation today?"

She sat across from me, her back methodically straight, trained to stay in command. I, on the other hand, felt my spine curve under pressure.

"Hello, Detective. Yes, that's fine." I looked down and cupped my hands around my eyes. I was good at crying on cue, but inconveniently, my tear ducts were dry.

She leaned and turned on the camera. "I'm sorry for your loss, Mrs. Moore." She readjusted in her seat. "Were you and Aaron close?"

I managed to poke my right eye hard before lifting my head. The tears began to form on my eyelid from the striking pain.

"Not as much as I would have wished to be," I sniffled.

As I looked at her, I noticed something unexpected. The signs were subtle, but I was a pro at spotting grief. The edges of her right eye were slightly pink, her eyebrows drawn low from constant tension. The under-eye bags looked fresh. I watched her as she watched me. Then, without a word, she began pulling papers from a folder. This woman was grieving. Heavily. Detectives had lives too, I realized. She might be dealing with something personal.

"It says here, you came to Vermont last week."

How do I phrase I need a lawyer without seeming suspicious? *I need a lawyer. Let me talk to my lawyer. I won't say a word without my lawyer. Bring my lawyer henceforth!*

I felt the heavy timidness of a kid asking to go to the bathroom to take a shit—in front of the whole class.

"Uhh."

Just fucking say it. *I need a lawyer.*

I cleared my throat and closed my eyes. "Yes. I came to see Aaron."

Fuck. Fuck. Fuck. Why did I say that?

"Do you come and see Aaron often, Mrs. Moore?"-

"Call me Margo, and not really. Listen, I think—"

She held up her hand.

"Let me get you a glass of water," she interrupted.

As she pushed back, the chair squealed and the noise boomed around the room, sending a shrill down my back. I felt my throat catch my breath and not let go.

Breathe, Margo, breathe.

I finally had my breath back to its natural rhythm when Sanchez walked in carrying a white cup. He placed it in front of me and turned to grab a chair from the corner of the room and sat next to Detective Gupta's vacant seat.

"Water," he gestured.

I looked down at the translucent pool of liquid in the cup, wishing I could shrink and float in the water, undisturbed. Instead, I took a big gulp and leaned back in my chair as the water lubricated my dry esophagus.

"Detective Gupta had to step out for a moment," he declared.

I wondered if it had anything to do with her eye bags.

"So, Mrs. Moore, I understand this is difficult, but we are trying to get to the bottom of what happened to your stepson."

His hands moved toward me, and I wanted to hold them. His words sounded genuine, his gaze empathetic, and his demeanor irresistible.

"I'm sorry, Officer Sanchez, but are you married?"

His head jerked back as though I'd just blown unsolicited wind in his face.

"Excuse me?"

"I'm sorry. I'm sure this may sound wildly inappropriate, but you have very kind eyes."

He looked at me for a prolonged moment, registering my words.

He placed his hands back on his lap and caved into himself enough to show his apparent discomfort.

"Thank you," he muttered.

He then looked at me and said, "No. I'm not married." His eyes flickered toward the video camera.

Somehow, making him uncomfortable made me feel powerful. He was not only a law enforcement officer—he was a human. A lonely human. The ball was back in my court.

"Mrs. Moore—"

"Please, call me Margo," I twinkled.

"Mrs. Moore," he insisted, "are you aware that your late husband—" He looked down at a sheet of paper, words too small to read from my vantage point. "Richard Moore willed his estate to his son, Aaron Moore?"

I was not aware.

"No," I said.

He shuffled another piece of paper and began reading off a column of numbers.

"Mrs. Moore, are you having financial troubles?"

I suddenly felt Sergio's cigar-ridden breath and heavy hands cuffed around my neck.

I shuddered.

"I mean, it's been a bit difficult keeping all of Richard's investments above water," I lied.

"I see."

"Where were you between 1 a.m. and 3 a.m.?"

"I was at home."

"Can anyone vouch for that?"

"No. I was alone."

"Mrs. Moore, are you aware that, following Aaron's death, the remainder of the Moore estate now transfers to you as the contingent beneficiary?"

My eyes widened. Aaron had no parents, no spouse, no siblings. That left me—the contingent beneficiary. I looked down. My heart skipped a jolly beat, but I quickly pressed my palms against my eyes to stifle the sudden exhilaration. I pierced my left eye this time, as I'd long mastered the trick of doing it subtly—just enough to jump-start the waterworks.

"I had no idea," I said between dainty sobs.

"Mrs. Moore." His voice was sharp, apathetic. "You had a lot to gain from Aaron's death."

I fixed my bloodshot eyes on his contorted face. His kindness was a ruse—a police tactic designed to make desperate women melt at his mercy. I saw it now. Beneath the gentle features was a savage determination: a goal to be met, a person to target, a promotion to attain. He needed someone to put behind bars—and he intended that person to be me.

The ball was never in my court.

"I want— I *need* my lawyer."

Chapter 7

Aleena

I knew of Aaron's stepmother. *"A gold digger. A whore. A murderer."* These were all of Aaron's vicious accusations toward Margo. But when I saw her, the persona I had concocted in my head dissolved. She looked terrified, with her uneasy doe eyes and tensed, thick eyebrows despite her ruse to seem unphased. She deliberately over exaggerated her wealth while undermining her own pretension. She didn't fit the profile of a vindictive person out for money. Aaron never told me how his father and Margo met, but one thing was clear: Margo was an outsider—and I had an affinity for outsiders.

My thought concluded as I approached the wall-hung landline. I had been pulled out because of a call, forcing Sanchez to return to Margo with her glass of water. I was steaming. To interrupt an interview for a call was inexcusable. Confessions were my golden ticket, my prize collection, my reputation—and an interrogation room was my incubator.

I shot a glaring look at the cadet who stood by the phone. She looked down immediately, ashamed.

"I'm sorry, Detective Gupta—they said it was an emergency."

"No shit."

As soon as I bit her with my words, I regretted it. She hurried off to her desk, and I wanted to run after her and hug her. Being the boss brought out the ugly in me. I couldn't find my footing as the leader I wanted to be.

But one problem at a time.

I reached for the phone and braced myself. "Hello?"

"Hello, Mrs. Gupta. This is Principal Calaver. I'm sorry to catch you by surprise, but you need to come pick up Shaan."

Fuck. What did he do again?

"I'll be right there."

I texted Sanchez with an emergency BRB message, grabbed my tan peacoat, and rushed to my car. Rahul was at least an hour away in Burlington, finalizing the details of an important solar panel contract. But if it were any other day, he would be the one picking up Shaan, as he frequently did.

Today, of all days, my child had to push his boundaries with me. As I drove out of the station, I couldn't help but fantasize about an alternate life. I rolled down the window and sped up. Trees zipped past one after another like a flipbook animation, while the familiar smell of cedar and brisk air tickled my nostrils. The exact amalgamation of senses I experienced on the many road trips with Aaron. Our secret getaways. Our lives, perfectly engulfed in one another, with no care in the world.

I turned to the empty passenger seat and watched as a memory was conjured. I observed myself in that seat—completely giddy, throwing popcorn kernels at Aaron as he drove. His laughter filled the car and fluttered my soul. With a mischievous smirk, I stroked my hand up his thigh, feeling him tense with urge, heightened by the anticipation of getting to our cabin in the forest to unleash the magic teasing between us. How life would have been, if the entirety of my reality was encompassed in that one snapshot. How much I craved for it to be that way. But it wasn't the case. Aaron couldn't uphold being the man in those special moments. I was his dirty little secret—solely privy to the woods in our hideout spot or late at night in his house. He made me feel whole only when no one was watching.

I was surprised by the tears streaming down my cheeks as I pulled into Lavisier Elementary School. I took a tissue from the console and wiped off the salty water and escaped mascara. I looked in the mirror and forced a smile before getting out of the car.

I walked through the open pavement parking lot and bus pick-up zone, rehearsing my plea to give Shaan yet another chance. I'd have to target Principal Calaver's soft spots. Her granddaughter was hospitalized with severe bipolar disorder six months ago. *Should I use this to my advantage?* I flinched at the thought and pinched myself in punishment. I was considering using a poor woman's granddaughter to help my fucked-up kid stay in school so he could continue terrorizing other students.

I'm a piece of shit.

I waved at Mark, a frail and elderly security guard, as I pushed the entrance door open to a freshly glazed terrazzo floor, exuding the smell of pines. Colorful billboards were plastered against the walls, signaling upcoming events— events Shaan may not be allowed to attend anymore.

"Hello, Mrs. Gupta."

Candace, the school's secretary, appeared from the side hallway. She guided me toward the principal's office.

"How are you doing, Candace? How is Thomas?" I asked with a smile but slowly curved my lips together as Candace responded with an icy glare.

What was her deal?

I walked through the tight hallway reserved for naughty kids. The smell was fresh of pines and disinfectant but the air was piercing. Dull brown plastic chairs were placed right below the vents, clattering Shaan's teeth. He looked at me pleadingly, holding an ice pack to his swollen purple cheek.

"What happened?" I hissed.

"Mom—please. It wasn't my fault."

"Shaan, quiet!"

I felt a burn stinging my eyes and a rush of heat shoot up my temple. I clenched my fist to subterfuge the threatening fury flowing through my veins.

"Mrs. Gupta, please come in," Principal Calaver said as she poked her head out of her office.

I walked in front of Shaan and bent down to make sure his cheek wasn't broken. His innocence stood out like a sore thumb, a hurt son pleading for his mother. I gave him a wry smile despite my rage.

"What happened?" I asked, as I stepped into her bright and vast office—a shrewd contrast to the rest of the administration area.

"Please, sit." She closed the door and clicked her heels back to her desk.

The room still held a faint smell of eggs and shallots. It made me want to retch all over her manicured desk.

"Mrs. Gupta, you understand we have a zero-tolerance policy for violence."

The image of Shaan's battered face flashed before my eyes.

"Yes."

"Shaan instigated a fight with a student today."

"Was he provoked?" I immediately asked.

"It doesn't matter," she sighed.

"Principal Calaver, we both know Shaan is working on his anger management—" I took a breath, "and provocation does matter."

"How has he been working on his anger management, exactly?"

I saw a glint of menace in her eyes.

"We do exercises at home."

She appeared unconvinced.

"And my husband and I have recently put him into counseling," I lied.

"Is that so?"

"Yes. We just started. I can send you their information as soon as I get home."

Anything to buy more time from the inevitable.

"That won't be necessary, Aleena."

Fuck, this kid is getting expelled.

"I will have to expel Shaan, effective immediately."

Noooo!

I stood up and landed off-balance.

"Please! We are working on Shaan's *tendencies*. We are both working parents, and he needs structure and stability. You are our only hope for—"

Don't say it.

I met her eyes. But she didn't seem to carry a hint of remorse.

"—for preventing the possibility of hospitalizing our child."

It was her turn to stand.

"Aleena, I don't appreciate the pressure you're putting me under." She looked down at her notes and took a breath. "Look, I tried. The superintendent is up my ass, and I can't give him any reason to cut our budget even more." She blew her brown bangs out of her face and squinted.

I really am a piece of shit.

She had given Shaan more chances than any other principal would, and I still tried to manipulate her by using her granddaughter's condition for my son's benefit.

Aaron was right about me.

I felt it rising. It was coming up so fast, I didn't have a chance. I exploded into tears and sobbed into my hands. My capacity for terrible news was full—from seeing Aaron dead on his kitchen floor, to yearning for the sweet memories of our time together, combed through with a slithering guilt for thinking about a man who wasn't my husband. And now, my son was sitting in a freezing hallway with a swollen cheek, expelled for beating up a kid.

From the creases between my fingers, I noticed a frail white hand come into view with a tissue. I looked up to see Principal Calaver standing next to me with a box of Kleenex.

"Who did he hit?" I managed to say between blowing my nose.

"Candace's kid."

"Fuck."

She sank into the seat next to mine and leaned back.

"Fuck, indeed."

I slowly sat back down.

"She threatened to resign and tell the press if I chose to keep Shaan in school," she said.

"But Shaan was also hit!" Anger befriended my grief.

"Self-defense," she remarked, sullied.

She leaned closer, and I smelled the resinous perfume on her wrist. "Look, you know I have a sweet spot for Shaan. But he did hit Thomas pretty hard."

"Is he okay?"

"He's at the nurse's office, icing a black eye."

"And Candace decided to keep working?" I asked.

"No. She only requested to bring you in."

I let out a manic laugh. "Pardon," I said, grabbing another tissue and placing it over my nose. "I should get going. Shaan may get frostbite from waiting too long in your Antarctica-simulated hallway."

She gave a wistful smile and stood as I did.

"Aleena?"

"Yes?"

"You should know—Thomas stayed late with Candace last Wednesday and saw a man sign in to pick up Shaan after wrestling practice." She crossed her arms and glanced at Shaan through the window. "Apparently, Thomas was teasing Shaan about it."

"Rahul?" I asked. He did have an unfortunate repository of bad dad jokes.

"That's what I thought. But I looked back at the sign-in sheet, and it wasn't Rahul."

"Last Wednesday, Shaan came home with Rahul," I remarked, puzzled.

"The name on the sign-in sheet was—" She strolled back toward her desk and looked down at a gridded piece of paper, holding her glasses in place.

"Aaron Moore."

Everything went fuzzy. My eyes locked on a sprawling philodendron resting on the windowsill. Then I was back—back to the ghastly impact of his fist against my lips, the sudden flush of iron flooding the hollows of my mouth.

Pennies. All I could taste was pennies.

"You piece of shit." His voice was low and rumbled against the shockwaves of my nervous system. Those words repercussed through my aching heart and throbbing face as the pea-sized miracle tousled in me.

"Aleena?" Her voice zapped me back to reality. "Do you know him?"

I touched my mouth, expecting the same trickle of blood. Instead, my lips were wilted and dry.

"Yes. I know him," I whispered, suddenly out of breath.

Chapter 8

Eva

The musk watered my eyes. The place was furnished with pine wood and washed with Pine-Sol. I got maybe an hour of shut-eye on Aaron' guest bed when Mr. Tahiti abruptly woke me up and escorted me to my new dwelling. I inhaled and slowly spun, I watched the room come into focus bit by bit: a queen-sized bed with a red rose duvet, a sturdy wardrobe offering only storage for one, a rustic table supporting a boxed TV, and a heavy door opened just enough to show a glimpse of the toilet seat. I could feel the countless souls who had passed through this confinement. I felt insignificant— just another inhabitant among many. It was comforting to feel this way, to have the weight of my tiny little life lifted from my shoulders, to disappear into the pool of millions of others with their own tiny little lives, as they resided at the Montpelier Inn.

The last time I stayed in a hotel, it was at the five-star Elysian Vale in Manhattan. I had just finished zipping up my black lace dress when he grinned, thirsty for more. I could feel my breath catching in my throat, in an effort to remain unfazed. Pounding spikes of pain kept shooting out of my neck from his recently suffocating grasp. I was afraid to pee, as standing made me wince. This is what rape must feel like: an unwelcome and despicable sanction to your body. However, I couldn't pride myself on being a victim, because I wasn't. It was me who approached him at the bar, right as his fourth Old Fashioned coursed through his veins. It was me who sat next to him— next to his wedding ring—and requested a drink. It was me who whispered in his ear, as he engulfed my pheromones, ripe and eager. It was me who told him I liked it rough, as I licked his neck. It was me who escorted him to my room—secluded, alone, and vulnerable. It was me who lay on an opulent bed as he strangled me while entering me in excruciating jabs, stabbing my self-worth over and over again. It was me who giggled as he slapped my face and nearly tore my breasts from my chest as I rode him.

I was far from being a victim. And I knew that as he got back up from the bed and began strolling toward me, ready to pounce again. I stood, frozen in place, deserving of whatever fate rested on the tribulation of my life. I remember seeing his wicked grin—a smile I knew far too well. I watched as his face changed into my mother's, with the same vigor to hurt, destruct, and control. I closed my eyes, ready for impact, when a loud knock reverberated in my ears.

I glared at his salt-and-pepper hair as it pivoted and bobbed toward the door. He cracked it ever so slightly, and after a moment, opened it wide with a smile on his face.

"Looks like you brought a friend," he nudged.

Aubree came in curtly, throwing concerned glances at me—at my body, and at whatever was left of my spirit.

"I would have preferred a more…" he gave Aubree a full look down, "appealing nurse's outfit." She had her mauve scrubs on, hair disheveled, and eyes fiercely wide.

He made his way to the perfectly polished pinewood wardrobe to fetch another condom.

As soon as his back was turned, Aubree ran to me, grabbed my wrist, and beelined to the staircase.

She was down two sets of stairs ahead of me before she realized I wasn't next to her. I heard her heaving breath as she marched back up and took my arm around her shoulder. I was hurt, struggling to move, with pounding pains in all corners of my body. I felt myself melt into her arms as she carried me down.

Aubree, my rescuer.

"What the fuck, Eva?" She hissed as she flagged down a cab expertly.

The autumn brisk titillated my skin as the sharp sound of chaos swam around me. Manhattan was the polar opposite of Sheneoik. Our small coastal town in Long Island had the Great South Bay and the rest of the Atlantic Ocean at our fingertips, but we didn't have this—the hustle and bustle of countless people, consumed in their own worlds while sharing what little space there was among skyscrapers.

In Manhattan, I could be anyone, but in Sheneoik, I was the daughter of the Golden Oyster's owner and chef. If anyone could make a delicacy as cheap as fast food, it was my dad, Jim. He made his living fishing his own oysters and selling them for a fraction of the price. Five-star chefs have made their way to our establishment, offering absurd amounts of money in exchange for his oyster recipe, but he always refused. *"Poor folks deserve quality food too"* was his slogan. He loved saying it so much that for his 60th birthday, I had it framed and hung on the wall next to the shack's entrance.

Dad is who he is because of Grams. She lived five minutes away from the Golden Oyster for the past fifty years. After World War II, Grams took it upon herself to disdain the central government and never be a slave to money. Granted, she was ten years old when she pledged, but once Grams made up her mind, nothing could change it. I loved her. She was a quirky conspiracy theorist and a collector of anything ceramic—a stocky woman with long lashes and even longer hair. She'd often give me ceramic angels purchased from secondhand antique stores because she believed I was an angel sent from heaven. *"Those eyes are proof enough,"* she'd twinkle after handing me my tenth angel in six months. Grams believed Satan drove the wheel when the jury gave Mom full custody, but God always had a plan and brought her granddaughter back to her. I admired her wholehearted faith and wished I could someday get there myself.

Sadly, I had found a home long ago in the devil's nest. I was cursed with Stockholm Syndrome after I moved in with my dad. The damage was done, the addiction had spawned, and I was forced to find my fix in other ways.

I was elated and giddy when Aubree gingerly placed me into a cab. The screeching pain emanating from my body, combined with the adrenaline of escaping a true menace, intertwined ever so sweetly with the comfort of Aubree's arms. It felt like pure ecstasy. It felt like home. She held me as she directed the cab driver where to go.

"How did you find me?" I inquired, enchanted.

"I finished clinicals at Bellevue Hospital and saw your location. I rushed over and asked the front desk for Amanda Armstrong's room."

I liked using my mother's name when I was being self-destructive.

"Are you mad, Aubree? Please don't be mad," I whimpered.

She kept looking ahead, expressionless.

"We need to get you to a hospital," she finally commanded.

The last thing I remember was repeatedly pleading for her not to be angry as I slipped into unconsciousness.

I opened my eyes to find myself sitting on a bed of painted red roses, staring at the hefty black box TV; my nostrils felt raw from the potent smell of musk. I took a long winded breath, settling back to reality. I grabbed my toiletries and headed for the shower. It was time I looked more like myself.

After adding the last of my mascara, my stomach couldn't take it anymore. I was depleted, running on nothing, desperate for food. I scooped up my purse and left, slamming the door behind me.

The hallway was painted maroon, with a matching Moroccan carpet splayed from one end of the narrow passageway to the next. The musk oozed from the dust bunnies on the carpet and the aging wood. *I guess this is the signature scent of Vermont.* In an effort to find reprieve from the smell, I hurried down the stairs to the lobby. The staircase was the main attraction of the Inn—grand and open, with an iron stair spindle railing. I felt exposed as I descended. Instead of scanning for faces in the lobby, I focused on the dupe neoclassical painting of Virgil reading the Aeneid to Augustus. It was massive and hung right above the front desk. I felt connected to Augustus, Livia, and Octavia, as though I was being told a tale that was my life. Unlike Augustus, I wasn't the protagonist of my version of the Aeneid. I was the subject of a cautionary tale.

I didn't notice when I collided into someone and fell hard on the step.

"I'm so sorry." I dusted off my backside as I extended a hand. She took my hold and swayed her way up.

She was pretty—universally pretty. Her thick, long blonde hair flowed past her waist, while her big, rounded green eyes tried to regain equilibrium. She looked to be in her early thirties with a slender and tall body, wearing a bright pink, tight dress and matching plump heels.

"Oh good, I thought I twisted my ankle for a second." She shook her heel and shifted her weight onto it.

She finally looked at me, and her jaw dropped.

"You have the most beautiful eyes."

"Uh—thank you," I stammered.

She rolled her head back and let out a guttural chuckle.

"I'm so sorry, how inappropriate."

"No problem," I said.

I resumed my path and began to descend when she touched my shoulder.

"Do you want to grab a bite?"

I looked back at her and noticed a heaviness in her eyes—a need for companionship.

"Sure," I acquiesced.

Her smile was vibrant, despite the despair painted on her face.

"I'm Bee." She held out her hand to meet mine.

"I'm Eva. Nice to meet you."

Chapter 9

Aleena

It felt as though a kingdom of flies had entered my cranium, buzzing around the open space in my head. I was unable to concentrate on anything other than the faded voice of Principal Calaver muttering the name Aaron Moore on a repetitive loop.

"Mom, watch out!"

Shaan's screech pierced through my haze as I swerved to dodge a car speeding perpendicularly—straight at us. I looked back in a panic, making sure Shaan was in one piece.

"You ran a red light, Mom."

He was out of breath, gurgling through his swollen cheek.

I pulled into a Valero gas station and tried to steady my breath. I couldn't allow myself to think of Aaron right now. I had a beat-up kid in the backseat, his father at least an hour away, while I overextended the meaning of BRB. I had to figure out what to do with Shaan.

"Mom, are you okay?" Shaan's tone was soft and childlike. His voice hadn't yet dropped, and the innocence in his words made me melt. But he also brewed a red temper and he already knew how to play with it.

"Shaan, I'm very disappointed in you." I glared at him through the rearview mirror, watching as his head dropped and his eyes sagged toward his knees. Luckily for me, he still had a fear of disappointing his parents.

Disappointing parents. The thought sparked an idea. I took a sharp turn out of the gas station and headed to Stowe. Shaan knew, as soon as I got onto 189-N, where we were headed. His plush baby butt bounced against the leather seat, excited to see Nana and Nani. I couldn't help but smile. I'd never felt unencumbered giddiness for anyone except... Aaron.

I shook my head, hurling his name out of my brain, and focused on the autumn leaves brightening the myriad small shops as we drove past downtown Stowe. I rolled down the window and put my hand out, making waves against the hard wind—grateful for fresh air in a polluted mind. Shaan dropped his ice pack and followed suit.

The car hopped over speed bumps and rocky gravel as it traveled further into the mountain. Mom and Dad bought a magnificent estate tucked in the woods after Shaan was born. They were happy to own a millennium mansion; I was happy they weren't in Montpelier anymore. They had sacrificed their future by leaving their home in India after marriage to move to the States, just so I could have a better life. There wasn't an interaction that went by without a rendition of their fortitude and grit. The guilt of their martyrdom constructed the earliest stepping stones of my identity—always aiming to be in the top 1% and never disappointing. I had to prove I was worth their sacrifice. I wasn't their daughter; I was their hefty loan. I began paying my dues in brutal languidness from the moment I was born. I detested my parents for viewing me as a return on investment instead of an inherently flawed human being.

I pulled into the manicured driveway, lined with a blossoming array of colors. Flowers were in season—a final hurrah before they perished. The house was custom-painted with light green stucco panels, merging in and out as they countered the giant windows and ample balcony. Their entrance was one to remember: columns of marble wrapped around the veranda, accompanied by plush outdoor seating, a fireplace and grill surrounded by terracotta sheepskin reading chairs. Mom must have flipped through a catalog, pointed at a pretty picture, and paid Dad's main qualifier—his money—to mimic the first thing people would see when they visited: a perfect, unblemished, beautiful front porch.

I think Mom still tells people I'm a surgeon.

Despite all their major screw-ups, they were amazing with Shaan. Dad somehow made time to play with him, and Mom embraced grandmotherhood as if she'd been waiting her whole life for it. They gushed over him like he could do no wrong. It helped that he was boyishly handsome—a nine-year-old with olive skin and hazel eyes. His hair wasn't jet black like mine or Rahul's, but a golden brown, like Dad's grandfather's brother. Apparently, he was the spitting image of the man—the Midas touch of good looks. A light-skinned Indian boy was, undeni-ably, a crown jewel in our patriarchal, fair-skin-obsessed Baby Boomer society. Unfortunately for Shaan, the pendulum had begun to swing the other way, and I, for one, looked forward to watching the world humble my son.

I took in a sharp inhale, unnerved by the upcoming trauma triggers, as it always was when conversing with my parents.

Just keep a cool head, Aleena.

As I began to get out of the car, my phone buzzed with a pop-up text from Officer Sanchez.

"Detective Gupta, quick updates: Margaret Moore wants a lawyer, and we'll be calling Eva in for interrogation after lunch."

The three typing dots appeared, disappeared, then appeared again.

"Will you be there?"

Shaan had already taken off his seatbelt and was reaching for the door handle when I told him to stop and give me a min-ute. He grunted, leaned back in his seat, and began playing Mortal Kombat with his two index fingers.

Okay. I'll have to drop Shaan off in a hurry. The drive back was about 30 minutes, and with a quick stop for a bite, I should be back at the station within the hour.

"Yes, I'll be back in an hour. Call Eva in. I'll interrogate her with you."

I got out of the car with Shaan's dainty hand in my palm and my phone in the other. As we stepped onto the veranda, Mom opened the door with exuberance. Shaan matched her energy and ran into her arms. My heart somersaulted. Against my will, I saw Aaron instead of Mom and me instead of Shaan, running into his arms. The purity of it all tackled me, pushing me back a step. Instinctively, I looked up at the heavens and prayed that the love between my son and his grandparents would never tarnish the way it had for Aaron and me.

"What happened, *beta*?" Mom gasped as she realized Shaan was being welcomed with a swollen face.

Her eyes darted toward me with an accusatory stare.

"He got into a fight at school," I said.

Shaan nuzzled his nose into Mom's baby pink cotton shirt. She wrapped her arms around him and caressed his head, shielding my own child from me.

Let's welcome our first trauma trigger, folks! My mother doesn't trust me.

I felt my diaphragm drop and my heart pang.

"Let's get you inside, *Raja*, and I'll make your favorite."

"Chole bhature?" His voice was muffled, pressed against Mom's shirt.

"Absolutely, my king!" she exclaimed.

Her teeth beamed as the sun reflected off her new veneers. She stepped aside and let Shaan gallop into the house, gone from my line of sight.

"Hungry for lunch, Aleena?"

She took a slow inventory of my outfit.

"I have to get going. Could I leave Shaan with you for the rest of the afternoon?" My voice quivered.

Her eyebrows contorted into concern. "Are you okay, *beta*?"

"Aaron's dead," I blurted out.

"What!" Her hands immediately covered her mouth as she convulsed.

Shit, why did I say that?

"I need to get back to the station," I said in a hurried hush.

Her expression was frozen in shock.

"I'll pick Shaan up later today," I concluded.

I jogged to her and kissed her on the cheek, and she nodded slightly, still baffled.

"Bye, sweetie—please tend to your face!" I called out to Shaan.

He came outside with Spider-Man and Iron Man figurines smashing each other in battle.

"Bye Mom—*bash vroom bash*—" Iron Man was flying victoriously, "I love you."

The way Shaan sounded when he said "I love you." If I could just bottle that up and keep it with me forever.

Spider-Man was already climbing up the wall for revenge.

"I love you too, pumpkin."

Chapter 10

Margo

The yellow lily wallpaper in my hotel room did it for me. I began heaving, mortified by the certainty in Sanchez's voice.

"You have a lot to gain from Aaron's death."

I hadn't put two and two together. I was next in line to Richard's estate. It was my golden ticket out of my atrocious debt, but like Richard, it proved to be the most conniving and twisted of options. I couldn't sell the estate without giving the cops the ammo they needed to arrest me. But the alternative was to be brutally tortured and killed by Sergio for not paying him.

Jail or death. Jail or death. *Jail or death.*

I felt the room closing in on me. I steadied myself by focusing on the wall—a wall full of washed-out yellow, spotted flowers intertwined in a hallucinogenic pattern. The Montpelier Inn and the McLanes Psychiatric Hospital must have shared the same designer. In an effort to distract myself, I lay flat on my back and watched the lilies dance on the ceiling. *Was this what Mom stared at, day in and day out?* I wouldn't know. I wasn't allowed to visit her anymore; yet I couldn't help feeling like I had abandoned her.

The only person I told about my whereabouts was Shannon. For decades, she served Richard as his housekeeper. Richard's ex-wife and Shannon had a special bond, so when I came into the picture, she welcomed me with distaste and pointed comments. She showed her loyalty to Richard in a way that made me the enemy. There was only space in her heart for one of his wives, and it was forever occupied by Aaron's mother. Although I was tempted to fire her after Richard's passing, I knew so little about the mansion's operations that letting her go would ultimately hurt me the most. She was now sewn into the property, and the luxuries of my estate depended on her. So I kept my smile wide and my gestures gentle. Even though I couldn't see it through the phone, I heard a smile creep across her papier-mâché-wrinkled face when I told her I'd be out of town—and stuck at the Montpelier Inn indefinitely.

The craving hit me like a ton of bricks. I was suddenly fiending for a looser state of mind—subdued and icy—hovering somewhere between consciousness and a velvety unawareness I could sink into.

I called Sally.

"Hello?" She sounded like she didn't recognize my number.

"Sally, it's me. Margo."

"Oh, hi sweetheart. Can I call you back? I'm in the middle of something."

"Aaron's dead."

Silence. Did the call drop?

"I'm sorry, what?" She sounded closer to the phone.

I couldn't speak.

"Margo, are you still there?"

"Yes," I said, trembling.

"Okay, don't worry. I'm flying out to Vermont first thing in the morning."

"Thank you, Sally. And—" I didn't know how to ask. "Could you please bring—"

"Of course, Margo. You and I are both in need of a Tranquility Hour."

I allowed my body to sink into the springy mattress. "Thank you," I whistled out.

"I'll see you soon, Margo."

She hung up before I could respond.

Sally and Aaron were close. He had always seen her as a stable part of his life. She'd gone into business with Richard when Aaron was just a toddler and remained partners until Richard's untimely death while Aaron was in college. Over the years, Sally kept in touch with Aaron more as a mother figure than I ever could. Although she built a fortune on her own two feet, Sally never started a family, remaining unmarried and childless. It seemed she found a sense of motherhood indirectly through her relationship with Aaron. And now, the closest thing she had to a son had just died. I was timorous at the potential of an unleashed and raw Sally. A heartbroken and enraged Sally. A vengeful Sally.

"You have a lot to gain from Aaron's death."

A drop of sweat trickled down my forehead as I sat up and scrolled through my contacts. I needed help—guidance, a shoulder to cry on—something. I dialed his number and listened to the deafening ringing, alone in an aged hotel room surrounded by a dizzying array of incongruous yellow lilies.

"Hello." His voice was raspy.

"Hi, is this Mr. Lebewisk?" I asked, trying to suppress the rising panic in my chest.

"Yes, this is he. Who am I speaking with?"

"This is Margaret Moore. The wife of the late Richard Moore."

"Ah, yes! Margaret. How are you?"

"Not too well." I cleared my throat. "Aaron is dead."

There was a brief pause.

"I'm so very sorry." He sounded trained to give condolences—sympathetic with a hint of opportunism.

"I need a lawyer, and I know how close you and Richard were."

"Absolutely, sweetheart."

I cringed. Richard and Mr. Lebewisk shared many of the same values.

"As soon as I get the retainer payment, I'll be on the next flight," he said.

"Oh. I thought Richard had an ongoing relationship with you."

"Yes, he did. But he *died*." He slowed his pace, as though explaining something of common sense to a four-year-old.

"I was under the impression your financial relationship hadn't ended."

The panic was beginning to uproar, sending bile up my throat.

"Listen, Richard was a dear friend of mine, and I watched Aaron grow up. I don't normally do this, but I will reduce the retainer fee to $30,000," he sighed. "I'm sure that's something you can manage."

Translation: Sweetheart, after your absurd payments on nails, makeup, boob jobs, lip fillers, Botox, and whatever else you women pay for, can you add up $30,000 for me? All you have to do is subtract it from the shitload of money Richard left behind for you.

"I'm a bit tight on money at the moment."

"I see," he said, his voice laced with disdain.

Translation: Of course a gold digger would use up all of her late husband's money.

"Please, Mr. Lebewisk, help me. I'm being accused of murdering Aaron!"

He cleared his throat and let a full second pass before saying, "I cannot give you any legal advice, but I—" He took a gulp of water. "I will pray for you."

What the actual fuck. You, me, and your neighbor know you won't pray for shit.

"Please!" I pleaded, my voice cracking as tears spilled.

"Don't cry, Margaret. You're resilient and resourceful. You'll find your way out."

He was silent for a moment, then sighed again. "Fine. I'll give you this advice: find someone with a greater motive, means, and opportunity for killing Aaron. Good luck."

Before I could speak, the line cut loose—a sudden, final whoosh.

Chapter 11

Eva

The scent of dewy grass tingled my senses as I looked up at the vibrant, cloudless sky. Children's laughter drifted from somewhere along the promenade. I couldn't help but smile at the sheer exuberance of being alive. Just after we left the hotel, I got a call from the police station asking if I could come in after lunch. Bee walked ahead of me as we reached the steps of a restaurant with a lookout. Black tables with matching umbrellas were arranged in a trapezoid formation on an elevated wooden porch. A few were occupied by brunch-goers: a cohort of youths deep in animated conversation, a couple covered in full-body tattoos, a polished family dressed up for a hike with their shepherding dog, and a transgender meetup group occupying a cluster of tables.

My phone buzzed. It was a text from Dad:

"The funeral is tomorrow. Where are you?"

"Inside or outside?" Bee asked, as a frail, cheery woman waited at the host stand.

I shoved my phone into my pocket.

"Definitely outside," I said, flaring my nose and drawing in a lungful of green air.

The frail woman guided us to a table furthest from the others but closest to the street. We were about four feet above the ground, altering the view completely. The ever-changing autumn leaves were extravagant from this vantage point, and the mountains appeared more domineering—colossal upheavals surrounding this small town of Montpelier.

I was thankful for the *plop* of water glasses. Our waitress was tan, young, and held an air of angst as she scanned our faces. I took a big gulp of water, shaking off the residuals of this morning.

"I'll have a Farmer's egg white omelet with a nitro brew," Bee said.

Both of them shifted their attention to me. I hadn't looked at the menu yet.

"Do you need more time?" the angsty waitress asked.

The last thing I needed was to nervously search for food items while Bee awkwardly waited. "I'll have the same."

"Good choice," they said in unison, letting out a playful snicker.

I chuckled along as though nothing gruesome had happened, and Bee was just a friend I'd made on my solo trip to Vermont.

"So, you come to this restaurant often?" I asked.

"I love their breakfast. It's to die for!"

Bee had a juvenile exuberance with an unlawful lustfulness. She could bring any man to his knees with her damsel-in-distress demeanor.

"So, are you from here? I haven't seen you before," she asked.

"No, I'm visiting from New York."

Her eyes widened with excitement.

"Oh my gosh! I love New York!"

Let me guess: the shopping, the men drooling over you, the fancy cocktail parties.

"I'm from Long Island, to be more specific," I said quickly, before she began her fairytale experience in New York City.

"I've never been to Long Island. What's it like?"

"It's nice. It's by the water, and it's quiet."

Her shoulders slumped, suddenly aware of our mismatched energy.

"You'd like it!" I exclaimed, trying to remedy my shit personality.

She took a delicate sip of water as her eyes flicked to the front door of the restaurant, hoping for the food to come faster.

"Are you from Vermont?" I asked, staring directly at her, bringing her back to our conversation.

"Yes! Born and raised." Her smile was unnaturally wide, delineated for boring conversations.

I opened my mouth to ask another get-to-know-you question, but she beat me to it.

"What brings you to Vermont, Eva?"

"I wanted a sweet and short getaway. I guess I was feeling a bit burnt out," I confessed.

"I know whatcha mean!" Her Northwestern New England accent crept up. "I work for my daddy's compostin' company." She snorted and sang, "Luckily I'm on the business side." Then she pinched her nose as a *pee-yew* sound came out of her mouth.

I couldn't help but laugh. She had the rhetoric of a kindergarten teacher in the middle of her lesson.

"I'm a thirty-six-year-old woman working for her father, but on the plus side, I consider myself his partner. Anyway, I'm guessing you're not in the composting business out in New York?" she inquired.

"No. I'm an accountant for my dad's business."

"I was always bad at math!" She giggled to herself. "I used to hate being called on to answer equations. I'd mess them up every time."

"Accounting does deal with a lot of numbers, but I like the no-bullshit aspect of it."

"What do you mean?"

"Math is objective. The answer never boils down to an opinion," I said.

"Facts are facts," she concurred.

Our food came out, and identical meals were placed in front of us. The plate was mainly covered with spring leaves and cherry tomatoes, with a small, thick, and soft omelet. It didn't look appetizing. But Bee was already a mouthful in, savoring her bite. I followed and dropped a piece of egg into my mouth. At first, my senses were overwhelmed with egg white and olive oil, but suddenly the flavor morphed into a slew of fresh pesto, enveloped in juicy mushrooms, green pepper, and bacon.

Bee had good taste after all.

"What do you think?" she asked, taking a gulp of her nitro brew.

"It's delicious," I muffled through my second bite.

The third sip of nitro brew sent me flying. Caffeine surged through my body like a live wire, crackling down my limbs and lighting up every nerve ending, my heart pounding in response. My face tingled in what could only be described as a botched facelift—raised eyebrows, wide eyes, and an unstoppable urge to move my mouth.

"Did you hear what happened?" Bee mirrored my expression, the coffee perking her up even more.

I did hear what happened. I was there when it happened.

"No," I lied, as I took another sip.

"Someone died," she whispered, her eyes wild, eyelids nowhere in sight.

I chewed on a massive bite of food and raised my eyebrows as high as I could.

"I know!" She was now speeding up her speech. "That's why I'm being asked to stay at the Montpelier Inn. Rumor has it, the cops want all potential suspects under one roof. How messed up is that? What about our safety? What about—"

I cut her off. "You're a suspect?"

She put her hands up in surrender.

"Woah, woah, woah. I didn't kill Aaron! But someone staying there probably did. I suggest we stick together for our safety during your rejuvenating vacation in Vermont," she grimaced.

"Maybe he committed suicide," I said.

She scoffed. "Knowing Aaron, he was likely killed."

In that case, sticking together might not be a bad idea. I needed leverage in case things went south for me. After all, I was the one who found him dead.

She looked down at her food and then back up at me. "I mean, I hated the guy, but I wouldn't kill him. That's a bit extreme, even for me!"

Who knew nitro brew doubled as a truth serum.

"How did you know this Aaron?" I asked.

"We were high school sweethearts. I loved him. He was the quarterback of the football team, he was homecoming king, and he was mine. Aaron was charming and sexy so much so that I lost my virginity to him, for crying out loud!" she yelled.

The tattooed couple glanced over.

I lowered my head and whispered, hoping she would do the same. "Why did you hate him?"

"He cheated on me." She shook her head, dismayed. "I didn't find out until freshman year of college, but apparently he had an affair senior year of high school." Anger washed her cheeks pink. "The same year I gave him my flower," she spat.

"That's fucked up," I said gently. I put my hand out to touch hers.

Too much? Maybe. But I needed her to feel safe with me.

Luckily, she squeezed my hand and smiled.

"Thanks, Eva. I know it's been forever, but it broke my heart."

"Heartbreak doesn't have an expiration date," I murmured.

"Amen. You want to know the worst part?"

She slid her hand out from under mine and leaned back in her seat. "He cheated on me with Andrew. His best friend."

"Oh shit," I gasped, almost choking on my salad.

"I know, right? Andrew left Vermont after high school and disappeared. But apparently, senior year, when Aaron asked Andrew to practice football drills, it was code for hooking up."

I covered my mouth, stunned. The whiplash Bee must have felt hearing this retroactively was enough to make anyone spiral.

"I found out by reading his text messages," she continued. "I know that's not the most ethical thing to do, but I was using Aaron's phone to text Andrew to come visit us when I scrolled and found pictures of Aaron naked and meet-up times—sometimes right before and after Aaron and I would get together."

"That's horrible."

"I slapped him across the face and left him. I got tested for an STD, just to be sure, and fell into a depression. I flunked out of college, and my dad took me in as an employee." She took another sip of her brew and fixed her gaze on her empty plate.

"This Aaron guy had some issues," I remarked.

Apparently, human decency isn't required to be a top-rated StayHere host.

"That's for sure! He offered me $20,000 to keep my mouth shut."

"Holy shit, that's a lot of money," I exclaimed.

"You have to understand, Eva, at that time our family business was struggling. Composting is a nasty job—and even nastier with the wrong equipment." She took in a breath to steady her tone. "We needed the money."

I gave her my napkin, and she dabbed away the crystal tears pressing against her underlid.

She then exhaled slowly and said, "Now that Aaron is dead, I can tell you about the hush money."

"Sounds pretty logical to me," I consoled.

The corner of her lips lifted into a shy smile. "It feels good to get it off my chest. Thanks for listening, stranger."

I nodded benevolently.

The angsty waitress appeared and asked if we needed anything else. I gestured for the check, and she sped back inside. A line was beginning to form by the entrance. She returned quickly with the card machine, and I swiped my card, determined not to be late for the police station. I pressed the button labeled: Pay the entire bill.

"Lunch is on me," I said.

"You shouldn't have. Thank you!" Bee smiled.

"You may not thank me later," I muttered under my breath.

Chapter 12

Aleena

I rushed back to the station from dropping Shaan off and felt moist spots under my armpits. This pantsuit had no breathability. I had gone to Giovando's Luxury to get it tailored specifically for when my first day as lead detective on a murder case would come around. I wanted to emulate authority and femininity—two forces pulled apart from one another for far too long. The hardy fabric felt symbolic, but now made me look like a wet gorilla. I adjusted my sleeves as much as I could before entering the station.

"Is Eva in?" I asked the cadet at the reception desk.

He flicked his eyes to the computer.

"Yes, Eva Armstrong checked in five minutes ago."

"Fantastic, thanks."

I puttered to the interrogation room and found Sanchez handing a cup of water to Eva. I remembered stealing a glimpse of her as the paramedic wrapped her in an aluminum blanket and checked her vitals. She had been fidgeting—distraught and in shock. Now, her appearance was entirely altered. Her hair was tied up in a long ponytail, and her face was composed of rosy cheeks and a pink gloss. She looked up at me nervously as I entered, and her eyes made me pause once again. Unlike her license photo, as the blues in her eyes moved, they sparkled like sunlight glinting off the surface of a turquoise ocean.

I couldn't help but grin as she submitted to my presence. I would have killed for a girl like her to look at me that way in high school—swelled with respect and a hint of fear.

"Hello, Eva. I'm Detective Gupta."

She lifted herself halfway out of her seat to meet my hand.

"Yes, I saw you at the—" she flinched, "at Aaron's house."

"Yes. Thank you for being here. I know this is not easy, but we have a few questions. Is it okay if I record our conversation today?"

She nodded obediently.

Other than finding Aaron's body, Eva appeared to be an unlikely suspect. Upon checking, she had no previous relation-ship with Aaron, her mother had died in a car crash years ago, and she was now living in the same town as her father in Long Island—not to mention it was her first time in Vermont.

"This is more so protocol than anything else," I said.

I glanced at Sanchez, who was transfixed on Eva—likely lost in her eyes. I took it upon myself to slide the folder from under him. He shifted immediately, straightening his back and clearing his throat.

"It seems here that you arrived in Vermont the afternoon before Aaron's death."

I was momentarily paralyzed by the forensic pictures of his twisted body, cold on the kitchen floor, and his cracked skull, scarlet with blood, wedged between the reports. I refocused on Eva as an avalanche of grief settled heavily on my chest. "Can you walk us through that evening? Any details—big or small—are vital here."

"Do you think he was killed?" she interjected. "I thought it was suicide."

"We are still looking into the cause of death," I said.

With sudden realization splayed across her face, as if my response confirmed he was murdered, she began breathing in short, rapid spurts."I can't believe someone would come in the middle of the night and kill him while I slept next door in his guest house."

She reached for her water and took a shaky sip.

"I wouldn't jump to conclusions, Eva. We're simply doing our due diligence as we find out more."

She wouldn't meet my gaze.

"Don't worry. We already have a lead," Sanchez's voice boomed from my right. "We just want to hear it from your per-spective."

Why the fuck would he tell her that? What did I miss during Marga-ret's interrogation?

"Whenever you're ready," I punctuated, trying to cease the fiery anger swelling up in my stomach at Sanchez's incompe-tence.

She fiddled with her ponytail and took a deep breath. "I came to Vermont for a weekend getaway and booked Aaron's guest house through StayHere."

"Why did you need a getaway?" Sanchez asked.

"I guess I was feeling burnt out at work."

"What do you do?" he followed.

"I'm an accountant for my dad's business."

Sanchez looked down at the other folder marked with her name, which held all of her personal information.

"Please continue," I nudged.

"When I arrived, he welcomed me in and asked if I wanted to come over for dinner. I appreciated his hospitality and said yes." I watched as her eyes sank and her cheeks reddened.

"It seems like"—Sanchez pointed at a note in her file—"you flew into Boston and then drove to Vermont. Why is that?"

"Tickets to Boston were substantially cheaper."

Sanchez nodded.

"Anyway," she proceeded, "he offered me wine, and we began flirting. One thing led to another, and we became intimate."

I felt tears spike the back of my eyes. I swallowed hard, using all my strength to hold them in.

"Did you notice anything out of the ordinary in his house or in his behavior?" Sanchez inquired expectantly.

"Not that I can think of. He was immaculate though—everything was spotless. But that was pretty much it. I'm sorry, the wine hit me stronger than I expected and my memory is hazy. The last thing I remember is waking up in his guest house."

I watched her as she picked at the nail on her right thumb.

"Did you at any point feel scared or in danger of him?" Sanchez asked, with a virile tone.

"No, not at all. Everything was entirely consensual."

"Everything you can remember," I remarked.

"Then what happened, Eva?" Sanchez delicately prodded.

"I woke up the next morning feeling terrible—by far the worst hangover of my life. I was somehow wearing his suit jacket, so I went back to return it."

She choked on her saliva and remedied it with three synchronized coughs. "And that's when I found him."

"Do you remember why you had his jacket?" Sanchez questioned as he took note.

"No. I've been wracking my brain, trying to piece the missing parts of the night together, but I'm falling short." She locked eyes with me. "I'm sorry."

She resembled Shaan so much at that moment—eyebrows knitted with sorrow, eyes wide with childlike innocence, and gaze soft with repentance.

I couldn't hold her stare, so I looked down at the open case file. Something caught my eye: a phone call transcript a cadet had with Mr. Armstrong.

"You said you work for your dad's business. What does he do?" I asked.

She scratched the back of her ear and shifted in her seat. "He owns an oyster restaurant."

"So you must be close to him to be working for him?"

I felt Sanchez looking at me.

"I guess so," she paused. "He's a good father."

"It seems like he was surprised to hear you came to Vermont."

She remained still.

"As a daughter and as an employee, you'd think to tell him before you left the state."

I could feel the adrenaline dancing in my chest.

"It was pretty last minute," she muttered.

"Why?" Sanchez asked. He had hopped on my bus.

I kept reading the transcript, but I had nothing. The conversation was short, and although her father was surprised, he didn't sound alarmed that she took a weekend getaway without telling him. *"Eva knows how to take care of herself. If that's what she needed, I'm glad she did it."*

"I felt burnt out and just needed some time to myself, away from the stress. I didn't think it was necessary to tell him," she said.

My gaze rose to meet hers, and her shoulders dropped, but her expression remained neutral.

"We all need self-care," I capitulated.

But I wasn't done.

"How was your relationship with your mother?" I asked.

She suddenly clenched her jaw as her eyes glazed over. She took a breath and reached for her water, buying time.

"It was okay," she threaded.

Although there wasn't much on Amanda Armstrong, and her criminal record was clean, the death of a mother was bound to activate some emotion.

"It says here she died from a car accident just a block away from your home," I probed.

She stared down at the Styrofoam cup, then yanked her ponytail tighter, pressing it hard against her scalp. It was clear she was uncomfortable.

"It was a hard time in my life." She flickered her head toward Sanchez, who must have held a blank expression. "I'm sorry, but what does this have to do with the case?"

"Just trying to understand you better," Sanchez said reassuringly.

Her right index finger jolted upward, as did her eyebrows. "Oh, I almost forgot, I met Aaron's ex-girlfriend, Bee."

Bernadette Wright. Aaron's first love.

I had watched them nibble at each other's ears by the lockers and hold hands between classes, day after day, like a nightmare on repeat. Years later, when Aaron and I got together, he told me how she had abruptly broken up with him in college and left him heartbroken. While we were in bed, he shared that he hadn't been able to open himself up to love since their breakup—until one day, I caught his attention. *"You make me believe in love again, Aleena,"* he had whispered in my ear as he kissed my neck.

Eva leaned closer to the table.

"Bee told me something that might help with the case. Aaron cheated on Bee back in high school—with his best friend, a guy named Andrew."

Air caught in my throat, and the pen I was holding fell onto the table with a *clang!* Andrew Styversant. The other heartthrob of Westwood High. Together, Aaron and Andrew dominated the school. Both were athletically built, with broad shoulders meeting at taller than six feet, charming eyes, and brilliant smiles. While Aaron's eyes were narrow and green against his ivory skin, Andrew's were large and topaz-hued against his deep brown complexion. Every guy wanted to be them, and every girl wanted to be with them.

When Bee started dating Aaron, I remember feeling the purest form of jealousy. I had the biggest crush on Aaron—a hormonal, fantasy-riddled, obsessive crush. But as he played football and went to parties, I played video games and went to math competitions. We were part of two different worlds; and no matter how much I wished to be a blonde-haired, blue-eyed cheerleader with a banging body, I would see a chubby brown girl with a bad case of cystic acne stare back at me in the mirror. I never told Aaron we went to high school together the whole time we dated—that we were in the same English class sophomore year, or about the countless love doodles I drew on the margins of my notebook as I stared at the back of his head. As far as I know, Aaron died only knowing me as an adult. As for Bee, I was sure she didn't even know I existed in high school.

Andrew, on the other hand, knew me. I tutored him in calculus senior year. He was flunking and on the verge of being kicked off the football team. According to Mrs. Styversant, Andrew's grades had dropped suddenly and significantly. So I was hired—as the top student in our math class—to help him get his grades back up enough to stay on the team. Andrew was smart and a quick learner, but his mind was elsewhere, anxiously focused on his phone. When I had his attention, he'd smile at me with those big, golden eyes as I explained derivatives. His tone was gentle, while his features were rugged with a strong jawline and bulging biceps. Despite his popularity, he was kind. I felt privy to a world I was denied access to, so I paid it no mind when I was often ignored for someone more interesting on his phone.

"Aaron's ex-girlfriend Bee told you this?" Sanchez asked.

We had Bernadette slated to be interviewed, but Andrew hadn't made the cut.

Eva nodded.

"Thank you for the information," I managed to spit out.

I was shell-shocked by Aaron's past—by how twisted it truly was, and by how naive I'd been. That is, if Bee was telling the truth.

Eva nodded and watched me for a moment.

I felt utterly exposed. *Could she hear my pounding heart?*

Sanchez took my cue as I closed the case file.

"Thank you for your cooperation today. We will be reaching out if we have any more questions. We do ask that you stay at the Montpelier Inn until further notice," Sanchez said in a monotone voice, clearly scripted for every interview.

Eva got up from her seat and shook Sanchez's hand.

I stood and wiped my hand on my pantsuit before extending it. She took it and smiled, holding on to my hand for an extra beat before she sauntered out of the room, closing the door behind her.

I pushed the chair back with an agonizing *squeeeeek* and leaned over to turn off the camera.

"Why did you tell Eva we already had a lead?" I jabbed.

"Margaret Moore did it," Sanchez interrupted.

"Did she confess?"

"No, but she has motive and no alibi," his eyes widened with excitement. "She's in some pretty bad debt and appeared skittish—like she was desperate enough to kill for money."

"I'll be the judge of that," I said, mentally preparing for a late night at the office to watch her interview recording. I didn't like how convinced he was to put Margaret Moore behind bars.

"You'll see," he muttered to himself as he began collecting his things.

"Either way, you can't go telling people we have a lead without even consulting me." I glared at him.

He nodded, deflated.

"At this stage, everyone Aaron was associated with is a potential person of interest," I said firmly.

His eyes dropped to his lap, avoiding mine. He had crossed a line, and he knew it.

Then he looked up. "You're absolutely right. I shouldn't have told Eva."

The way he looked at me—full of regret—gave me the urge to put a hand on his shoulder and tell him everyone makes mistakes. But I held back, reminding myself Sanchez was a grown man, capable of handling feedback. I cleared my throat to break the cold silence echoing off the stale walls, just as a knock sounded at the door.

"Come in," I yelled.

A cadet opened the door slowly. He was skinny and short, with a butter face and thick brown hair. He looked like a college freshman, with his rounded cheeks and youthful eyes.

His gaze flitted between Sanchez and me, clearly nervous. "Sorry to interrupt, but the autopsy report is here."

"Thanks," I nodded. "We'll be headed to the coroner's office. Make sure Dr. Waltz is in."

"Yes, Detective." He gave a salute and instantly regretted it as he pivoted on his heel to leave.

"Cadet Stevens," Sanchez called out.

He spun back around, his cheeks flushed.

"Get Andrew Styversant to Vermont. Now."

Chapter 13

Margo

The hotel's continental lunch was malodorous, almost nauseating. But it was the perfect opportunity to scope out someone who appeared guiltier than me. Different faces were lazily making their way to the lobby and the food. Vermont was an eclectic place: nature-seeking, hygiene-avoidant residents with overgrown hair and remarkable body odor. But on the flip side, they were some of the most hardy and alluring people I've ever seen—the epitome of natural essence. I scanned for my target. Preferably a shifty woman with something to hide.

Families streamed in one after another, with a few sightings of single men moving toward the meatloaf. I watched as two women came down the stairs, both stunning. They paused by the entrance and scanned for an open table. They stood oddly distant from each other, seemingly acquaintances yet compatible enough to be best friends. I could slip into their orbit and become friends with them. I should have people in this town know I existed, in case I was whisked away.

I decided to get up and introduce myself. As I got closer, my knees buckled and my head jerked. *Was I having withdrawals? A panic attack? Or both?* My vision began to blur, and I took a sharp right into the restroom. The last thing I needed was to be coined as the crazy lady.

The restroom smelled of fresh bleach and lavender. The dark granite countertop had been recently wiped, leaving streaks of soap. I placed my hand on the edge of the counter, the coolness easing my frenzied state of mind. My face was disoriented in the mirror, as though a ghost had blown fog on it. When I felt confident enough that my knees wouldn't give, I reached for the faucet and turned on a heavy stream of cold water. I splashed the water on my face and observed my mascara melt down my cheeks as my skin grew taut from the cold. As my vision cleared, I noticed my baby hairs had clung to my skin from the water, and my lips sat in a perpetual frown. I looked like a sad clown.

I felt like a sad clown.

I took three long, tempered breaths and waited for my heartbeat to steady. I forced my mind to focus on the white stream of running water. Once my pulse evened out, I grabbed a paper towel and wiped the smeared makeup from my face. As I worked to fix my hair, an elderly woman walked in and offered me a gentle smile.

"Are you doing okay, dear?" her reedy voice asked.

"Just fine. Thank you," I said as politely as I could.

She nodded slowly and moved toward the stall right behind me.

I may have to remain in the shadows. If I couldn't walk up to two human beings and introduce myself without having a meltdown, then I sure couldn't befriend them.

Suddenly, Karen's bright smile and high cheekbones flashed in my mind—a specific memory of her on our childhood balcony. I saw the sun's rays glowing behind her, a golden halo around her jubilant expression. A woman with onset schizophrenia was capable of giving me my most cherished memories and the happiest time of my life. If she could do that for me, then I could do this for me. And if not for me, then for her. I control my emotions, not the other way around.

I grabbed my purse, straightened my back, and rolled my shoulders. Deliberately turning my frown upside down, I pranced out of the bathroom like I was stepping onstage as a pageant winner—beautiful, confident, approachable, yet unattainable. I scanned the lobby, ready for a second chance at making friends but the crowd had dissipated. *How long was I gone for?* Most tables were vacant, with sporadic seats filled by disparate faces and the two women were nowhere to be found.

My stomach growled. It rumbled so hard that the old lady—who had just made her way out of the bathroom—did a double take.

"Good thing there's food here!" she quackled.

"Sure is!" I flashed my teeth in a wide smile.

"Have a good day, young lady." She waved me off before I could thank her.

Bet your wrinkly ass I will have a good day.

Making friends aside, I had more pressing matters on my agenda. I had to find someone more suspicious than me in this eclectic town, so I could get the cops off my back.

But first, food.

I wasn't going to attempt to eat the scraps of mushy meat and stale bread of the buffet. I turned toward the hotel's entrance and stepped outside and was in direct view of the mountains, bright from the overhead sun. The air was crisp, with a hint of bite. I loved this weather—it was the perfect sweater weather. The autumn colors were in full bloom as I twirled to take in my surroundings. Although the mountains were majestic on their own, the brick-lined streets, polished and clean, felt almost utopian—untouched by the erosion of life's grimmer parts. I ended my twirl and fixed my eyes on a sign three blocks ahead: a grocery store. *Perfect*. All I needed was caffeine and probiotics. I might even indulge in a croissant. My mouth salivated at the thought, and I headed straight to Ranger Groceries.

The parking lot was small, with a few pickup trucks sprinkled among family-friendly SUVs and sprawled grocery carts. Although the day was bright, the closer I got to the grocery store, the duller everything seemed—like the sudden onset of a storm. But when I looked up, there was nothing but blue sky. *Was I hallucinating?* It felt like my subconscious was bleeding into reality, and I was doing a convincing job of it. The terror of Officer Sanchez's accusation was affecting me more than I realized. I wanted to vanish. I sucked in a cool breath of air to withstand the titillating excitement of running away—of being a fugitive of the law, disappearing into the forest forever. Just me and Mom, dancing around trees in our flowery, flowy dresses, making headbands from leaves and branches. Gypsies of the night.

But Karen was locked up in a mental asylum, and I might be on the hook for murdering my stepson.

I forced my mind blank and made my way inside. The grocery store was basic, with a few aisles filled with only the essentials. The produce section took up half the store. An old Bohemian woman with long silver hair, a flowy skirt, and layers of jewelry browsed alongside a young couple dressed for a hike, sniffing their way through herbs and cruciferous vegetables. I headed straight to the dairy section in the back and grabbed a vanilla bean yogurt—my favorite sustenance. I grew up hating the sour taste of bacteria-infused dairy, but as my days grew shorter and my nights stretched into endless despair and self-deprecation, my stomach cried for help. The probiotics temporarily remedied the poison. Unfortunately for my gut health, I could never part ways with coffee. I liked my coffee black: strong, pungent, and acrid. It was the only way I could feel the effects of caffeine. Part of me needed pain to feel good. I couldn't fathom a life in which good came as its own wrapped gift, without any contingencies. Coffee had to taste like ass, so I could rejoice in its stimulants.

My hotel room had a kettle and a mini fridge, so I grabbed some instant coffee, two individually wrapped croissants, and a yogurt, then made my way to the register. The self-checkout lane was closed, so I had to stand in line behind the hiker couple. They had filled their cart with broccoli, carrots, potatoes, meats, and dairy but most of it was lined with protein bars. I now noticed the rows upon rows of stacked protein bars by the front entrance: a hiker's fuel. I nodded at the cashier when my turn came up. She had dreadlocks but was pale like concrete, with small muddy eyes and dark eye bags. She looked like an unkempt mouse—and she spoke like one, too.

"Good afternoon," she said, barely making eye contact.

"Good afternoon."

She couldn't find the barcode scanner for the yogurt.

"I guess many people don't buy yogurt," I joked.

She looked up and took in my face, starting with my jawline and making her way up to my forehead. She looked dazed and half-asleep.

"Oh," she grunted, still twirling the yogurt.

Her eyes shot back up.

"Are you Margaret Moore?"

What the fuck?

"Who's asking?" I demanded. I wanted to snatch the yogurt from her hands and run out.

Her lips spread open, showcasing her teeth. Many were missing, and the others were stained brown.

"I'm Carla."

"How do you know me?" I asked again, anger creeping up my neck.

She itched her dreadlock, inserting her index finger deep into her bushy hair.

"I'm a friend of Aaron's."

Aaron would never be seen with the likes of her.

"Is that so?"

She let out a giggle and twirled her dread. *Did I see a twinkle in her eye?*

"Well, I'm a fan of his," she said through gritted teeth.

Goosebumps rose on my arms, and my chest went heavy. She gave me the creeps.

"Find someone with a greater motive, means, and opportunity for killing Aaron."

The concoction of fear, anger, and suspicion that had painted my face began to melt. This woman looked textbook crazy, and I needed textbook crazy. She already frightened me and was clearly infatuated with Aaron. If I could get the police, especially Officer Sanchez, to experience her firsthand, maybe— just maybe—I could pass the guilt baton and walk away a free woman.

I took a soft breath and smiled. "It's always nice to meet one of Aaron's friends."

Her eyes shrunk as her smile deepened. "Yes," she purred, "Aaron's friend." She glanced around, then down at her watch. "My shift is ending. Would you like to come over for lunch?"

I looked at her. Her cheekbones were high with anticipation, and her eyes glistened—not just with desire, but with a raw, disarming innocence. If she killed Aaron, there had to be a reason. And what reason would she have to kill me? Unless, of course, she was simply unhinged and found some twisted thrill in ending a life.

She waited for my response, eyes wide with the giddy impatience of a child. I could take her if things went sideways. If she tried anything, I'd kick her in the crotch and run. I just needed to keep my guard up, that's all.

I should be fine.

All I needed was incriminating information—just enough for Officer Sanchez to leave me alone. And the best chance of getting that was in her safe space. Her lair.

HER CAR REEKED OF BURNT CIGARETTES AND STALE BEER. THE backseat was buried under a mess of unwashed clothes, piled high enough for a family of guinea pigs to nest in. She blasted AC/DC the entire ride. Before I knew it, we were out of the quaint town of Montpelier and climbing into the mountains. The sun had vanished, leaving us on a dark, winding path, deeper and deeper into the trees. I studied her as she drove. Beneath the wear and tear—expedited aging from drug abuse and a lack of hygiene—her features were striking: naturally arched brows, a button nose and thick lips. She was skin and bones, her cheeks hollowed out, but when I glanced at her hips and strong legs, I could picture the hourglass figure that once defined her. She must have once been beautiful.

I turned and looked straight ahead. It's sad how we ruin ourselves.

She took a sharp right onto uneven dirt. The car jolted upward, crackling and groaning, forcing me to grip the grab handle.

"Sorry it's a bit bumpy, but we're almost there."

She was leading me somewhere secluded. Panic began to bubble up. Maybe I wasn't fine after all. Maybe I'd become just another fatally gullible adult, blind to the glaring signs of my own imminent death.

She finally pulled up in front of a large wooden shed. It leaned off balance, like it had been punched repeatedly by the wind. A blue corrugated plastic sheet was poorly plastered to one side, flapping rhythmically in the breeze. At first glance, the shed looked abandoned, standing alone in the middle of overgrown grass and ancient trees. It had taken us three minutes from the winding road to get to the shed. Two miles on foot, give or take. If I ran, I could be out in fifteen minutes. Fifteen minutes to escape. Fifteen minutes at the mercy of century-old trees and an invisible trail. Fifteen minutes between life and death.

The engine sputtered to a stop, and she motioned for me to get out. She was electrified, skipping in tiny jumps toward the shed.

"Come on in!" she burst, like fireworks.

I stepped delicately onto the cold dirt, clutching my bag of coffee, yogurt, and croissants. My heart hammered. My stomach twisted into knots.

Leave, Margo. Leave.

As I glanced at Carla—still holding the door open for me—I suddenly saw Officer Sanchez's menacing grin, the same one he'd wear when opening the gates of prison for me.

I had to get the cops off my back or die trying.

Chapter 14

Eva

As soon as I got out of the station, I felt my pulse hammering against my ears, washing out the noises around me. All I could hear was the quickening of my breath as I felt the warmth of his body pressed against mine. Now, he lay cold on a slab of metal, forever unconscious. As expected, the police were suspicious of me—but for a different reason. I had no idea the police had called my dad. I had to call him and clear things up. I rushed to my rental car and slammed the door shut, pushing the rest of the world out.

"Eva?" His voice was hoarse and distracted.

"Is this a good time?" I asked, knowing it wasn't.

"Any time is a good time for you, sweetheart. Are you doing alright?" I heard his heavy feet shuffle away, likely to the storage closet.

"Yeah, I'm fine, Dad. Sorry I didn't get a chance to call you. I came to Vermont for a short break. Unfortunately, my experience has been anything but."

"I know. The police called me asking questions, something about someone dying," he said, lowering his voice.

"What did you tell them?" My knuckles whitened as I tightened my grip around the steering wheel.

"I told them I knew nothing—and I don't. What's going on, honey?"

"I booked a StayHere, and the host was found dead the following morning." I sank back in my seat.

"That's terrible! I'll book a ticket and come to Vermont."

I could hear him pacing. My father hated flying, and he still had tomorrow to endure.

"I'm okay, Dad. The police just want me to stay in Vermont for a little longer, but I'm safe."

"Eva, the funeral is tomorrow." His voice was shaky, and my heart sank. Without my permission, tears leaked effortlessly down my cheeks like a waterfall.

"I won't be able to attend. I can't leave," I choked between sobs.

"They've detained you?"

"No, but if I leave, it will look bad." I held my breath, and so did he, letting a whole minute pass.

"That's understandable, honey." He cleared his throat. "Please don't harbor any guilt for not making it home by tomorrow. I love you, and I'm here for you, whatever you need."

I wanted to wrap my arms around him and lay my head on his chest. I wanted to inhale his idiosyncratic scent of salt water and cheap cologne. For the first time in my life, I yearned for my father instead of my mother.

"Thanks, Dad. I love you."

"I love you more. Stay safe and be careful."

"Also, Dad, did you mention the funeral to the police?"

"I didn't say a word."

The last thing I wanted was for the cops to find any reason to bother those back home while they were grieving. The less they knew, the better.

Chapter 15

Aleena

"I have to make a quick phone call before we go meet Dr. Waltz for the autopsy." I nudged Sanchez as he grabbed his coat.

"Sure."

He draped his coat back over his chair and moved toward the coffee pot.

I slid into the bathroom and made sure no one was in the stalls. The last thing I needed was for a cadet to eavesdrop on a detective's family troubles.

I rang Rahul.

"Hey, sweetie." His tone was muffled.

"Driving back home?" My voice reverberated in the empty air around me.

"Yeah. Today felt long and draining."

I could hear the traffic in the background.

"It's about to get a bit longer," I said.

"Oh no, what's wrong? Is it Shaan?"

I caught myself gnawing at the inside of my cheek. "He got expelled."

Silence followed, then a *swoosh* from a motorcycle.

"Are you serious? What happened?" Rahul always made every situation more manageable. There was a gentleness in his tone regardless of the circumstance.

"He punched a kid."

Silence again.

"Fuck," he blew out.

"I know. We need to figure out what's going on with him." I deliberately skated around the root cause of Aaron appearing at my son's school asking for him.

"Where is he now?" he asked.

"He's with my mom. Can you pick him up?"

I heard him ask Siri to re-navigate.

"Also, I'll be at the station late today. I'm so sorry, baby." I felt my eyebrows crease and tension pinch my forehead.

A long sigh came through the other end of the line.

I'm an inadequate wife—and an even worse mother.

"It's no problem, sweetie. I know this is a big case, and I understand if you need more time at the station."

He deserves so much better than me.

"I love you, Rahul. Thank you for understanding." My heart ached.

"I love you too. Also, I think we'll need to bring Shaan to your parents while we figure something out," he said circumspectly.

I was afraid of that. My therapist had been adamant about setting boundaries with my parents. We'd discovered that the main triggers for my panic attacks were rooted in how they'd made me feel my entire life. I took up therapy like one takes up rap music—because it was trending—but I was glad I did. I made headway with my anxiety and overall sanity. But as soon as I got involved with Aaron, I stopped going. I didn't need a professional telling me what I was doing wasn't good for me. In an effort to live out my adolescent fantasy of being with Aaron, I diluted the progress I'd made in therapy about my parents. Was I healed from my parents' controlling tendencies? Could I allow my son to be repeatedly exposed to a similar environment? Did I have a choice?

Rahul took my pregnant pause as ambivalence.

"I know it's not ideal, Aleena, but we don't have much of a choice. I can't take leave from work, especially not right now, during a critical merger, and you can't either."

"I know, but maybe we—"

Any options I could think of wouldn't work. Even if Rahul and I alternated days off, we'd both end up playing catch-up at work, leaving us useless. We also didn't have close friends we trusted enough to watch over Shaan. But in reality, we didn't trust Shaan to be under anyone else's supervision.

"You're right," I surrendered.

"It won't be for long. With the merger finally in motion, I should hit some downtime soon and take time off."

"And hopefully we can close Aaron's case, and I can also take time off."

"It was Aaron? Like Aaron Moore, who was found dead this morning?" Rahul exclaimed.

"Yes."

Rahul and Aaron bumped into each other once. It was at the grocery store, when Rahul was making a quick stop for diapers. He took Shaan with him to give me time to rest. Rahul came back home irritated—Rahul's version of irritated—still gentle and caring, with an undertone of perplexity. He told me he'd run into a guy I used to know, who was asking pointed questions about me. He said his name was Aaron and that he acted cocky, as though he held a sense of authority over Rahul. I tossed in bed, my back to Rahul, feeling ashamed. Rahul took it as disinterest and never spoke of it again.

"Oh," he said.

For the kindest person I know, Rahul's reaction was surprisingly flat. The man was dead, and Rahul still couldn't summon much empathy. Maybe more had happened that night between him and Aaron, or maybe Rahul just didn't forgive easily. Either way, it was a topic I sprinted away from.

"I'll call Mom to let her know you're on your way," I finally said.

"Sounds good. And do tell her that we're planning to drop him back first thing tomorrow."

"Will do," I grimaced.

I peeked out of the bathroom and watched as Sanchez leaned back in his chair, sipping from his mug and laughing with Cadet Stevens.

Great, he's still distracted.

I went back into the bathroom and dialed my mom.

"Hello?" She sounded confused. Did she not have my number saved?

"Mom, it's me," I said.

"Aleena! How are you?"

I heard cartoons in the background and could almost smell the *aloo parathas*—a childhood tradition of mine: Spongebob and flatbread stuffed with spicy potatoes.

"Rahul is on his way to pick up Shaan."

"Great!" Mom said. "I'm making aloo parathas. Rahul can stay for dinner."

"That's nice, Mom. Thank you."

"What else are moms for?"

A kick straight to my aorta. I cleared my throat and kept myself focused, pushing the trigger bots away.

"Mom, can you take care of Shaan for a few days?" I asked.

I heard her place the rolling pin down and grab the phone. Her voice came through clearer, louder.

"Why can't you, Aleena?"

"I'm in the middle of solving Aaron's death," I jabbed.

"I understand but your main priority is your family." She clicked her tongue. "I'm the one fulfilling your responsibilities."

My blood began to boil. My eyes stung as tears pooled on my eyelids.

"I'm a detective." I was suddenly out of breath, my words a weak whisper.

"You're a mother and a wife first, Aleena," she declared with a magisterial pronouncement.

I turned and looked at myself in the mirror. I saw a little girl with no voice to stand up for herself and no idea who she was in this world. I saw my mother towering over her, commanding her. I blinked hard, allowing the tears to make their way down. As I looked at the mirror again, the image morphed. This time, it reflected reality: a grown woman, wearing a slim-fit navy pantsuit in a bright bathroom. I was at my workplace, in the middle of solving a potential homicide. I'd worked tooth and nail to be here—and if I had to compromise a bit, then so be it. That's what support was for.

"Mom, will you support me or not?"

She resumed flattening the dough with a hum, placing me back on speaker.

"Of course I will, beta. Shaan can come anytime."

"Great, thanks."

"No problem. I will make extras for you too," she said, intoning a Lata Mangeshkar song.

That was it. The call had ended. The roller coaster of emotions was over. My mother would always be oblivious to the damage her words caused, and I would always be triggered by them. But I found my footing and weathered the storm. I'll take that as a win.

I turned on my heel and left the bathroom, wiping the tears off my face in one quick sweep.

"Ready?" I poked Sanchez's shoulder.

He stood up immediately while making a final smug comment about the New England Patriots to Cadet Stevens and met my stride as we walked out the station.

We reached the coroner's office in under five minutes. The parking lot was empty, and the air was crisp. It hit me then—I was about to see Aaron again. Well, Aaron's corpse. Would he still have that shiny brown hair and those soft, pink lips? Would his jaw still look as defined as it did when he clenched it in desire for me? I could almost feel his fingers tracing the places where my body curved. I shook my head in quick movements, lurching the thoughts out of my mind and onto the lined gravel. *Rahul, Rahul, Rahul.* My husband Rahul was the man I vowed to be with—the man who loved me for me. His deep, dark eyes were framed by gentle, beautiful contours, his thin nose, immaculate facial hair, and radiant smile. My handsome husband. Rahul is alive and well—stable, secure, and best for me. Aaron was now just a memory.

Formaldehyde swarmed my nostrils as Sanchez opened the door. The smell of death. Rather, the smell of scientific death. I remember running to the bathroom and regurgitating my lunch the first time I smelled formaldehyde. It was in my college Biology 101 lab, when we were dissecting thick worms. Before class, I was convinced I'd pursue my parents' vision of becoming a doctor. But as I watched misshaped crumbles of pasta floating in toilet water, I knew I couldn't do it. I couldn't stomach being so close to ill bodies. Now, standing in a purposefully chilled hallway incubating countless corpses, I questioned why I got into law enforcement in the first place.

I turned to look at Sanchez. He was wincing, his lips wired tight and his nose flared.

Two large door flaps swung outward from the far right corner. Dr. Waltz clipped toward us, removing his contaminated gloves.

"Dr. Waltz," I said, while he was still six feet away, signaling a no-contact greeting.

"Detective Gupta and Officer Sanchez. Pleased to see you both," he nodded.

His voice was deep and gravelly, as if his vocal cords were out of practice. His face was clean-shaven and slick, resembling a wax figure. He was a stocky man with large limbs and even larger hands. I often wondered how he managed delicate examinations. Still, he was the best in Vermont.

"Follow me," he gestured.

The long charcoal flapping doors were designed for easy gurney access. Thick rubber seals framed them, and a small peering window was set high. I didn't want to enter purgatory. I wanted to go home—to be the wife to Rahul and the mother to Shaan that everyone expected me to be. I wanted to run far away from the painful ache in my stomach and the sharp thorns of unbearable grief. I shuddered in disbelief and pushed the doors open.

It took a second to readjust to the light. It was bright, with dark sore patches. The brightest part of the room was in the center, above a still body. The translucent toe was looped with a single string and paper. Aaron Moore was inscribed neatly across the top of the slip.

What if he fidgeted? First his fingers, then his toes. What if he was in a meditative trance this whole time? What if he got up and pierced my soul with his knowing gaze and slick grin? What if he glided off the slab of metal like water and flowed into my arms? What if this was all a dream, and I woke up in the car, riding with him to our secret spot in the woods—happily in love? What if everything else since was just a figment of my imagination?

I'm a terrible person. Truly.

"Detective Gupta?" Dr. Waltz prodded.

"I'm sorry, what was it that you said?" I flickered to Sanchez, who was eyeing me.

"Don't worry, Detective. Death is uneasy for most," Dr. Waltz said, his reassuring words wrapping around me like a protective cloak. "Now, I asked if you're ready to proceed?"

He was positioned over Aaron with a file in his hands.

"Yes," I said, moving closer.

Just then, I noticed human-sized black bags sporadically placed on stainless steel slabs around us, like a nightmare.

"Typically this takes a few days but I ensured expedited results based on the notion that this may be a potential homicide." Dr. Waltz recited expertly.

"Thank you Doctor," Sanchez said.

I sucked in a mouthful of disinfectant air and forced myself to look at Aaron. He resembled a male rendition of a haunted sleeping beauty, particularly his mouth. His lips were parted and slightly asymmetrical. His tongue was nowhere to be found.

"We took tissue samples from his oral cavity and from the blunt force trauma to his head." Dr. Waltz sounded distant as my mind processed the lamented version of Aaron.

"At first, it appeared as though the cause of death was his fall, as fragments of granite were found in his brainstem. But after reading the forensics report—which expressed doubts about a fatal fall due to the angle at which he had landed—I ran a toxicology screen just to be sure."

Dr. Waltz was the best in the state for a reason.

He slid his glasses down to the bridge of his nose and read the chart. "Elevated levels of opioids were found in his blood, as well as in his oral cavity."

Only his eyeballs shifted upward, toward us.

"Aaron Moore died from an overdose of fentanyl."

What!?

Aaron despised hard drugs. He would scrunch his nose and purse his lips every time we saw a homeless person in a hallucinated state. He believed drugs were reserved for *"repugnant people"* and proclaimed that only the weak were susceptible to addiction.

"Is there a way of knowing if he was a user of fentanyl?" Sanchez asked methodically.

Dr. Waltz looked down at his paperwork again. "There were no signs of extended opioid use in his system. This man kept himself healthy."

Aaron was obsessed with his physique. The last thing he'd do was voluntarily take opioids. Whoever poisoned him was counting on it looking like a run-of-the-mill rich boy overdose.

"Thank you," I said, swallowing the rocky buildup in the back of my throat.

"As for next steps," Dr. Waltz said, placing the file on the table behind him, "a family member can proceed with funeral arrangements."

What's left of him, soon to be buried, swallowed whole by earth's core.

"Let's get Margaret Moore back to the station," I muttered, still looking down at Aaron, allowing my words to float away.

Sanchez snatched my command and responded with a triumphant, "Certainly."

Chapter 16

Margo

The inside of Carla's dwelling was more spacious than I expected. My eyes landed on what looked like a blown-up version of a KidKraft kitchen set, outfitted with basic home goods. A black, stained futon sat in the back right corner, in front of a makeshift window—her living room. Against the back wall stood a foldable table with a portable stove, a microwave, and a mini fridge buzzing beneath it—her kitchen. Nearby, a large gray bucket, a bar of soap, and an old shampoo bottle served as her outdoor shower caddy. On the far left was a twin-size mattress topped with a galaxy-patterned comforter—her bedroom. She stood to my right, smiling ear to ear. Behind her was a blue tarp draped over what looked like a large rectangular structure. I wondered what she was concealing.

"Would you like to eat your breakfast here?" she asked, pulling out two metal folding chairs and placing them in the middle of the shed.

She gestured for me to sit as she plopped a frozen pizza into the microwave. The smell of government cheese and pepperoni quickly flooded the space, making my stomach groan. I unwrapped a croissant and took a heaving bite. As I chewed, the sunlight caught the end of something outside, sending a sharp twinkle of light into my eye. Carla was singing the rest of Witch's Spell as she waited by the microwave, her back to me. As though called to approach the light, I placed my bag of food on the chair and walked toward the window. The floorboards creaked with every step I took.

Carla threw a sharp glance from the corner of her eye but remained in the kitchen. I smiled at her as I took another step around the futon.

"I like your view," I said, before even seeing it.

My comment was drowned out by the loud *beeeeeep* of the microwave.

A sunray touched the top of a gray porta potty. It stood in a bed of verdant grass with a red sign stuck to the front: PRIVATE PROPERTY.

"Hot, hot, hot," Carla whimpered, now standing next to me, jamming a steamy bite into her mouth.

She must have floated over; I hadn't heard her approach. My heart fluttered with fear.

"Oh yes, if you need to use the bathroom." She pointed at the porta potty, her nail browned with dirt and greased with oil.

Something else caught my attention. Right behind her finger stood a house. From my vantage point, all I could see was the top corner of it, with trees covering the rest. I tilted my head and caught a glimpse of the siding: mustard yellow. I held in a gasp.

We were about half a mile away from Aaron's house.

"So, how do you know Aaron again?" I asked, making my way back to my designated chair.

"Oh," she said, fluttering her gaze toward his house, "we were friends in high school."

She shuffled over and joined me as she took another bite. "I had a huge crush on him. He was the quarterback and the most popular guy in school."

I didn't know Aaron when he was in high school. I only got to know him afterward, right after Richard and I got married. I knew he had been a quarterback, though, because one night Richard got off the phone, walked over to where I was reading a magazine, and slapped me across the face. Then he started pacing, sputtering rage-filled phrases: "*My fucking son didn't get a scholarship. What an impudent boy. The one thing going for him is gone. What's the point of being a quarterback in high school if you can't do anything with it?*" It was the first time he hit me.

Later that evening, I was crying in the bathroom, icing my bruised face, when Richard knocked delicately on the door and apologized. He said he'd been furious at his son, ashamed of him, and had taken it out on me. Then came the make-it-up-to-you monologue. He told me he was going to buy me a diamond bracelet and book us first-class tickets to Bora Bora. Just me and him, on our honeymoon.

I was trapped. I couldn't go back home to Roxden, and I couldn't reject him. I had become a damsel in distress, and my savior was also my captor. I opened the door and flung my arms around his neck, hugging him. I remember it viscerally, as if it were yesterday: the wave of terror that washed over me as he hugged me back.

"Are you out of it or something?" Carla asked, watching me.

I caught myself staring at my feet, frozen in torment. I cleared my throat and pinched myself back to the present.

"Sorry about that. So, how was he back then? I only met Aaron after high school."

"He was amazing. We would flirt sometimes at parties..." her voice trailed off. "The way he could make you feel like you were the only girl in the world," she swooned.

I couldn't picture Aaron ever flirting with the woman sitting across from me. But it had been over ten years, and the chasm of an unhinged woman was apparent.

"Did you end up going to the same college?" I inquired.

When did Carla go from being at preppy high school parties to this?

"Oh God, no! School was not for me." She looked down at my lap. "Do you want a spoon for your yogurt?"

I didn't want my lips on anything in this shed, but I had to make her think I was comfortable.

"Sure."

She got up and grabbed a plastic bag from a cheap drawer unit tucked in the dark corner. In the plastic bag, she fetched a plastic spoon. She handed it to me and waited as I opened the yogurt.

"I got in with a bad crowd after high school," she admitted.

Her downfall.

"I tried to get my act together after a few years and got a job at Rangers Groceries."

She dragged her chair closer to me, instantly tightening my nerves and stiffening my back.

"Please don't be scared, Margaret," she pleaded.

I saw it then—the pain in her eyes, like a dog waiting for their owner to come back.

"You loved Aaron, didn't you?"

"I did," she said with a sigh. "I've been trying to figure out what happened to him."

She pulled herself upright, absently tapping her fingers on her shins as she moved slowly toward the blue tarp.

"Me too." My voice came out like a fleeting thought—a whisper of desperation.

She grabbed a handful of the bare blue tarp covering the rectangular apparatus and swished it off, leaving it limp on the floor. But what the tarp had covered wasn't bare in the slightest. It was a large cork board pinned with pictures, timestamps, and labels. An entire investigation board. My gaze bounced from one photo to another, until I saw my own. A photo of me entering Aaron's house a week ago. *Shit.*

"Carla, I would never kill Aaron," I declared.

"What were you doing here last week?"

I could lie, but she'd see right through me.

"I'm in some serious debt." I couldn't bear to look at her as shame flushed my cheeks. "I came to Vermont last week to ask Aaron for money." The words spilled out of my mouth like screws stuck to my tongue—harsh and excruciating.

She bit her nails, glancing at the photo of me on the board and then back at me. "Did he give you any money?"

"He basically told me to fuck off."

She didn't seem convinced.

"You have to understand, Carla. I was desperate enough to ask my stepson for money, and I lost my dignity in doing so. And as soon as he rejected me, I went home embarrassed and ashamed."

If I could see myself, I'd hope to see the eyes of a pleading woman, someone honest and hurt. I met Carla's gaze and saw that expression on her.

She believed me. *Thank God.*

She took the pin that held my photo against the board and moved it. She placed me under a category she'd labeled Not a Suspect.

"Can I come see the board?" I asked, still glued to the hard metal chair.

She motioned me over.

Photos of Aaron's driveway were splayed across the board, each taken at a different time, showing different people coming and going, different parked cars, even different weather.

"Where do you take these pictures?" I asked.

I was skating on thin ice. A swipe too hard and she'd close up shop.

"From my roof," she said grimly, with no sense of pride in her innovative tactics.

I didn't recognize most of the people. Men in suits, families in kayaking gear, and women in pencil skirts. But one woman did catch my eye. She was dressed casually, in slacks and a white top. The photo showed her shaking Aaron's hand next to a Toyota Corolla. Her eyes, even from a distance, gleamed. Ocean-blue irises—the same eyes I saw at the Montpelier Inn. The same girl I was going to befriend.

"She's Eva Armstrong. The last person to see him alive," Carla mentioned, following my gaze.

"Do you know anything about her?" I asked.

Now, she was Aaron's type.

"Not really. She had booked his guest house, and she's still in Montpelier." She nibbled on her cuticle. "I hate that I didn't catch what happened last night."

She pointed at another picture. This one was chaotic: red and blue flashes, people everywhere, and Eva in an aluminum jacket, looking up at the sky and straight into Carla's focal point. Her eyes were wet, her jaw stiffened, and her eyebrows raised. She looked petrified.

I thought back at all the candid shots displayed at the Beacon Hills Boutique Art Gallery. I'd watch characters dripping with money, stroll in and pick enlarged photographs of mediocre and uninspired subjects, costing them $20,000 a pop. Those prized frames evoked a sliver of what Carla snapped.

"You're a talented photographer," I said.

She was taken aback.

"Thank you," she giggled.

"You should keep these photos. Especially this one." I pointed at Eva's shiny, saddened eyes.

A hue of confusion and flattery showered her face.

"But I digress," I waved. "Do you have any leads?"

"Not yet," she said, taking a step toward her kitchen. "It could be anyone."

Leave it to Aaron to make enough enemies that anyone could end his life.

A particular photo stood out. I hadn't noticed it before, but now it seemed impossible to miss. It showed Aaron's driveway with a car parked out front. What caught my attention, amid the sea of other photographs, was the way the car was parked: pretentiously, parallel to the house rather than in the designated guest spot. A shiny silver Audi GT.

Sally's car.

Carla's curvy handwriting postmarked the photo: September 21st. Two days before Aaron's death.

What was Sally doing at Aaron's house?

I snuck a glance over my shoulder and saw Carla working on the kettle, her eyes turned away from me.

I couldn't help it. I slowly unpinned the photo and slipped it into my pocket.

"Would you like some tea?" she called, still with her back to me.

"Uh—" My heart pounded.

Then my other pocket sprang into a sudden vibration, sending shockwaves through my body.

A call from the Montpelier Police Station. Were they calling to arrest me?

Fuck. Fuck. Fuck.

"Are you going to get that?" Carla was now watching me suspiciously.

I forced some color back into my face and smiled. "Yes." I gestured toward the front entrance. "Could I step out for a moment?"

"You don't need to ask for permission," she chuckled.

Right. I wasn't being held hostage.

As soon as I stepped outside, I inhaled the fresh, wooded air. It was cooler in the woods, the trees blowing me kisses.

"Hello?"

"Mrs. Moore, this is Officer Sanchez."

My heart dropped to my stomach.

"You had a lot to gain from Aaron's death."

"Yes, hello. Any news on Aaron's case?" I asked as my voice trembled.

"Mrs. Moore, we need you to come down to the station," he said apathetically. "We need you to collect Aaron's body."

Great. Now I was responsible for burying the man, with all eyes on me.

"Can you get here first thing tomorrow?" His voice was growing impatient.

"Yes, I'll be there."

Chapter 17

Aleena

I clicked stop on the videotape. The end of Margo's interrogation took me by surprise. When I left to pick up Shaan from school, she had seemed nervous and even a bit misplaced, but by the end of her interrogation, she was completely depleted. As Sanchez pressed forward with his questioning, her demeanor began to unravel until it became entirely disparate. I watched as another person surfaced from beneath her façade—one of fear, loneliness, and estrangement.

"You have a lot to gain from Aaron's death."

Sanchez's menacing tone as he uttered those words gave me goosebumps. I had never heard him hiss that way. He was determined, like an arrow in search of a bullseye. I had paused the tape on Margo. She looked ossified. I could envision her heart pounding, slamming against her chest cavity with full force, while her face glistened with sweat. As her eyes drooped under the fluorescent light, so did her confidence. This was the face of damaged goods. My vision tunneled as I focused on her visage, slightly pixelated and cinematic. I felt like I was the camera lens, sitting in the interrogation room, watching her shed her outer skin and expose her true self.

As the clock ticked to 10 p.m., I began diving into her background. She intrigued me. After an hour of reading through a web of related reports, I started connecting pieces of her past. I found out that Margaret Moore—formerly Margaret Vessel—grew up on Skid Row with a severely mentally ill mother. Roxden was a tough neighborhood, and McLanes was a swanky mental hospital. Margo had been desperately poor and married rich and *old*.

A sharp sound bounced me out of my intimate time with Margo and back to the dark and deafening station. It was just me in the station, Margo in the camera, and Rahul ringing my phone.

"Hello," I said.

"Sweetie, when are you coming home? It's late."

"I was actually packing up, babe. I'll be on my way," I reassured.

I heard a soft sigh. Rahul was tired. Tired of a demanding job, tired of Shaan's outbursts, and tired of me.

"Okay. Drive safe." His tender voice hugged me as I got up and turned off all the buzzing electronics.

"I will."

I hung up and made my way out of the station.

I SLEPT LIKE A LOG FOR THE FIRST TIME IN MONTHS. MY BRAIN, body, and soul work on their own schedules, charge their own rates, and deliver their own reports. I expected to toss and turn all night, replaying a series of horrific snapshots like a business presentation: Aaron's bloody body on white tiles; Sanchez's steely tone as he scared the living hell out of Margo; Shaan's swollen cheek after hitting a kid; Mom's judgmental gaze as I dropped him off; Aaron's body again, cold and motionless on the metal slab; Rahul's drowsy eyes watching me fall asleep; and then back again to Aaron's crushed head on the kitchen tiles. But no. All I saw was blissful darkness. I slipped past REM sleep and plunged into deep, unbroken rest, waking with a fresh sense of renewal as the sun perched over the mountains in our backyard, casting a honeyed glow across the bridge of our bed frame.

A new day, and a new me. I would no longer allow myself to be the grieving ex-girlfriend, holding back tears every other minute. Instead, I was going to embody the lead detective I'd always dreamed of becoming—in what I believed to be a homicide.

Rahul took it upon himself to drop Shaan off to Mom's on his way to work. He truly was the perfect husband and father. I added a mental note to buy him a thank you card on my way home tonight.

Thank you for loving me despite not knowing the type of woman you married.

I was left to my own devices, with a piping-hot thermos of coffee and a gray pantsuit on. This outfit wasn't tailored to fit me just right, and it showed. But the first day was over, and now we were expected to look rumpled in honor of solving a case.

What I didn't expect today was to see Andrew Styversant.

When Sanchez got a hold of him, he noted Andrew's arrival for tomorrow, and I had planned to call in sick with food poisoning. Although I looked substantially different since high school—with a clearer face, years of practice in makeup and hair, as well as a new physique thanks to academy training—I couldn't risk it. Neither Sanchez nor anyone else in the department knew I was previously connected to Aaron or had attended high school with most of our suspect list. If they did, I'd be kicked off this case, or worse.

I'd spent my entire life skating around sin—so focused on being perfect that I never learned from small mistakes, leaving me unprepared for life's unavoidable transgressions. What was left was a deeply flawed, regretful woman. A saint until I wasn't. An honor-roll student and devoted daughter until I became a cheating fiancée. A faithful wife until the man I once called mine was found dead—and all I could think about were his hands on my waist, his body pressed close, his sugar lips tickling my neck. I was a detective with strong ethics until I found myself tangled in a case I had no business touching. So when I saw Andrew Styversant sitting at Sanchez's desk, bathed in morning light, I felt the fragile world I'd built come crashing down.

I scrambled to hide from his sight. Ducking behind the other officers waiting for their morning drug of choice to brew, I went in for my second cup of the day. Peering over Cadet Stevens's shoulder, I watched Andrew answer questions. He carried an amorous air of ruggedness that could make anyone fall desperate for him. Although cute in high school, he was downright gorgeous as an adult.

"Detective Gupta," a whimpered voice called my name from the lobby entrance.

I turned to see Margaret clutching her Chanel purse, leaning on her right heel. For a second, all I could see was the tormented face from the video recording. But as I watched, her expression softened ever so slightly. She appeared smoother around the edges and a bit lighter. Yet she still held an impending fear in her eyes — like a kid caught stealing candy but accused of looting heroin.

I approached her with a final glance over my shoulder at Andrew and Sanchez, still meandering, unaware of my presence.

"Hello, Margaret." I extended my hand, and she shook it delicately.

"Hi, detective," she said, tilting her head toward Sanchez. "I was told to come to the station regarding Aaron's body." She looked down at her feet, and so did I. Her manicured French tips were edging forward as her nail beds pushed them out, a slow expulsion of a carefully manicured lifestyle.

"Yes, we won't take too much of your time." I gestured for her to take a seat on one of the waiting chairs, away from the crux of the station. I sat next to her.

"Aaron's autopsy came in, and we received news that his cause of death was due to an overdose of a potent opioid called fentanyl."

She was aghast. "But! Aaron hated drugs!

The protocol was to bring Margaret into an interrogation room before the conversation continued. I was then to turn on the video camera and have the red light record all her words and expressions onto a file that could live on a compwuter forever. But if we moved even an inch, I would lose whatever fizzing connection I felt sitting next to her, away from everyone else. I had to continue our conversation here.

I was already breaking so many rules.

"Is there any reason why you think Aaron would overdose?" I asked empathetically.

She looked down at her purse and back at me. For a moment, she appeared inflated and ready to pop, but she finally shook her head.

She had soft rouge freckles lining her cheeks and nose, previously concealed with expensive makeup. She was beautiful, with her red hair and fair skin. Her amber eyes still held a glimmer of youth despite her hollowed eye bags. I could smell the acetaldehyde from a night of drinking on her breath. It was clear this woman had years of suffering under her belt.

"Okay," I said, "if you think of anything, please reach out to me directly." I felt for a business card in my pocket and handed it over. I wanted her to feel comfortable with me as a refuge from the big, ugly monster of Sanchez's accusatory words. I wanted her to come running to me when whatever she was cooking up failed miserably.

Our eyes locked, and for a moment we disappeared into a parallel universe, floating as two broken souls intertwined by a common thread. Maybe I was too close to this case and couldn't see clearly, because in that fraction of a second, I felt deeply protective over the stranger sitting next to me.

She was the first to break the spell. "With regards to Aaron's body?"

"Ah, yes." I shuffled back into my pocket for another card. This one was glossy. "Please have the funeral home you choose pick up his body as soon as possible."

I sounded curt and transactional as I handed her Dr. Waltz's card. She looked down at the two names printed on two different cards—two people she wished she'd never met.

"Yes. I'll work on funeral arrangements right away."

And with that, she stood, tossed the cards into her lavish handbag, and walked out of the station.

Before I could process my next steps, Sanchez tapped me on the shoulder.

"Detective Gupta, we have Andrew Styversant here."

I turned to face him with a gentle smile.

"Fantastic," I said.

Fucking fantastic.

"He's ready for his interrogation."

"I think you can handle this one on your own, Officer Sanchez. I've been impressed with your interrogation style, and I think it's time you ran point on one."

I hoped he couldn't sniff the bullshit on my words.

He was surprised. "Detective Gupta," he started, "as much as I appreciate the vote of confidence, I think you should join." He glanced around and lowered his voice. "I shouldn't have divulged confidential information about the case to Eva when I assumed we already had a lead." He shook his head. "I'm not ready yet."

He wasn't ready. His impetuousness with Eva and his threats to Margaret were rookie mistakes.

But who am I to talk?

"Let's go then," I motioned to him with a pat on the shoulder.

I hoped Andrew didn't pay me much mind when I tutored him.

The interrogation room felt colder than usual. Maybe it was the first one of the day, and the lingering body heat and human emotions hadn't built up yet. Or maybe it was just me, sitting across from Andrew Styversant. He smiled at both of us as I extended my hand and introduced myself as Detective Gupta. He shook it but quickly diverted his attention to Sanchez. He felt more comfortable with him.

We were off to a good start.

I let Sanchez lead the interrogation, so as to keep myself in the shadows of Andrew's memory of this experience. All the questions were being answered; all the details of his friendship with Aaron were being discussed, until Sanchez prompted, "Did you have a sexual relationship with Aaron Moore?"

This is when everything went to shit.

Andrew's face dropped. He was both shocked and horrified. Suddenly, he was more comfortable with me. He proceeded to speak to me as though Sanchez was the bully and I was the principal.

"Aaron came on to me senior year of high school." He was distant, his memory sucking him back in time. "We used to practice scrimmages together and talk about girls and video games. Until one day, he started talking about me instead of his girlfriend Bee. He would say things about how I looked and how I made him feel. I brushed it off, but he continued to make those types of comments." He took a shaky sip of water. "Then he started asking me if I ever saw him as more than a friend. He had this look. A look almost impossible to say no to."

I knew exactly what that look was: the twinkle in his eyes, the slight lift of his posture, the subtle curve of his grin. It was the look of a master manipulator.

"I also knew if I didn't say what he wanted to hear, he would turn me into a complete outcast at school." He fiddled with his thumbs. "I know high school is nothing compared to the rest of your life, but back then, it was everything to me. When you're seventeen, you have no clue about the world. You barely know anything about yourself. Maybe I did like him in that way? I didn't know. I was clueless."

I nodded, giving him the validation he needed to continue.

"Aaron used to tell me that this was what I was missing in my life. That as my best friend, he knew me better than I knew myself."

I saw his Adam's apple move in a heavy gulp.

"He was wrong. I wasn't interested in men—not in that way. Not even a little. But it was too late." He took a quick, shameful glance at Sanchez and rested his sorrowful eyes on me. "I know you think I could've said no, but I couldn't. He had a hold on me, and I was too weak to break it. So we kept it going." He winced. "I felt trapped and taken advantage of by my own best friend."

When Andrew's grades suddenly dropped and he was often distracted by his phone during our tutoring sessions, it wasn't due to the usual popularity habits; it was the result of a complicated form of coercion.

"When high school finally came to an end," he said, "I left with no intention of coming back. Until today."

Sanchez's tone was uneven. "Where were you between 1 a.m. and 3 a.m. on September 23rd?"

"I was asleep at my house."

"Can anyone attest to that?"

Andrew scratched his head. "My dog," he said with a faint chuckle.

Sanchez looked at Andrew with discomfort and scribbled in his notebook.

Andrew shifted in his seat, aware his joke hadn't landed. "I got home around six and stayed in for the rest of the night. I have security cameras at all my entrances that can confirm that. I can send you the footage from that night."

I saw Sanchez smile and nod, making another note.

Andrew moved his gaze to me, studying me with growing perplexity. "I'm sorry, but… are you Aleena Gupta?"

I immediately shut off the camera, sensing Sanchez's suspicious glances cutting through me.

I couldn't speak. The ground beneath me felt like it was trembling—an impending earthquake. All I could do was nod. A simple, perfunctory gesture that became the catalyst for an avalanche: my career, my reputation, my relationships, my integrity—all tumbling down.

Andrew beamed. "Oh my! You look so different, Aleena. I almost didn't recognize you."

Almost.

Sanchez looked between us like a spectator at the world's wildest ping-pong match. "Please fill me in," he said flatly.

I shot an icy glare at Andrew, then at Sanchez, still unable to get my larynx to cooperate. If only they could understand nonverbal communication as well as I did.

"We went to high school together," Andrew said, with some respite from his grueling past.

I didn't need to look at Sanchez to see his head boiling. The way he hissed at Margaret, seeped in a murmured undertone of mistrust in women, was now being validated once again.

Time froze. I felt myself detach, hovering above the scene like an eagle surveying wreckage. There I was: stiff in my seat, anguished and paralyzed; Andrew, buoyed by the recognition of an old classmate; Sanchez, simmering with fury. This moment would be seared into my memory, branding me forever.

Chapter 18

Eva

I left Aubree a voicemail.

Hey, sista from another mista. Sorry, these past couple of days have been INSANE. Since I last updated you, I've been stuck in Vermont. They want everyone associated with the case to stay nearby until further notice. So here I am, burning precious oil. I'll be missing the funeral because of it. I cried in my hotel room for five hours last night. Five hours. It was 8 p.m. when the bulb of sadness reached my throat, and then midnight when the entirety of it soaked my bed sheets. Talk about a grieving evening.

A knock interrupted my flow.

Oh shit, someone's here. But I should be back home soon. I'll call you later, love you!

I hung up the phone and jammed it in my back pocket. Before opening the door, I took a quick glance in the bathroom mirror to make sure no apparent residues of last night's cryfest were stamped on my face. My eyelids were puffy but tenuous enough for the general population.

I swung the heavy door open to see the Barbara Millicent Roberts version of Barbie in the flesh, standing with two cups of coffee in hand. It was uncanny how much Bee resembled the infamous plastic doll. Her blonde hair, long and straight, was pulled up in a ponytail, and she was dressed in a baby blue halter tank top and jeans. She stood taller than me, wearing white pumps and carrying a matching handbag.

"Has anyone ever told you you look like Barbie?" I said with a giggle.

"Why do you think I dress like this?" She smiled and handed me a cup of coffee.

"You shouldn't have," I said, hugging my fingertips around the heated cup.

"I owe you for lunch," she bowed.

She then pushed past me and sat on my unmade bed. Her eyes scanned the room, soaking in the blemishes of my inhabitancy.

"How did the interrogation go?" she asked, taking a cautious sip of her steaming coffee.

"It was a bit tense, but overall fine."

Fine, because I gave the cops a new lead—thanks to you.

"Why was it tense?" she asked.

"They're just sussing everyone out." I paused, thinking back to Officer Sanchez's kind voice. "But it seems like they already have a lead."

She placed her coffee on the corner table and jumped up from the bed. "Hurray!"

She came back to me and put her arms around my shoulders. "Any idea who the lead is?" Her breath was caramelized, and her perfume floral.

"No idea," I remarked with a smile. "When are you going in for an interrogation?"

"I'm still waiting on a time," she said as she spun around. If I didn't know any better, I'd think she was drunk.

"You've got brandy in your coffee?" I teased.

"I wish," she laughed. "Come with me. I want to show you something."

She looped her arm through mine and opened the front door with her other hand, leaving her pink, lipstick-smudged coffee cup on my corner table.

She drove a custom-painted periwinkle Mini Cooper with the roof peeled back. The air flew through my hair like a blow dryer set to cold. The sensation was healing the soggy corners of my misery. I closed my eyes and sat back for most of the ride as the radio played Katy Perry. Bee was also in her own trance, driving deep in thought. There was something impeccably detoxing about riding in a convertible, in a capital town predominantly forest.

I lifted my sun-sunk eyelids when we parked. The smell of brisk, fresh air instantly morphed into something more acrid. She had stationed her car in front of an oak fence enclosing a red brick house with an expansive backyard. The backyard had its own fence, topped with coiled wiring. Jutting out from behind were massive steel containers. I saw nine, spread out asymmetrically.

"Welcome to my home and—" she stretched her hands up, "our family business!"

Her father's composting business was smaller than I imagined. With the 20 grand they accepted as hush money from Aaron, my mind had architected a factory. But there was something nostalgic about their setup—the raw grunt of a family business. I'd come here to throw away my orange peels.

She opened the fence latch in one quick motion, and I followed her in. Wild bergamots were overtaking the outskirts of the home, adding a touch of femininity to an otherwise primitive property.

The screen door swung open, hitting the brick wall with a loud *clang!* A heavy-set man in a hunter-green flannel shirt, with a sandy, tangled beard and pearly blue eyes, stood at the footsteps like a bouncer to a hillbilly nightclub.

"Who is this!?" he roared vehemently.

The hairs on my arm stood up in command.

"Daddy, stop! It's *ma* friend," she pleaded.

"I told ya, Bee, you must be tellin' me when ya bringin' folks 'round here." His accent thick as wood, voice loud as thunder.

"But Daddy! It's *ma* house too!" She kicked her right heel against the ground in frustration.

"But honeybun, you know why—" he stopped himself and scratched his balding head.

"I can leave," I muttered.

I want to leave.

Bee took me by the arm and shook her head. "You're not going anywhere, missy."

She dragged me forward and into the house, forcing her father to move aside. I looked down at my feet the entire second it took to get inside her home, avoiding eye contact with the other, galled and averse host.

"Daddy, can you please get us some water?" she yelled over her shoulder.

I heard heavy steps move away and into the kitchen.

"Sorry about that," she giggled. "Daddy can seem scary, but he's harmless."

We sat at their dining table, covered in a plastic tablecloth. The wood under the tablecloth was authentic, and so were the sturdy chairs we sat on. Framed photos of Bee at different ages were propped up on all four walls. The room toggled a thin line between a shrine for Bee and a display by a doting father.

The sound of crackling wood grabbed my attention. To the right, a fireplace was working overtime, enclosed by a beige mantle. Apart from a fascination for warship collectibles, a photo with a golden-glitz frame sat in the middle. It was a family photo with Bee as a child, a different version of her father, and a woman I could only assume was her mother. She had Bee's blond hair and slender build, tall and graceful, but her sharp jawline and smoldering gaze made her look like a Scandinavian model.

"Is that your mother?" I asked, pointing at the photo.

Bee nodded ardently. "Yes. She died when I was in middle school from cancer."

I reached for her hand. "I'm sorry for your loss." I looked at the smiling woman again. "She was beautiful."

"Thank you." She took a quick look at the kitchen and whispered, "Daddy hasn't been the same since."

I glanced over at the picture again and analyzed her almost unrecognizable father. His tangled beard was replaced with a chiseled chin and smooth cheeks. His head of hair was ample and slicked back, and his smile was wide and vibrant.

Bee's dad entered the dining room with two clinking glasses of ice water. He placed one in front of me and the other in front of Bee, reaching for her shoulders and planting a kiss on her head.

"I'm sorry for how I was earlier," he said, scratching his head. "We're not used to company at the house." He pointed to the giant cylinder bins. "Over there, that's a different story. The more the merrier!"

"No problem," I reassured him. "I'm Eva, nice to meet you."

"I'm Frank." He awkwardly reached his hand out for a shake.

I took it, and my hand was immediately engulfed in his. I gave it a stern movement, like I did with Dad's customers.

Bee was smiling ear to ear. "Eva is from New York. She's the one who found Aaron dead." The way she said those words—like she was talking about the weather.

"Good riddance," Frank said without a stutter.

"Daddy! Have some compassion," she nudged him.

"Why should I?" he said, turning up his nose. "He was scum of the earth with how he treated my lil' girl."

He removed a stainless steel flask from his back pocket and took a generous swig. Bee didn't seem to notice.

No shame in the whiskey game, I guess.

"Do you know anything about the composting business, Eva?" His words slurred ever so slightly as the dark poison kissed his tongue.

"No, sir."

"It's a nasty job," he said, shaking his head in disarray. "But it also requires acute attention and precision."

He lifted his flask to his mouth, emptying its contents. "Best be sure, I'm the best in town." He dropped the flask on the table and crossed his arms. "Fun fact. The human body is also compostable," he scoffed.

"Daddy!" She slapped him on the bicep. "Stop." Her voice had gone down a couple of octaves, and her words were sharp.

A wave of fear washed over me.

"Daddy is going senile! Sorry, Eva," she shrugged, giving her father a menacing glance.

Frank babbled something about how it was a father's duty to protect his family while walking out of the living room and toward the backyard.

"Gotta get back to work!" he yelled from outside, the sound seeping through the semipermeable backdoor and straight into my fight-or-flight limbic system.

"I am *soooo* sorry," Bee's words fluttered around me. "My dad gets super weird when he's drinking."

She let out a chuckle and shook her head, like a mother watching her toddler trip over its own chunky feet. She wasn't fazed by the oddity of what had transpired.

I shifted in my seat, contemplating an exit strategy, when curiosity got the best of me.

"Why did your dad mention composting bodies?"

"Oh, that!" She shook her head and laughed. "Since I dropped out of college, he's taken on dark humor. He's always trying to be morbidly funny, but never succeeding at the funny part."

She took a sip of water, lost in thought. "I think it's been his coping mechanism—trying to find humor in the grimmer parts of what life handed us."

My heart panged for the loss of a good mother.

"You know what?" She pushed her chair back and stood up. "Let's get out of here."

I looked around her quaint family home one more time. It truly felt like a blast from the past—a rendition of a 2001 Wright household. A moment of life frozen in time, when Bee was a child and Bee had a living mother. Frank's favorite memory, trapped in these four walls.

"Was there anything you wanted to show me?" I asked.

Why the fuck did you bring me here?

"It must be hard being stuck in a place where you know no one, and I wanted you to know you have a home in us." She smiled wryly. "I didn't expect Dad to be like this, but he is truly harmless."

I felt bad about spilling the beans to the police about Andrew. She shared her past in confidence, and I turned around and abused her trust for my own safeguarding. At the time, I assumed I wouldn't spend time with her again. But now, standing in her childhood home, I felt a tinge in my chest.

"This is very kind, Bee. I'm glad I met you."

Bee's home was the first one I'd been in since Aaron's. I never used a hotel room for more than one night, and it was already beginning to feel suffocating. I missed having compart-mentalized rooms—different spaces for different thoughts. I was thankful to be welcomed into a home, far from my own.

But something nagged at me. I couldn't shake the feeling that she was hiding something. Maybe she was compensating for her father's bad decisions. Or her father was compensating for hers.

Chapter 19

Margo

I didn't need to pick up Sally from the airport, because Sally had a whole team of hyperactive, busybody squirrels working on her every need. She showed up at the Montpelier Inn, right in front of the very room I was staying in. I had just come back from the station, still processing my conversation with Detective Gupta. How was I supposed to take care of all of Aaron's funeral arrangements when I couldn't keep my own shit together?

I heard a perfectly pitched knock on my door.

"Margo, it's Sally. Open up."

I reached for my handbag and grabbed the photo I stole from Carla. Another knock—harder this time.

It had to be her car. It was the same exact brand and model, with identical curves and shine. Sally kept all her possessions in tip-top shape, like her touch couldn't blemish. Never did I see her car unwaxed or dull—nor her—except for once. Even at Richard's funeral, she wore Christian Dior from head to toe, with a lace headband covering her face just enough to shade the grieving streaks. The closest I've ever seen her be human was when she decided to once over on Tranquility Hour, taking another snort of the iridescent snow powder, a magical blend with traces of fentanyl. We never took another snort. That was the whole point of micro-dosing: staying within the limits of what was formidable for a woman of great wealth. *"I need to dissociate for a moment,"* she had said, licking the rest of it from her gums. She slumped back on her Italian bouclé wool sofa and began removing her hair extensions and peeling off her eyelash extensions. It was the closest I'd ever felt to her—high and unhindered.

What was she doing at Aaron's two days before he died?

Any idiot would know that Sally was shady but to go as far as to murder the very man she thought of as a son? A glacier sweat ran down my spine.

And here I was, opening the door for her.

"I hope I'm not disturbing you," she said as she pushed past me.

She was holding a burgundy Saint Laurent tote bag, with a matching pantsuit and dusty pink Jimmy Choo Bing 100 heel mules. She looked like a real estate agent for the rich and famous.

"I took care of all the funeral arrangements." She approached me with the intention of a hug but settled for a hand on my shoulder.

That was Sally in a nutshell. Just when I started to doubt her, she'd swoop in like a fairy godmother, wand at the ready to clean up whatever mess I'd gotten myself into. But I'd also learned she could double as the evil queen at a moment's notice.

"You shouldn't have," I said.

Still, I couldn't help but feel a heavy weight roll off my back.

"My team also secured a marble mausoleum at Green Mount Cemetery."

"Richard would have liked that," I murmured.

He always said he wanted his legacy to be planted every-where. Boston for Richard, now Vermont for Aaron, and hope-fully somewhere far away for me.

"That's incredibly thoughtful, Sally. Thank you." I raised my hand to meet hers.

"The funeral home will be picking up Aaron's body today." She looked at her oyster Rolex. "We are printing invitations for Wednesday's memorial service as we speak."

Sally's team was good — overworked and underappreciat-ed, the cornerstone of corporate America. That is, if you con-sidered Sally to be corporate America. I, for one, certainly did.

"Phew," I exhaled. "I don't know how I would've done it without you."

While there was some truth to it, if the decks had been stacked differently—and Sally had never returned to Urban Roast that cloudy late afternoon—I believe my nightmares would have been shaded differently. A slightly lighter gray. No Sally meant no Richard. No Richard meant no Aaron. No Aaron meant no dead Aaron. And no dead Aaron meant no Officer Sanchez accusing me of murder.

I can finally attest to the infamous wisdom that money doesn't buy happiness. I had clung to the idea that the golden ticket out of misery was, quite literally, gold—cash flow, and an endless supply of it—for as long as I could remember. I held on to that belief even after being abused by a husband old enough to be my father, even after I needed drugs to escape my elite lifestyle, and even after my stepson, nearly my peer, was found dead. Now, as I held Sally's cold, manicured hand, I felt the entire life I had built—one where happily ever after was hidden behind the sparkling gates of Beacon Hill—collapse in on itself.

I don't know what moment finally cracked the illusion. Was it the constant push and pull of keeping my ideologies firmly planted? Was it the self-destruction and hurt that were so easily swept aside because they didn't fit my narrative? Or was it simply Sally and all of her poisonous deeds, often coated with decadent sweetness? I wanted to break free from these golden handcuffs I had voluntarily submitted to. I wanted to disappear and never come back. All I wanted was peace.

"For Aaron," she said, raising her pinky, embroidered with a diamond ring.

"For Aaron," I said, with a broken spirit.

My phone dinged.

We both shot a look at my handbag.

It dinged again.

"You get that. I need to run to the loo." She delicately walked toward the bathroom, as though she were nervous about contracting an STD.

It dinged a third time, before I could snatch it.

From: an unrecognizable number.

"Hi!!! Carla here. I had a gr8 time wit u. I hope ur back does not hurt from sleepin on my futon."

Then:

"I wuld have made breakfast if u did not have to leave in a hurry. How wus the police stazion? Any news on Aaron?"

And finally:

"Also, did u take a pic from my investigazion board? I think there is a pic missin."

Fuck. I totally forgot I gave Carla my phone number as a parting gift. I didn't even know she had a phone. She must've memorized my number. For a woman who can't spell for shit, she had the memory of an elephant.

After my unpleasant call with Officer Sanchez, demanding my presence first thing in the morning regarding Aaron's body, I went back inside the shed where a shot of whiskey was waiting for me.

If I ever wrote a memoir of my decrepit life, I'd title the chapter with Carla as *The Shed*. A vagrant woman, with an underlying sense of beauty, made an abandoned shed her home—right on the outskirts of her obsession's property line—on a self-proclaimed investigation to uncover what happened to the man she stalked and loved.

As ridiculous as it sounds, Carla reminded me of Mom: eccentric, lost, yet tender and innocuous. Most astonishing of all, she reminded me of me: misguided and determined.

When I got back inside, Carla was dancing to music in her head with a bottle of malt in hand. She poured us another. Then another. And another. Until day turned into night, and awareness turned into fog—while the picture of Sally's car rested safely in my handbag.

The liquor twisted and turned in my mind, leaving gaps in recollection. But I do remember haphazardly setting an alarm to make sure I woke up and showed up at the police station on time. Even my inebriated self knew better than to risk a hiccup with the cops.

The sound of the toilet flush interrupted my reverie. I quickly punched the keys on my phone: *Thank you for the ride, Carla. It was wonderful meeting you, and I appreciate our time together. I am not aware of any picture you're referring to, but we will be holding a memorial service for Aaron this Wednesday at Green Mount Cemetery, if you'd like to come.*

A diplomatic response molded by a dismissive reaction to our newfound bond, with a sprinkle of white lie and a cordial invite.

Sally groomed me well.

As the bathroom faucet turned on, I closed my eyes and was transported back to sitting in Carla's car as she drove me to the station earlier this morning. The feel of dawn's wind blasting through her open windows, the dew moistening every green surface as we bumped along the gravel, felt like pure ecstasy. But I was spoiled. I couldn't wait for serendipity to randomly sprinkle its fairy dust on me. I needed to feel that way again—now. And my only form of instant tranquility was fabricated, packaged, and illegally sold on the market.

Sally had nearly opened the door when I slid the phone back inside my handbag and zipped it shut.

"Tranquility Hour?" she asked, as though she read my mind.

"Yes, please." I'd stopped hiding my yearning for it a long time ago.

Sally and Richard earned a handsome sum over the years by hosting art exhibitions and entertaining the world's one-per-centers. But that wasn't where the bulk of their wealth came from. As Sally's receptionist at her Beacon Hill location—and the scapegoat for her paper trails—I was well aware of the real reason behind their absurd fortune. That knowledge inducted me into her inner sanctum. I had the privilege of marrying her business partner… and getting high with her.

She kept me close.

As routine would have it, we settled near the closest surface, which happened to be a gray desk, supplied as essential furniture in my hotel room. There was a thin layer of dust settled on top. I hadn't had a reason to touch it, until now.

It didn't take long to realize what kind of paperwork I was signing. She was using me to cover up her drug operation. Sally Beaurshop—the Griselda Blanco of Beacon Hill. She supplied top-tier opioids, available only to the highest bidder. Her art exhibitions brought in pennies compared to the drug money, but they made the perfect front. *"Rich people do pay a lot of money for art, after all,"* she'd often say. She was a problem solver—always two steps ahead, finding solutions before anyone could sniff out the rot. I, for one, presented myself as a young and dumb solution. An anguished and desperate girl like me would do just about anything for financial freedom. And she was right. I had gladly sold my soul to Sally.

When Detective Gupta handed me her card, every bone, muscle, and fiber in my body wanted to grab the photo of Sally's Audi parked outside Aaron's home two days before his death and shove it in her face. I wanted to tell her everything. *Cut me a deal* — that's how I would have started. Immunity for information. She would have nodded her pretty head, and I would have told her that Sally had been running an underground opioid cartel for years. And that I believed she might have been responsible for Aaron's death. *"Do you have evidence?"* she would ask. And I'd simply say: *Tranquility Hour.*

Alas, the cookie hadn't crumbled that way, and I stood next to Sally in my quiet hotel room as she crushed a pill on a slit of marble, surrounded by a thin layer of dust.

I'm chicken shit, and Sally knew it the second she laid eyes on me.

Her dark brown bangs fluttered as she took a sharp inhale, flooding her nostrils with a state-of-the-art fentanyl concoction. One and done. She stepped away and splayed herself on the bed's duvet. I glanced over to see her eyes closed, a blissful smile painted on an otherwise plastic face. I wondered where she was. Maybe she was her child self, trapped in her favorite memory, replaying it in an ardent cycle. Or maybe she was reliving the first time a million dollars hit her offshore accounts—the catalyst of it all—rewiring her brain like a new discovery: the heightened potential, the impossible made possible, the goal to be anew, the one million becoming two.

I shifted back toward the desk. The powder looked like baking soda, but I knew all too well it felt like sugar. My nose flared as I kept staring. The temptation kicked into high gear, the devil inside pushing hard on my shell of a body to bend. *Bend, bitch. Bend. Closer to the table, that's it.* The tip of my nose tingled at the magnetic pull of the marble slit. I was so close to the table, I could sense the dust bunnies entering the openings of my ears.

When I had jammed my phone back into my handbag while Sally was coming out of the bathroom, I grabbed something else: a tricked lipstick. That's how she traveled. She had lipstick for her lips, and lipstick for her nose. She re-engineered the means of transporting drugs by designing a storage compartment inside what looked like a luxury lipstick. She built a slit at the tip, exposing a hollowed compartment. At first glance, the outer shell looked normal, a combination of wax, oils, and pigments, but the inside held nothing but drugs. She outsourced the production of 500,000 tricked lipsticks. *"Just in case,"* she had said once, with a sparkle in her eye and a smirk that could ruin a nation. The brilliant and sadistic Sally was scaling, fast.

One night at her house, I carried myself into her room and into her glamorous en-suite bathroom. High out of my mind, I mistakenly took her lipstick as mine. I had strolled in with nothing, but for some reason, I was sure I had left my lipstick on her counter. *It has to be mine*, I remember whispering to myself. The tricked lipstick had sat in my purse ever since.

Now, as I took another peep at a sullied Sally—still frozen in time, embraced by her own mental rapture—I grabbed the tricked lipstick from my pocket, slid the tip to reveal a dark hollow opening, and proceeded to drag the powder off the table and into the hole. I was immaculate. My accuracy was aided by the long acrylic French tip glued to my thumbnail, like the perfect spoon. Once the lipstick was secured, I turned my entire body and faced Sally.

As I watched her lie there, blithely unaware of my gawp, I knew the fire was starting to burn too close to her operation. And I'd be the one condemned for her actions. Even though she terrified me and had the means to cut my life short, I couldn't go down without a fight. It was time I earned my freedom.

This was my shot; her guard was down. It was just me and a dazed version of her.

"Sally?" I stayed put. I was close enough to run to the door if things went south.

"Hmm?" she murmured.

I clutched the tricked lipstick, locking it in the palm of my hand. "Why were you at Aaron's two days before he died?"

As if my voice had traveled slower than the speed of sound, Sally didn't react at first. She just lay there. I sucked in a puff of breath to repeat myself when she slowly rose from the bed. She looked like a possessed marionette, her upper body pulled up by an invisible string while her feet stayed planted on the floor. She slowly inched her head 90 degrees, using only her neck as a rotator, and locked eyes with me. Her glare blazed.

"What the fuck did you just say to me?" she shrilled.

My blood ran cold.

Chapter 20

Aleena

anchez took the lead, wrapping up Andrew's interrogation seamlessly while I stood beside him like a lost little girl. Andrew didn't seem to notice the shift in the air—or the storm about to hit me. He was escorted out of the station by Sanchez, leaving me alone in the interrogation room, teetering on the edge of a panic attack. My heartbeat quickened. My eyes brimmed with tears. Then the hyperventilation hit me like a punch to the gut. I was going to lose everything—my job, my reputation. Once the news broke, I'd lose my family and friends too. I'd be publicly, brutally canceled. Without work, we'd lose the house. Our lives would unravel. Rahul would leave me and take Shaan, and my parents would dedicate their lives to shaming me. I'd spiral. Fall into drugs. Die the same death as Aaron. Burn in the same eternal fire. The room began to spin. I lost my footing.

I expected the fall to hurt. But instead, I floated.

For a moment, I pulled my attention from the tornado of devastation swirling in my mind and focused on the source of my stability: two hands pressed gently into the dip of my shoulders, steadying my stance.

"Come with me."

Sanchez nudged me outside of the station like a choo-choo train and steered us sharply to the right into an alley, away from eyesight.

"Calm," he said gently as he let go of my shoulder and slowly padded my back.

I felt like throwing up. What was coming up my esophagus was not food but guilt, like millions of different viruses waiting to be expelled. I pushed myself against the brick wall, ready to hurl when nothing but gag came out. A sharp and mean gust of air. It was only then, I could catch my balance again.

"You good?" Sanchez looked concerned as he watched me finally compose myself. I still needed support, so I leaned against the wall like we were high school kids ditching class and bumming a cigarette.

"I'm so sorry Eric."

I've only called him by his first name when alcohol was present and the stress of law enforcement was subdued by pints of beer.

"So, did you know Aaron?" His eyes squinted.

I felt like regurgitating again, but this time, it was words and phrases and full sentences, explaining it all. Coming clean.

I nodded.

His eyes left mine as he stepped back, took an aggravated spin, and flicked his gelled hair back. "Aleena, what the fuck?"

He hadn't called me Aleena since our last happy hour. For some reason, it calmed me. I watched as a dark cloud grinned from the mountaintop.

"Aaron and I went to high school together," I began. "We didn't know each other much back then." *Well, he didn't know me much.*

Sanchez planted himself in front of me like a sprouted tree, unwilling to move or interrupt.

A gust of wind washed through my hair with a cooling remedy. I sighed and looked up at the steely sky, ready to atone.

"Aaron and I dated," I said. I couldn't bear to see his disappointment, so I looked down at the concrete, fixing my gaze on an oil spot. "We dated nearly ten years ago. I was a cadet, and he had just bought that house."

"Did you love him?" A hissed, low-tuned voice danced toward me.

"I did."

My eyes began to sting, and the only way I could alleviate the pain was to blink the salty drops down my cheeks. I kept my head down, making laps with only my eyeballs around the circumference of the oil spot. It was a perfect splash—rounded and splattered. I felt ferociously splattered. All the rounded, tight-knit seams of my life were being completely unraveled.

"I have to ask." Sanchez paused. I forced my head up to meet his eyes. He looked disturbed. Panicked. "Did *you* kill Aaron Moore?"

Every cognitive system in my body knew he'd ask. Still, when the words spilled from his mouth, my veins bulged, and my blood turned to ice. I looked up and exclaimed, "I did not kill Aaron Moore!" I said it with such force that the tightness around my temples sent sharp pains shooting to the back of my skull.

He watched me. He watched me like I was a cobra at a zoo—unnerved and perplexed.

My head spun again; the silence between us was agonizing. What was he thinking? Was he plotting his grand entrance back to the station with me in handcuffs? Was he replaying Aaron's death like an old tape recording, watching as I murdered him and convincing himself it was the truth? I felt a gush of heaviness wash over my face, my blood pressure dropping. I felt faint—another fall making it onto the agenda—when he twitched his lips to form a word.

"I believe you," he whispered.

My eyes widened.

Can this all be remedied?

"But you can't be on this case any longer. You're too close to it," he said.

My breath caught in my throat. Although it was protocol, I felt the floor fall from under me.

"Are you going to report me?" I managed to ask.

"Listen, Aleena," he sighed. "I respect you a lot, and it hurts me that you couldn't trust me with this information from the start." He came closer, grabbing my hand. "But we are in too deep now. I don't want to report you, but how are we supposed to get you off this case without raising suspicion?"

I knew what I had to do.

"I'll email Captain Warshburg, letting him know that Shaan was expelled for punching a kid in the face, and that I need to stay home and care for him."

A half-truth and a half-lie. It pained me that the fabricated part was taking care of my own son.

"Was that your emergency during Margaret's interrogation?" he asked.

I nodded.

"Is Shaan okay?"

I nodded again.

"And I'll tell Captain to put you in charge of the case," I said.

He didn't want to show it, but I could see a glint in his eye.

"Do you think he's going to give you leave?" he asked.

"He'd practically do anything for Shaan."

I still remember when the Captain came to the hospital after my delivery. The perks of a small town: coworkers feel like friends, and bosses feel like family. When he held Shaan, tears welled up in his eyes, lighting the crow's feet at their corners. Shaan, less than a day old, and Captain Warshburg, pushing sixty, became bonded at that moment.

Captain Steven Warshburg and his wife, Melissa, were never blessed with children. Every avenue they tried turned out to be a dead end. Steven eventually became captain of the precinct and played a vital role in launching specialized schools. His ribbon-cutting ceremony for the Vermont School for the Blind was the only other time I saw tears in his eyes. Melissa started a nonprofit donation bank, helping underprivileged children with

clothes and accessories, while also providing formerly incarcer-
ated individuals with jobs and stability. They were the humblest
power couple in north-central Vermont—two philanthropists
with a large and tender soft spot for children.

"It's settled then," Sanchez said.

I filled my lungs with damp air as mist began to fall from the
sky. "Thank you," I breathed out.

"Aleena, I want you nowhere near this case. Do you understand me?" he bellowed. "If anyone else finds out, you'll be
fired."

I nodded obediently.

And with that, we marched back inside. I began drafting my
email to the Captain, relieved he wasn't in yet. Sanchez grabbed
a cup of coffee and returned to work, now single-handedly solving a potential homicide.

I tried to let go of the case, but I couldn't. Sanchez had stuck
his neck out to save my career, and still, I couldn't walk away.
The problem was, he had a target on Margaret's back. And
something in the pit of my stomach told me she wasn't the killer. Although her eyes didn't tell a story of murder, she certainly
wasn't prudent. She had information, and I needed to find out
what she knew before Sanchez zeroed in on her. I couldn't wait
for her to run to me anymore. I had to think hard, and act fast.

As soon as I finished drafting the email to the Captain, I
looked around to make sure no one was watching and pulled
out my phone. I snapped pictures of reports, crime scene photos, suspect contact information, anything I could access. Rahul
taught me this trick when he snuck a photo of me on our second
date: *"pretend you're doing something else on your phone."* Apparently,

when he took that photo, I was debating what to get for lunch while he pretended to look up the menu online. *"I can't seem to find the menu,"* he had said, adjusting his camera lens. One silent click led to another, and now I was harnessing confidential information, officially tampering with evidence in plain sight. It's incredible how deceiving one can be, with just a little effort.

The email to Captain Warshburg was professional enough in its directness but layered with sadness: *I'm lost with Shaan. I think he needs his mother.* Coupled with: *the investigation has been moving forward, and I believe Officer Eric Sanchez is capable of taking the reins while I'm on leave.* I grimaced as I wrote the last of my email. *I will be taking my leave effective today, but you know where to find me.*

"MOM! CAN I HAVE A GRILLED CHEESE SANDWICH?" SHAAN'S VOICE echoed from the living room.

I found myself pacing in the kitchen. When I had gone to pick up Shaan unexpectedly, Mom didn't let me off easy. *"I want to spend more time with my son!"* I had finally yelled after the eighth accusatory poke of *"What did you do, Aleena?"* The more she repeated the question, the more her eyes narrowed. Shaan was by the porch with his backpack on before Mom could inquire for a ninth time.

Shaan always heard the pain in my voice. It starts early, this connection between a mother and a child. For us, it began during labor. I was nearly at the end of my rope, sixteen hours in, when the doctor proclaimed it was time for an emergency caesarean. *Rip the stomach open and pull the baby out* was all I comprehended as my vagina throbbed. I must have told them to wait, because all I remember is whispering to my unborn child that Mommy was in a lot of pain and really needed him to come out now. "*Wait!*" I had heard the doctor's voice. "*She is ready.*" Shaan was born a minute later.

As I plopped a buttered toast on the skillet, I felt a wretched dump of guilt in my stomach. I'm only here because I was forced out. Why wasn't I capable of being the mother Shaan deserved? How did my decisions catapult so miserably that I became this type of person? There are women who know, at their very core, that motherhood isn't written in their hearts—but that wasn't me. As an only child with overbearing parents, I collected a laundry list of things I'd do differently when I became a mother. Even as a child, after my parents would yell at me for one reason or another, I'd lock myself in the bathroom with my dolly, Vanessa, and whisper into her smooth plastic ear that she and I would leave this home one day and start fresh. I guess a child fantasizing about motherhood hadn't yet experienced the downfalls of adulthood.

Cheddar cheese, then American cheese, then cheddar cheese again—Shaan's favorite grilled cheese sandwich recipe. As I added the last slice of cheese, I heard a loud *squeak!* from the living room, followed by an eruption of laughter. I hadn't heard him laugh so openly in a long time, partly because he was getting in trouble, and partly (and more likely) because I wasn't around him as much. I felt my heart melt as the cheese did. Shaan was my child. He grew in my body and was now out in this world as his own human being. Why did I have such a hard time connecting with him? Who am I kidding? I knew exactly why. I took a deep breath as I placed the crispy sandwich on a plate and decided it was finally time to come clean.

I told Rahul to come straight home. By the time he pulled into the driveway, Shaan was taking a sweet nap inside our built-in fort. I'd had more fun these past few hours than I had in the past few years. After grilled cheese sandwiches, we settled into a Teen Titans marathon and built a fort with every cushion and blanket we could find. The result was more of a pillow play-pen, but cozy enough to fit both of our warm bodies together. Rahul walked in to find Shaan purring against my chest while I scrolled through my phone, analyzing the quality of all the pictures I'd taken at the station.

The look on Rahul's face was new. His shoulders slumped, dragging his laptop bag down, while his closed-lip smile creased the sides of his eyes. He was smitten.

"Look what we have here," he said.

I watched Shaan's furrowed face for a minute longer, sound asleep in his mother's arms. I finally found the courage to wiggle myself out.

It was now or never.

I braced myself. "Babe, can I speak with you in the kitch-en?" I asked in a hush.

He tiptoed back to where he came from. Shaan shifted and moaned as he lost my grip, then slumped onto a white, fluffy throw pillow. I stole a last glance at him as a tiny stream of drool seeped from the corner of his mouth, fully enamored in a dream. My hands involuntarily grasped my heart, with an aching fear that it might be the last time I saw him so at peace.

"Are there any grilled cheese sandwiches left for me?" Rahul asked mischievously as he placed his laptop bag on the counter and fetched us some water.

"Absolutely," I smiled back.

"So what brings you home earl—" he started.

"I need to talk to you, Rahul," I interrupted.

If we continued with small talk, I'd lose my nerve.

He leaned over the counter, concerned.

"I was kicked off the investigation," I said.

He choked on the water, and I squeezed his hand from across the counter until his throat was clear.

"I got kicked off the investigation because of my romantic past with Aaron Moore."

He straightened his back and crossed his arms. His eyes held a glassy sheen, but he didn't say a word.

That wasn't even the worst of it.

I looked down at my leopard fuzzy slippers and wiggled my toes—just to feel something.

"When Aaron and I were involved…" I paused, my voice catching in my throat. My heart pounded so loudly I could barely hear myself speak. Then I looked up—only for a second—and said the words that would change everything. "Aaron is Shaan's father."

Chapter 21

Margo

The clock gleamed its brilliant red at 5:03 a.m. The crust in my eyes pried open as I saw the time. The room was dark, but my head gyrated. I didn't know if I had even slept, because the images in my mind were on an endless loop: Sally as she glared at me. The panic in my heart. The sweat on my face. The sound of my stertorous breathing as I watched her delineate how to kill me. She was a different person then and there—one possessed by greed and power. One who punished all who questioned her. Questions like:

What were you doing at Aaron's two days before he died?

I tossed the covers off, suddenly feeling a hot flash creep up my legs.

"The cops." Was all I was able to say.

Her eyes—ever so menacing—were glued on me.

"The cops told me." I had lied.

I believe a person is made up of many different entities—like a single soul is the bark of a tree, with countless branches of personality. Somewhere deep in my membrane, one branch lit up—the branch that knows what to say and how to act when you're in deep shit. I couldn't process a word of what was coming out of my mouth, but somehow, I managed to get myself out of it.

Lying on my back in a dark, musty hotel room I hadn't yet grown accustomed to, I stared into the abyss above. I was shell-shocked by how smoothly the conversation with Sally had sunsetted. Once I mentioned the cops, she shifted her stance and reverted to her usual self. *"What exactly did the cops say?"* she asked carefully. I went on painting her a picture of a fabricated dialogue with Officer Sanchez, in which he claimed to have reasons to believe my friend Sally Beaurshop might be connected to Aaron's untimely death. *"He divulged that you were spotted at Aaron's home two days before he was killed."* Like liquid flowing into a cup, my tone was immaculate. A professional con artist like Sally couldn't detect the bold-faced lie I spat. But then the playback would restart in my head — how could I be sure Sally believed me? What if she was playing me just as much as I was playing her? What if she pretended to believe me only to buy time... to end me? And then it would begin again: Sally's distorted, evil glare as she stared at me after I asked a question I shouldn't have.

Somewhere between the second or third cycle of rumination, I dozed off. The alarm jolted me awake but something more sinister pushed me out of my subconscious. *Stop, please stop!* I could feel my neck compressing, fast. I was choking under someone's heavy hands, determined to squeeze the life out of me. I forced my eyes open and saw the flowy silhouette of Sergio, like the ghost of hell's past. I reached for my neck as it lay under the covers, smooth as ever. Although Sergio was a figment of my imagination, the alarm clock didn't just sound the 7:00 a.m. mark—it sounded a rude awakening yet to come.

These past couple of days have felt like a vacuum, as though I've been sucked into a parallel universe. But to Sergio, it was just another day. A day closer to collecting his debt. A debt I put myself in by gambling all of Richard's money away. Sergio Marino was still expecting one million dollars by the end of the month—which I didn't have. Officer Sanchez was still expecting an alibi—which I didn't have. Sally was still expecting my obedience—which I didn't have.

Everything seemed to be leading me to the Grim Reaper.

The alarm's deafening blast ripped through the room again. This time, I silenced the snooze, pulled the sheets off my body, and shifted upright, planting my feet firmly on the floor. I shook my head, trying to clear the fog lingering in my mind, and forced myself to focus. There should be only one thing on my mind— Aaron's funeral today. I'm a grieving stepmother, and that's all I'm going to be. Many skeletons from Aaron's closet may meander to his grave—and who knows, maybe the odds will finally be in my favor and someone unexpected will show up.

And maybe that someone will also hand me a million dollars.

Margo died the wishful thinker.

GREEN MOUNT CEMETERY WAS BREATHTAKING. SET ON THE ROLL-ing hills of Vermont, the gate to the deceased gave off an air of ethereal serenity. Leaves were beginning to lose their chlorophyll, with yellows, oranges, and reds brightening the foliage. There was a nip in the air, forcing a constant readjustment of my scarf. I was directed to the far east of the cemetery by an old white man dressed in black. He resembled the transition between life and death—of old age withering. I had chosen a black A-line chiffon dress with black tights and ballet pumps. I'd had three different outfits to choose from: One, for a grieving, judicious stepmother. Two, for a high-end grieving stepmother. Three, for a bombshell grieving stepmother. With cops sniffing around the funeral service attendees, the best I could do was blend in, and hopefully be forgotten. Option one was a no-brainer.

As I marched across the pristine grass toward the head-stone marked *Aaron Moore*, something off to the right caught my eye—a life-size sculpture of a little girl. I felt instantly drawn to her. As I moved closer, I understood why. She looked like Mom, with her slick curls and a heart-shaped nose.

When Karen went down memory lane, she always flipped through the same photo album—pictures of herself at seven years old. I never knew my grandparents, but in those photos, it was clear they loved her deeply. My grandmother used to dress her in garden-print dresses and pose her in front of their porch. In one picture, Mom looked so much like Shirley Temple I half-wondered if it had been copy-pasted.

The sculpture leaned against a floral railing, its surface etched with a name: *Margaret Pitkin*, died 1900. If irony ever played the cruel bitch, today was the day to prove it—a little girl with my name, who looked like my mother, memorialized in the very cemetery where I was about to bury my stepson—the same stepson whose murder I was being accused of.

My heart hurt, and my face sagged at the thought of my mother. I missed her so much. It's one thing knowing you could never see someone again because they're dead but it's a whole other level of torture when you can't see someone just because their mental hospital said so. *I'm sorry to inform you, your mother, Karen Vessel, has lost all visitation rights indefinitely due to an incident violating our code of conduct.* Years later, that letter still burned a hole in my wallet.

Without composing myself, I turned back toward Aaron's grave. Never in a million years could my body produce this gravity of emotion for Aaron, but luckily, I had Mom on my mind. Like a VIP section at a Miami club, Aaron's funeral plot was over-the-top luxurious. It was decorated with Sally's signature flowers—black dahlias—arranged around a sunset-bronze casket. The flowers were fresh and in full bloom. Sally's team must have imported them from the mountains of Mexico just hours ago. The mausoleum looked like an opulent barn, its white marble exterior and dark oak door shielding the vault that would enclose Aaron forever. Two Roman pillars stood on the stoop—something Aaron would have liked: an unnecessary display of ostentation.

Familiar faces began to trickle in as I stood rooted near the casket. From the corner of my eye, I spotted Sally, greeting everyone as if it were her own dinner party. I watched her shake hands with Aleena, who wore a sleek black satin dress. She looked stunning—her long black hair framing her large, expressive brown eyes. Beside her stood her partner, well-built and smooth as caramel. They made a striking pair, accompanied by a fairer-skinned boy with hazel eyes. He looked more Middle Eastern. Then again, India had been colonized for centuries, and genes had an unpredictable way of making their way down the line.

Aleena looked depleted, while her husband was clearly uncomfortable, almost standoffish. He kept holding his son tightly around his arms, as though someone might push him down the casket hole. Aleena and I met eyes, and she smiled at me. *"My condolences,"* she mouthed, and I bowed my head in gratitude. I noticed how she also kept throwing suspicious glances toward Sally. A detective never sleeps—and a good one knows when something doesn't smell right.

Sally moved on to shake hands with a handsome Black man. He looked rugged yet put-together, his charcoal suit stretching tight over his biceps. As he stepped past Sally, I noticed his attention shift elsewhere. Following his gaze, I spotted the woman I was meant to befriend at the Montpelier Inn—before my ill-timed panic attack. Her eyes. I remembered those ocean-blue eyes, large and charming with thick lashes, staring sorrowfully into Carla's camera. Eva Armstrong—the one who found Aaron dead. She stood beside the same friend, also beautiful; blonde and slim, wearing black pumps and a matching cocktail dress. The blonde whispered something into Eva's ear while glancing toward the rugged man.

Next thing I knew, Carla was standing beside me. She'd managed to make herself presentable, tying her jungle braids into a ponytail and wearing an oversized black blazer with matching pants. She must have noticed me eyeing her outfit.

"The blazer is from Goodwill," she said, while tugging at the bottom of it.

"Glad you could make it," I said.

"Cut the shit," she hissed.

I turned to look at her, and her eyes were wide with rage. She shifted her body toward me, ready to lunge.

The last thing I needed was for Carla to cause a scene. But before I could say anything, the priest began his sermon.

Sally stepped up to give the eulogy—her words dripping with poetic prose about her time with Aaron, painting herself as a pseudo-mother. Some anecdotes were clearly fabricated, especially the parts about the emotional availability she claimed to have shown him. Emotions, to Sally, were as foreign as the Chinese language was to me. But she was a great actress. Her performance teetered between genuine testimonial and calculated theatrics. She kept rotating her glances, often lingering on Officer Sanchez, who had arrived just after the first passage of the Gospel.

Sally had to make her mark among the people of Vermont—portraying herself as a loving friend and role model to the deceased, not a conniving criminal. As she gave her final thanks, I searched desperately for an organic exit for Carla and me. That's when I noticed Officer Sanchez approaching Sally. He leaned in close, near enough to smell her breath, while she stood cool as a cucumber. In reality, Officer Sanchez had nothing on Sally. But from her perspective, it was a different story. She believed he knew she had visited Aaron just days before his death and had even questioned me about it. I had planted a spoiled seed in her mind, hoping this otherwise innocent interaction would sprout into paranoia—temporarily distracting her from me and redirecting her focus toward saving herself.

I was forced to let go of my sightings and shake hands with the line of people walking to Aaron's grave. With every person giving me their condolences, Carla stepped back. She wasn't comfortable confronting me within earshot of other grieving visitors.

Wonderful.

She knew I stole the picture from her investigation board, and I needed time to come up with an explanation.

After the Montpelier Public Library's librarian gave her respects—unsure if she even knew Aaron or was just already at the cemetery—Carla whispered in my ear.

"I know you took the picture of the Audi parked outside of Aaron's house from my investigation board." I turned to face her. Meshed with the anger in her expression was a streak of sadness. I had betrayed her trust.

Carla wasn't the type to toy around with. She had a sharp memory and an even sharper tongue. The best way to keep her as an ally was to tell her the truth.

"I'm so sorry, Carla," I said in a low-pitched tone, blowing the words into her face. "I know whose car that belongs to, and I had to make sure."

Her arms were crossed, and her face was still, like porcelain.

"*Please*, you have to trust me," I urged. "We're on the same team."

Her eyebrows arched. I was cracking her, but I had to give her proof.

"You see that woman over there?" I pointed to Sally.

"Yeah, the one who gave the eulogy?" she asked.

I nodded.

"It's her car."

She watched Sally for a moment, contemplating.

"I guess it makes sense. It seems like she was close to Aaron." she said.

"You're telling me someone who's tracked Aaron's every move and has never seen her before just coincidentally stopped by his house two days before he died?" My whisper was aggressive and a bit of spit landed on her cheek.

"First of all, I didn't track his *every* move," she huffed. "But I get your point."

"Listen, Carla, this woman is dangerous." I looked around and caught eyes with Aleena. *Fuck*, she was making her way over. "You have to believe me. I'll tell you more once I know more." I placed my hand on Carla's shoulder and felt it relax. "Remember, we're on the same team," I managed to say before Aleena made it around the casket.

"I'm sorry for your loss," Aleena said.

Up close, I saw how her scleras were ruby red, and the haphazard attempt to conceal her hollowed eye bags.

I turned and Carla was gone.

"Thank you, Detective Gupta," I said as I settled my gaze on her.

"Call me Aleena," she smiled. "I took leave from work to spend more time with my son," she nudged her head toward her family. Her husband still looked uneasy—the way Sally did when she came to Roxden for the first time. He clung to his son the way she clutched her purse.

"I understand," I said.

"Listen," she bent her head close to my ear, the smell of jasmine fluttering into my nostrils, "I don't believe you killed Aaron, but I'm not so sure others on this case agree with me."

Fucking Officer Sanchez.

"Let me help you…unofficially," she asserted.

I looked over Aleena's shoulder and watched Officer Sanchez chatting away with Sally.

"Do you still have my card?" she asked, still close to my ear.

"Yes."

"Okay. Call my personal cell and let's grab coffee," she whispered, before straightening her back. "My condolences again, Mrs. Moore," she said loud enough for others to hear, but looked me in the eye and mouthed: *"coffee, soon."*

Aleena's condolences must have grabbed Officer Sanchez's attention, because the next thing I knew, Aleena was pacing back to her family, Sanchez was giving me a conspiratorial glance, and Sally was as white as a lab mouse.

AFTER WHAT SEEMED LIKE AN ENDLESS STREAM OF THANK YOUS over sad eyes and awkward hugs, I finally made my way back, completely depleted. I gave Sally a wonderful performance of gratitude and appreciation as I hugged her tight, for the first time ever, in front of an audience.

On my way out, Officer Sanchez met my pace and gave his sorrys, but before he could take this opportunity to investigate me further, I forestalled by telling him I was tired and needed to rest. He bowed and walked off, throwing glances my way until he disappeared in his car.

On my way back, I had a sudden craving for a cheeseburger and had the taxi driver make a stop. As a thank you, I ordered him a Mcdouble meal as well.

Finally, in bed after a steamy shower—hair dripping with shampooed water and body smooth with lotion—I sank my teeth into the burger while flipping through cable channels, feeling the early sweetness of gluttony embrace me.

As I got under the covers, happily bloated and lethargic, my phone buzzed. I reached for it with a heavy hand and saw a text message from 24371:

Bank Wire Transfer Alert (R): Margaret Vessel sent you $1,200,000.00. It's ready now. Reply STOP to cancel these texts.

The account for Margaret Vessel was run by Sally. Technology had seeped into our lives and numbed it all— even life-changing events were delivered via text message. *Ding!* Your Postmates is here. *Ding!* Sally wired you 1.2 million dollars.

Chapter 22

Eva

Bee insisted we attend the funeral together. After our rendezvous at her home, I'd hesitated to spend more time with her—mostly because of her father. Her hospitality and infectiously warm personality had touched my heart, but I couldn't risk ending up on their bad side. Maybe old-timers like Frank Wright—the mountain-man type—were just naturally abrasive, blunt, and contemptuous, but ultimately harmless. Maybe he just hated Aaron's guts and was all talk, no hands. Still, I had to be careful. If he found out I'd slept with Aaron the day before he died, he might see me as the enemy.

I had hoped Aaron's funeral would be the tail end of my time in Vermont. I yearned to go back home, breathe in Dad's cheap cologne, and play chess over Dos Equis.

The whole time at the cemetery, I kept staring at Aaron's stepmother. She was much younger than I expected, and beautiful. I had seen her around the hotel, but I had no idea who she was. She always seemed worried and withdrawn, as though she were accompanied by an abusive ghost ordering her around. When I paid my respects, her eyes were lost and her smile was weak. She appeared to have reversed in age right in front of me—a sad little girl looking for refuge. Every cell in my body wanted to hug her and tell her everything was going to be okay. Instead, I settled on grazing her hand and walked off with a heavy heart.

"He keeps staring at you," Bee was in my ear again.

When we arrived, she gave me a rundown of all the visitors. The man she labeled as Andrew Styversant was the same one whose eyes kept lingering on me.

He was stunning—better looking than Aaron, at least in my eyes. Where Aaron had the polished veneer of a conventional model, Andrew carried a quiet kindness beneath his barrel-chested frame. He was the definition of tall, dark, and handsome. As I felt his gaze, a low tingle stirred deep in my core. Uninvited, wicked thoughts surfaced—fantasies of his strong arms pinning me down, one hand wrapped around my neck, my body dwarfed beneath his.

I'd be his servant, forced to do anything he wanted, and I'd oblige, terrified and aroused. That terrifying sweet spot. The tyranny of my mother, paired with my distorted understanding of my own sex appeal, had created something twisted in me. My beauty had only ever served one purpose: to be exploited. Aubree tried to save me—fending off predatory men, offering hours of pseudo-therapy—but the damage had already been done. My mother's voice had carved itself too deeply into my psyche. Nothing ever managed to unwrite it. So instead of mourning a man who had been inside me just days ago, I sat there—aroused by the same man Aaron had betrayed Bee with—wishing I could feel his weight pressing into the hollow that still ached between my legs.

I didn't hear when the phone rang.

"Fuck, I have to go," Bee said, glancing at her phone. "My dad needs help with a new compost deposit," she added with a sigh—one tinged more with pride than frustration. "He conveniently leaves all the finances to me. He can't even send a simple invoice." She took my hand, eyes softening. "Will you be okay?"

"Oh yes, don't worry," I smiled. "I understand the demands of having a family business."

"That's right! The Golden Oyster," she said, marking the words in the air like a Broadway performer. "I'll have to come down to Long Island and try your dad's famous oysters."

"That's a must! Now go before your dad blames me for your tardiness," I laughed.

Luckily, she took that as a joke, and not as a blatant apprehension toward her father, and strolled off to her Mini Cooper.

I stood firm as people trickled out, keeping my eyes fixed on Aaron's photo. It was a black-and-white portrait. He wore an alluring grin, his long brown hair pulled into a manicured bun. Just beneath his thick neck, the edge of a suit collar peeked through. He was looking straight at me, as if I'd been the one behind the camera. He was handsome, and he knew it. He understood the power of his grin—how it worked like a weapon of seduction. His hair looked effortlessly voluminous, yet neatly trimmed to frame his sharp features. He must have gone through life with glitter-filtered glasses, always seeing himself as the star of the show. The world was clay, and Aaron believed he could shape it however he pleased. There were telltale signs, even for a stranger in his life like me. I remembered the way he watched me, like a prize to be won. The way he grabbed me—with victorious force—when he did me. He moved like a predator, and I strolled into his cave, an ignorant deer. Even with his body in a coffin, I still felt his pull. As if any second now, he might appear behind me, tap my shoulder, and whisper *"Round two?"* with that same crooked grin. Just then, I felt fingers press lightly on my shoulder.

My heart thumped.

I spun around, half-expecting to lock eyes with Aaron's corpse. Instead, I was met by a gentle smile from a rugged man. Up close, his features were unexpectedly soft. Though he had a sharp jaw and broad shoulders, his large brown eyes held that elusive kindness. When he smiled, his cheeks lifted, casting his face in a compassionate demeanor.

"I'm sorry!" he exclaimed. "I didn't mean to frighten you."

The juxtaposition was also apparent in his voice. The sound was deep and guttural, but the words were gentle and tender.

"That's no problem," I said, sucking in a breath. "It's a bit overwhelming being here, that's all."

He nodded earnestly. "Tell me about it."

He extended his hand. "Andrew."

I extended mine. "Eva."

I had finally introduced myself to the infamous Andrew Styversant. The man Aaron had an affair with, leaving Bee to drop out, lose herself, and solicit a bribe.

I suddenly didn't feel comfortable talking to him.

"I'm sure Bee has told you about me," he said, as though I had transferred my thoughts to him.

"A little," I shrugged, leaning back to create a slightly larger gap between us.

"She has every right to feel the way she does about me." He looked down, arms crossed.

For a man of his size—with arms big enough to throw me with one easy motion—he looked fragile and delicate as he surrendered to his past.

"But I would like to share my side of the story," he finally said.

"With *me*? You don't even know me," I gasped.

"I know it may sound odd, but you being a stranger makes it easier for me to share. Montpelier is a small town, and everyone has already made up their minds about me. But if I could share it with someone who hopefully hasn't yet, it would mean a lot." He cleared his throat. "And it helps that you are absolutely breathtaking," he mumbled.

I gave Aaron's photo another glance. Although Aaron and Andrew were counterparts in many ways—two peas in a handsome pod—they belonged to different worlds when it came to character. Aaron was cocky, exuberant in his self-importance, while Andrew exuded a timid humility, unaware of the power he possessed.

I was intrigued. "Coffee?" I asked.

He shifted on his feet, surprised I agreed.

"Coffee would be great."

WE DROVE IN HIS HYUNDAI PALISADE. IT WAS WELL CARED FOR, with a clean throw blanket on the backseat, two Yeti bottles in the cup holders, and the congenial scent of cotton and pine. We didn't talk much on the five-minute drive to the nearby café, except when he mentioned his trip back to Vermont. He lived in New Haven and had driven five hours overnight to get to the police station earlier rather than wait for a flight. *"I wanted to get this shit over with,"* he said, staring straight ahead, misery etched on his face.

Once we settled at a secluded wooden table by the far window of the refurbished mansion–turned–café, I cradled my warm cup of coffee and offered, "I also live in a coastal town."

He lifted his own mug, took a careful sip, and asked softly, "Where are you from?"

"I live on Long Island."

And just like that, I told him about The Golden Oyster, my father's form of activism for ocean-to-table decadent oysters at a bargain price, my grandmother, my best friend Aubree, and my career as my dad's accountant. It was his eyes. They held nothing but empathy as he gave me his undivided attention and showed genuine interest in my life. It was physically hard not to spill all my beans.

"I'm guessing your trip to Vermont did not turn out the way you expected," he said when I told him how I knew Aaron.

"Not by a long shot," I said, and a manic laugh bubbled up.

I prompted my mind to shift gears and asked Andrew to share about himself.

He told me about his English Springer Spaniel, Roxy, whom he adored. He spoke of his love for hiking, something he'd acquired growing up in Vermont. He now lived in a small community mostly occupied by retired couples, including Roxy's sitter. He told me how he taught himself to code instead of going to college after he moved away. He invented a calendar application that color-coded events by location, sold it for millions, and now consults for startups. He told me he works two hours a day and spends the rest hiking, volunteering in the community garden, or running a bouldering center for youth that he founded with his app earnings.

"Sometimes I feel like I live in a little bubble, away from the rest of the world," he noted. "But I like it that way. It helps me displace my past and focus on what makes me feel at peace."

I hadn't realized my jaw had dropped until my tongue went dry. "You are not what I expected," I said.

"I hope in a good way," he smiled.

"He cheated on me with Andrew! His best friend." Bee's voice suddenly interrupted my flowery stream of thoughts the way a spiked speed bump stops a car in its tracks.

"Listen, I'll be direct for a second," I began, my chest tightening. "Bee told me Aaron cheated on her with you. Was she telling the truth?" Even as the words spilled out, I felt my diaphragm drop. Our eyes locked, and for a moment, I wished time would freeze—just a man and woman in a coffee shop dipping their feet in the water, unaware of how deep the plunge could be.

"Bee was telling the truth."

His words shattered the crystalline glass holding my fantasy.

He went on to explain how Aaron had convinced him to explore a sexual relationship, even though he wasn't receptive. But Aaron held a cloak of power over him, and fear got the best of him—the fear of rejection, isolation, and desolation. He confessed that the experience was traumatizing, leaving him with PTSD not only from being pushed into a sexual dynamic he didn't explicitly consent to, but also from the shame of not standing up for himself and the guilt of feeling complicit in breaking a relationship.

"I haven't dated anyone since," he concluded.

My heart dropped. I understood better than anyone the pressure of having to live under someone else's control—the power they wield over you and the fear they amplify just to keep you on a leash. It's demoralizing and suffocating. I found myself sharing it all with Andrew: how I grew up, how abusive and jealous my mother was, how she died in a tragic car accident, and how, even though I was given a second chance, I still struggled to unlearn the "truths" she told me about myself—while simultaneously feeling guilty for that struggle.

This time, his jaw was left hanging.

"I would have never thought—" he stopped, then rephrased, "Thank you for sharing."

"Back at ya," I smiled.

The only person I'd ever been this open with was Aubree—and that had taken years. Letting my guard down now felt both exhilarating and terrifying. In that rustic coffee shop, beneath the afternoon gloom, Andrew and I forged a connection by revealing our raw, unfiltered selves. To do that with someone I'd just met felt almost sacred. Whatever the future held, a bond had already formed between us.

Chapter 23

Aleena

I woke up wrapped in my handsome's arms. The last twenty-four hours had been a roller coaster of emotions. What started as a confession for my sins led to a revelation I never saw coming. The night before Aaron's funeral, I stood in front of Rahul, hands clasped behind my back, finally atoning for my indiscretions. I told him everything: the unhealthy crush I'd harbored for Aaron in high school; our encounter in Vermont a couple years later, which led to a romantic relationship; the way he carried me forward, shackled to his every need by my fairytale delusion; how he reacted when I got pregnant and the throbbing pain on my lip after he hit me; the shame I felt seeing Rahul, already engaged and visiting from California; how my mother had convinced me to keep the baby and expedite our wedding; and the way the truth had caught in my throat every day until, years later, my husband still had no idea his son wasn't his. As I let my heart take over and the words flowed out like a painter with a canvas, saline streams poured down my face and knots tightened in my stomach. I was heaving around every sour corner of my past. I remember steeling myself when I finished explaining, like standing before a hundred-foot tsunami, ready to be engulfed by Rahul's wrath.

Instead, he came to me and hugged me.

My eyes nearly popped from their sockets. I couldn't believe I was feeling his arms grip my waist as I melted into him.

"I know, Aleena. I've known for a long time now," he whispered in my ear.

I leaned back, his face stolid. I puffed ragged breaths out of my mouth like someone expelling a demon in a horror movie. It was a demon indeed—one of shame, guilt, and fear; one that kept gnawing at me, chipping away at parts of my soul.

"I didn't know he hit you, though," Rahul said softly, as he replayed my words in his mind.

I watched his calm expression morph into anger as a pronounced vein pulsed down his forehead, and his jaw clenched. "I can't believe he hit you when he found out you were pregnant," he snarled.

"How did you know?" I asked, still wiping my face.

He shook his head and took my hand. I loved that about Rahul, how easily he could shake off his anger. The compassion in his heart was so strong that he forbade himself from projecting his rage for someone else onto his wife. I'd never paused to internalize the magnitude of his goodness. For years, my mind had been distracted, and my heart was still recovering. Even something like this was a sign of his character. That's how it worked, wasn't it? Actions, when done in the purest way, added up to someone's character. Rahul shook off his anger and refocused on his love for me, while Aaron harnessed his anger to punish me.

Rahul proceeded to guide us to our dining table and we sat side by side, still holding hands.

"Do you remember when I ran into Aaron at the grocery store when Shaan was an infant?" He inquired.

"Yes."

"Well, he said more than I led on." He brushed his thick hair back. "Aaron pointed at Shaan in my arms and smiled coyly, saying the kid was actually his. He also said you were still in love with him and I was just a bandage to save face."

"Oh my God," I whispered, lowering my head into my hands, anguish flooding my system. "I can't believe he said that."

"I mean, no one deserves to be murdered for being a jerk, but he sure was one," Rahul punctuated.

The only person Rahul ever judged was Aaron—and even then, he just called him a jerk. I'd missed yet another sign of his character. While the world often encourages men to be like Aaron, it's the gentle, kind ones like Rahul who are the real prize. And I was beyond blessed to have married one.

"I didn't believe him at first," he said as he rose to fetch our waters. "But when someone says that to you, it sticks."

We could still hear Shaan's low hum of snores in the next room.

"I got a paternity test," he said. "I took Shaan to a clinic while you were napping, and a cheek swab later, it was confirmed that Aaron was Shaan's biological father."

Rahul's tone was even, almost transactional, but in his eyes I saw grief. He was a man mourning the loss of what he believed was his own blood, betrayed by the one person who had vowed to care for him.

"Rahul, *you're* Shaan's father."

"I know," he muttered.

"How did you forgive me?" My voice broke as tears welled up again, the ache in my chest rising with them.

He locked eyes with me, and for a second I thought he would say, *because you're my wife*, but instead he said, "I spoke to your mom."

Great. The last person I'd want my husband to consult about our marital problems was my overbearing, disapproving, opinionated mother.

"Before you say anything," he added, "she really was the reason I forgave you."

I sat back in my chair, ambivalent.

"One day, while you were at work, I went to your mom's to drop off Shaan. She saw it on my face. As much as I tried to hide the betrayal and heartbreak—"

My stomach dropped. I reached for his hand, and he took it.

"Your mom kept asking me what was wrong. Part of me thinks she already knew. Finally, I told her once your dad took Shaan to the living room. She told me how you came crying to her, and how she was the one who pushed you into having the baby—and to keep it quiet."

He twiddled his thumbs for a moment. "She didn't make any excuses for you. She agreed that what you did was wrong, but that you regretted it. Then she asked a question that changed my perspective: 'Is it worth throwing an entire marriage away because of it?'"

Yes. It is. Rahul deserved better.

"She explained how you were seeing Aaron on the down-low when we met, and how we got engaged so quickly while I was still across the country. You hadn't yet caught up to your new reality. Then it was too late. You were pregnant with his child, and the wedding date was set with me."

I stood and moved behind him, wrapping my arms around his chest and burying my head in the dip of his neck. "I'm so sorry, Rahul. I'm so, so sorry." I began to sob into the warmth of his body.

"It took time, but I forgave you and promised myself to raise Shaan as my own." He reached around and gently freed my arms. "I also decided to let you come to me in your own time." He took me by the waist and swung me onto his lap.

Nose to nose, bodies pressed together, he said, "I'm happy you finally told me."

The timeless adage had merit after all. The truth did set me free.

"You have no idea how happy I am, too," I whispered, sending a slight breeze through his beard.

I leaned closer and kissed him. For the first time, my mind simply received. I felt his soft lips press against mine, his hand trailing along my back. I welcomed his tongue as it danced with mine, and his other hand as it gathered my hair. I noticed his short breaths between kisses, his body growing, yearning for mine. I received my husband wholeheartedly—and it was the best feeling in the world.

I pulled back and placed my hand on his cheek. He was gorgeous, and even though Shaan wasn't his, their cheekbones were the same. Moments like these proved that miracles exist. Shaan resembled Rahul in subtle yet unmistakable ways, despite sharing no genes. It was a divine confirmation of a father and his son.

"Do you remember why Shaan got expelled?" I asked, brushing my lips against his cheek.

"For punching a kid, right?" he replied.

"Apparently that kid saw Aaron trying to sign Shaan out after school last Wednesday."

Rahul gasped and pushed his chair back with heavy hands. I lifted myself off his lap.

"What?" he hissed.

"I don't know, Rahul. That's what Principal Calaver told me. Apparently Thomas, the secretary's kid, was teasing Shaan, and he punched him."

"What was Aaron doing at Shaan's school, trying to pick him up?"

"By the time I found out, Aaron was already dead."

Rahul stood and began pacing. After a minute or two of circling the table, he stopped abruptly and placed his hands on its smooth surface.

"We should tell Shaan," he said.

"What? That's risky, babe."

What if Shaan sees Rahul as an imposter? Or despises me for ripping his biological father away from him?

"I know, Aleena, but he deserves to know."

Rahul took a breath and began pacing again until he turned to face me. "It could help with his anger."

"Or make it worse," I countered.

"We have to trust," he whispered. "We are his parents, and that's never going to change. All we need to do is reiterate that to him and be there for him as he works through his emotions."

Rahul was the inherent optimist. The path to success seemed so simple when he explained it that way. I, on the other hand, was a natural pessimist. Shaan's biological father suspiciously died just days before he learned the truth. That's bound to mess *any* kid up.

But as I looked at Rahul, a face twinkled with hope and geared with determination, I

folded.

We have to trust.

"Okay," I said. "Let's tell Shaan."

SHAAN TOOK IT WELL. HE SEEMED DETACHED FROM IT ALL, THE way you tell a kid a distant uncle passed away. To Shaan, his parents were Rahul and myself. He was overall unphased but he did want to attend Aaron's funeral to say his goodbyes. He proceeded to hug us, one arm around each of our shoulders, tucked in the cocoon of his protectors. He apologized for hitting Thomas and promised not to use violence next time he got angry. He also chuckled in the same breath and said, "I guess Thomas was right after all."

I took Shaan into my lap, as he wiped the sleepy drool from the corner of his mouth, and caressed his hair. "How do you feel about being homeschooled for a while?" I asked.

Rahul wrapped his arms around my waist, watching Shaan in a huddle.

"What's homeschool?" he asked, in his teensy way.

Rahul's breath warmed my ear. "We were thinking Mom could take some time off to help with your schoolwork."

He craned his neck and jumped with excitement. "I would love that! Mommy and me!"

Now that I was on leave, I could teach Shaan the rest of the syllabus in the mornings, and my parents could take him for creative afternoon sessions. Rahul would pick Shaan up from my parents after work, and we'd spend the evening cooking dinner and building pillow forts together.

"What will you do while Shaan is with your parents?" Rahul had asked as we worked out our game plan in the dining room before waking Shaan from his nap.

"I still have a case to solve," I had said decisively.

Chapter 24

Margo

I wasn't sure if it was impulsivity or survival instinct, but upon receiving the text message alert from the bank, I transferred one million dollars to Sergio Marino. A clean wire transfer to Saloon Car Wash.

As soon as I sent it, I received a phone call from an unknown number. "Got it." His voice rang in my ear, and before I could acknowledge him, the line cut out.

I slumped head first onto the bed. Relief washed over me like a second chance at life. I was free from debt — one I had put myself in — and I didn't want to go back. I didn't want to go back to Beacon Hill, to my abusive late husband's mansion, right in the bee's nest of the dirtiest queen of all. I wanted to break my mother out of her own prison and drive to where flowers bloom year-round and a kaleidoscope of butterflies flapped their pretty wings around us.

"You have a lot to gain from Aaron's death."

Alas, with one problem solved, another crept on my doorstep. This was all a tease. I still had $200,000 from Sally's wire transfer, more than enough to start a new life, but I couldn't escape without giving Sanchez the ammo he needed for an arrest. A second chance was simply an illusion — one that would land me a life behind bars. But if I didn't run, I'd have to answer to Sally about the missing million dollars. And without a clear and plausible explanation, I was as good as turkey on Thanksgiving Day.

Jail or death. Jail or death. *Jail or death.*

I curled into a fetal position and let my stomach contract and my lungs expand. I gave myself permission to sob, after so many years. What has become of my life? Where did I go wrong? When was the last time I felt at peace? When did I lose myself? As I looked around the dark room, with the low murmur of the television, I was struck by a sudden urge, a need for change. I couldn't allow myself to live like this anymore. I'd had enough. I was sick of being in a chokehold, clinging to whatever delusional shortcut I could find. It didn't pan out after working for Sally, it didn't pan out after marrying Richard, and it surely didn't pan out after getting high and gambling my life away.

I slid off the bed and landed on my knees. I placed my elbows on the mattress and prayed. *Please, God. Please help me right my wrongs. Show me a path to salvation. I don't want to be here anymore. Please, God, help me find my way back to myself and to You. Amen.*

And with that, the pillow called my name, and the only thing left in me was sleep.

I woke up, sundering my eyes open. My body reacted to a good cry like an allergic reaction. My eyelids were swollen, and my mouth was impeccably dry. The morning sun had just hit the green mountains, illuminating a pastel canvas of blues and yellows. As I stretched, a judder of pain rose from my neck. I was sore, swollen, and thirsty. My body had finally caught up to my state of mind.

The sound of a telephone reverberated through the room. It was deafening and misplaced in an otherwise quiet atmosphere. I dove for it on the side table, eager for the ring to stop.

"Hello?" I murmured.

"Mrs. Moore?"

"Yes."

"Good morning! This is Amy from the front desk." She paused, and when I didn't respond, she continued, "We have a package for you."

Blood rushed to my head, and my heart began to pump abrasively.

What package? Please, don't let it be another gift from Sally.

"Mrs. Moore?"

"Yes, I'm sorry. I've just awakened."

"Oh! My apologies!" Her perky voice felt like nails on a chalkboard.

"I'll have someone bring it up to your room, no problem!"

"Thank you, Amy."

"My pleasure. Goodbye!"

I was able to get my face washed, my teeth brushed, and my clothes changed by the time I heard a knock on the door. I watched through the peephole until a right-out-of-high-school boy with shaggy blonde hair, dressed in a Montpelier Inn hunter-green uniform, dropped a white box and walked off.

The package was light and addressed to Margaret Vessel. *It's going to be those damn lipsticks.* Sally must have gotten nervous after Officer Sanchez's, albeit innocent, interest in her during Aaron's funeral, and began her slow descent into planting evidence on me as her glorified scapegoat.

But it wasn't from Sally. The package was from McLanes Psychiatric Hospital, with a yellow sticker forwarded to the address of the Montpelier Inn. Shannon must have rerouted the package here. With all the cold shoulders, dirty looks, eye rolls, and crude responses — she did have a heart after all. Richard spent years raving about Shannon as a fantastic housekeeper, and I finally understood why. She didn't have to go through the trouble of sending this package my way, but she did, knowing it came from the same hospital that housed my mother.

I grabbed my cuticle cutter from my handbag and slowly ripped the tape. Overlaid was a letter, floating halfway in the box because something else was hidden beneath it. I grabbed the letter, opened it and upon reading the first sentence, my heart sank.

It is with great sadness that we inform you of the passing of Karen Vessel.

I slumped to the ground, my buttocks hitting the hardwood floor with a clunk. It felt like a flood had broken loose in my abdomen—I was underwater, unable to breathe, crushed by the weight of shock. My body was drowning from the inside out, and the only way to survive was to let it all out. Thick tears streamed down my cheeks as my lungs worked overtime, trying to match the erratic rhythm of my convulsive gasps. My mother was dead. The only person I loved with my whole heart was no longer part of this world. I tilted my head back toward the ceiling and screamed.

Why, God — WHY!?

Day turned to dusk, and dusk to darkness. Time blurred, accelerating around me as I surrendered fully to despair. Hours passed before I could bring myself to look at the package again. What had once surged through my body like a flood was now drained completely; my organs had entered a sudden season of drought. My skin wilted under the weight of it, dry and limp, while the tears kept streaming like an open hose I couldn't shut off. Worried I'd end up hospitalized for dehydration, I dragged myself to the bathroom. The fluorescent light stung my eyes. I bent over the sink and drank straight from the running faucet, desperate for something to anchor me. Then I rested my cheek on the cold, slightly grimy colonial-white granite and stayed there for what felt like another hour—waiting for muscle memory, for something inside me to return.

As I made my way back toward the bed, I sucked in a heap of air and read the rest of the letter. The hospital had taken care of it all. No mention of a cause of death, only that she left peacefully. *My ass.* The letter ended with the location of her burial and a request for a referral.

Fucking pricks.

I fetched a manila envelope from the bottom of the packaging box. I felt around for a small object, the size of a nail clipper, a metal double-sided flat piece, and a paper. I dumped the contents onto the bed and found another letter, a monarch butterfly brooch, and a flash drive wrapped in bubble wrap. I grabbed the letter and immediately recognized my mom's handwriting, written in orange crayon. The letters were big and rounded, but her g's were the same curly ones I used to copy as a kid.

My sweet Margo,

I write this letter to you in a hurry. I will place it in my safe, if God forbid my escape plan fails and I don't make it out alive. These fuckers (except for Max — I like Max) told me to put anything I want sent to you after I die in the safe. Yesterday, Richard visited me. He told me he was terrified because Sally Beaurshop was plotting to kill him. Richard is part of some crime organization with Sally and wanted out. Did you know this, sweetheart? Are you safe? Don't worry, I'll send Larry to watch over you. I told him to hide in the shadows so he's not caught, even though everyone keeps telling me they can't see him. Anyways, Richard gave me a flash drive with… EVIDENCE!

Be careful, pumpkin.
Love, Karen (Mom).

I read her letter ten times before I put it down. Is this why Mom lost visitation rights? Did she try to escape after Richard visited her? Why would Richard confide in my mother and give her evidence? Did Sally murder Richard? Was his fatal car malfunction rigged on purpose?

If Sally had no problem killing her business partner and friend of over twenty years, killing me would be a walk in the park.

I felt goosebumps as I shuddered.

I took my laptop out of the suitcase and plugged in the flash drive. It was an audio file. I clicked on it and waited, impatiently, as it loaded.

"Listen, I need you to do something for me." —silence— *"Discreetly. I need you to invite someone to the Fuchsia Summit, okay?"*

"Yes, ma'am. Who's going to the summit?"

"Richard Moore."

"Affirmative."

A low swoosh, followed by a clink, like ice in a glass, and then the recording was over.

I recognized Sally's voice immediately. But she was speaking to a man — a man with a low-pitched tenor. Who was it? He sounded familiar. I replayed the audio recording on repeat, and each time, the fog in my brain cleared ever so slightly, until it clicked. It was her bodyguard. The one with the thick mustache like Luigi from Mario Kart. I hadn't seen him in years. He must've gotten promoted from an entry-level bodyguard. I remember when he came into Urban Roast, he had a peculiar accent. It was subtle, only noticeable when he asked a question. His whos and hows were elongated, the way a child mimics an owl. I replayed *"who's going to the summit?"* a dozen more times, until I was sure.

What was the Fuchsia Summit? Why was Richard being asked to attend? Was there even a summit or was it code for something else entirely?

I felt an abrupt dizzy spell and nearly lost my balance. My head was throbbing, leaving me no choice but to tend to it. Then I realized the heavy growls in my stomach. The day had escaped me entirely, and I hadn't eaten since McDonald's, over 24 hours ago.

I ran my fingers through my hair, grabbed my handbag, pinned Mom's butterfly brooch to my gray T-shirt, and stepped out into the chilly night.

The streets were quiet, save for a few dive-bar goers. There was something cathartic about walking up the hilly town of Montpelier. No graffiti. No potholes. Not even a homeless person in sight. Montpelier held a nostalgic charm untouched by time's erosion. I wandered to a few restaurants glowing with LED lights, only to find them all closed. I was ready to turn back when a 24-hour diner sign caught my eye a few blocks down. The taste of cheap coffee and overindulgent Belgian waffles lingered in my imagination. I curled my middle finger over my index finger, hoping this diner also served breakfast in the middle of the night.

As I plopped into a booth seat, I was welcomed with a hot pour of coffee by a woman in her sixties. She had a pixie cut and a missing tooth.

"Nice brooch, darling," she said, placing a basket of bread next to my coffee.

"Thank you," I bowed. Suddenly, my chest tightened, and I used all of my might to hold back tears.

She cleared her throat and said she'd give me a minute.

I nodded, my eyes filled with water. I redirected my emotions toward the audio recording. What was the Fuchsia Summit? How could I find out without Sally noticing? Richard was scared for his life and he did, ultimately, die in a suspicious way. I guess Aaron was right about his father being murdered, just wrong about me being the murderer. Also, what was Sally doing at Aaron's house two days before he died? Did she drug him with her fentanyl and make it look like suicide?

"Are you ready, sweetheart?" Pixie-cut asked.

I pressed my temples. "Yes. Do you have Belgian waffles?"

"We sure do," she smiled.

"Perfect. Thank you." I gave her a gentle nod before she carried herself back behind the counter.

I was happy to see only a few other patrons. A group of college students sat on the opposite side of the diner playing cards, while a rotund couple covered in tattoos and piercings sat at the counter. Then there was me, a deranged-looking, sad woman.

I sunk my teeth into a piece of bread as I tried to piece my scrambled thoughts together. This was all too overwhelming. I had to be smart about my next move. If I said too much, I might get myself into trouble. But if I said too little, there might not be enough to go off of. I needed someone with experience handling crime — and someone I could trust.

Aleena Gupta.

I dug into my handbag to fetch her card. My fingers caught Dr. Waltz's glossy card first, and I chucked it back in. I was about to spill all my contents onto the table when I felt the pointy corner of another card. As I took it out and placed it on the table, Pixie-cut returned with a heavy plate of sweet-smelling food.

First waffles. Then a phone call.

Chapter 25

Aleena

I was awakened by my phone. At first, the ring sounded like a circus—an invitation for Rahul, Shaan, and me to watch the show of the year. But the ringing didn't stop once we were seated, and it didn't stop as the performers came out in acrobatic displays and extravagant outfits. The show turned into a haze, my mind fixated on the sound. Then my eyes opened, and the source of the ringing became clear: a number I didn't recognize was calling me—at four in the morning.

"Who is it?" Rahul muttered, still caught between two worlds.

"Not sure," I said, rubbing my eyes.

"Hello?" I murmured, speaking into the space between myself and a stranger.

"Detective Gupta?"

I knew that voice. It was Margaret. I pulled myself out of bed, suddenly alert, and stepped out of the room.

"Margaret?"

"Please, call me Margo. I'm sorry for calling you at this hour, but I need to talk to you. It's about Aaron."

I started pacing, passing Shaan's room in slow increments.

"Absolutely."

"Are you free this afternoon? 1PM?"

"Yes," I said quickly. I didn't want her to lose her nerve.

"Great. I'll see you at the 24-hour diner."

I paused. I hadn't been to the diner since Aaron and I shared an apple pie under a full moon, one breezy late night. My heart fluttered, but this time, I didn't hold on to it. I let the memory pass me like a cloud in the sky.

"I'll see you then, Margo. Get some rest."

"Thanks."

She sounded utterly depleted. Whatever she needed to share must have been gnawing at her.

Homeschooling Shaan turned out better than I expected. I had initially pictured a frantic woman chasing after a mischievous child, burned out before noon. But Shaan was a great student—attentive, patient, occasionally distracted, but eager to learn from his mother. As someone who had always prided herself on being career-driven, I was surprised to discover an untapped love for teaching my own child.

Yesterday afternoon, I reviewed the remaining syllabus and mapped out the rest of the school year. I was surprised to see multimedia and basic computer programming listed as core subjects. The entire climate of our future was shifting before our eyes, and technological competency became as essential as algebra has been for a century.

I decided to start our academic relationship by teaching a skill we often learn only retroactively, after a myriad of adult mistakes: emotional intelligence. If there was one thing I could teach well, it was the gold medal of my professional success. We spent the entire morning focused on a soft skill in articulating feelings. *Name three feelings you feel when you're angry.* He was a quick learner, and soon he understood that anger was just a bundle of feeling mad, hurt, and disrespected. His homework was to journal his feelings every night for the next week. At-home schooling and at-home therapy. Two birds, one stone.

After lunch, I dropped Shaan off at Mom's, planting a quick kiss on his cheek and thanking her for setting up an afternoon gardening class. Then I hurried back to meet Margo. Arriving ten minutes early, I treated myself to a slice of apple pie and a much-needed coffee. This time, I savored the sweet, nutty pie—the sharp, familiar tang of Granny Smith apples—alone. With each bite, I began to rewrite my story. This diner wouldn't just hold memories of soft giggles and light, fleeting kisses between Aaron and me, the full moon rising behind us. No. Now, it held this moment—me, savoring dessert in peace, grateful for a husband like Rahul. It was time to reshape what this place—and half of Montpelier—meant to me.

The bell above the door chimed, and Margo shuffled inside. She was wearing canvas shoes, jeans, and a white hoodie. She looked transformed, the way a celebrity does when you spot them running a drugstore errand. She scanned the diner and spotted me in the far-right booth as I waved. She looked around conspiratorially before sliding into the seat across from me.

"Thanks for meeting me," she said quietly.

Her eyes were swollen, and so were her cheeks. She appeared unsheathed, as though layers of her had been peeled off unwillingly. The Margo I first saw strolling into the station with her red-bottom heels and Louis Vuitton carry-on felt like a distant memory.

She signaled the waitress over.

"Can I get a cup of coffee and a cheeseburger, please?"

"Sure thing, darling," the woman responded.

She craned her head my way and waited.

"Just a refill on the coffee, thanks."

Margo proceeded to tell me about her tumultuous relationship with Aaron—and her even more bitter one with his father. She said Aaron had blamed her for Richard's death, when in fact, it was Sally Beaurshop. *"I have proof!"* she nearly squealed. She also spoke of her mother, whom she loved dearly, and her struggle with mental illness. *"Schizophrenia is no joke,"* she had said. The way Margo shared her story, I couldn't help but reach for her hand. This woman had been through the wringer, time and time again.

After I assured her for the third time that our conversation would remain confidential, she revealed Sally's underground drug operation. As a young woman, Margo had agreed to be the face on any paperwork associated with Sally's dealings in exchange for a high-paying receptionist job at her art gallery. *"A ticket out of poverty,"* she said shamefully. She also described a trick lipstick invention Sally used to traffic drugs. Then she told me about a woman named Carla—formerly Aaron's stalker—who had been photographing people entering and leaving Aaron's house for almost a year. And she had a photo of Sally's car parked outside Aaron's house, taken two days before he died.

"Wait — slow down," I gasped. My mind was racing, and I needed a moment to digest an entire dimension of Aaron I had never known.

"I know, it's a lot." She tilted her head as she bit into a fry. "Wait... why aren't you working with Officer Sanchez?"

I expected her to ask. And after all my dishonest, carefully-crafted brainstormed versions, I knew there was only one answer I could give.

"I was suspended."

The truth.

Her mouth dropped, exposing the buttery mash of potato on her molars.

"I had an affair with Aaron when I was engaged," I confessed.

"Wow," she gulped.

"Only Officer Sanchez and my husband know. To the rest of the world, I took time off to care for my son."

She took another fry, now slumped in her seat like a teenage girl.

"No wonder your husband seemed uncomfortable at Aaron's funeral," she muttered, thinking out loud.

I searched for her eyes until they met mine. "I'm going to solve this case, Margo. I know I shouldn't — and it'll probably get me fired — but I can't leave it up to Officer Sanchez now, can I?" I felt a grin form on my lips.

She straightened her back and furrowed her eyebrows. We both knew Officer Sanchez was gunning for Margo.

"You certainly cannot," she said.

She then revealed the reason behind her swollen appearance. A package had arrived from her mother's psychiatric facility, notifying her of her mother's death. Inside were a butterfly brooch, now pinned to her shirt, a letter, and a flash drive. She glanced around the diner before reaching into her handbag and pulling out the letter and flash drive.

"Sally murdered Richard?" I asked, after reading her mother's letter. I was taken aback by the innocence of its making. It resembled the love letters I used to get from Shaan when he was six years old, with slightly better handwriting.

"The flash drive has audio. It's a conversation between Sally and her bodyguard."

"Does she admit to killing Richard?" I could feel my body leaning in.

"Not exactly." She nibbled the skin on her thumb. "She talks about a Fuchsia Summit but I think that's a code."

Fuchsia Summit? If it was a code, we had no way of decoding it without a warrant for her or her possessions.

"I was thinking of dropping it off to Officer Sanchez so he can look into it," she said.

But I could tell by the way she shifted in her seat, she didn't want me to agree with that idea.

Luckily for her, I didn't.

"Listen to me carefully. You can get yourself into deep shit if you don't tread lightly."

She leaned closer, and suddenly, we were two girls gossiping about the pretty boy next door.

"Your name is on every incriminating piece of paperwork," I began. "You need to make sure you're protected — at all costs."

"How the *fuck* do I do that?" she wheezed, clearly frustrated by the dead end.

"Are you willing to testify against Sally?" I asked.

She took another bite of her cheeseburger, and I watched as she digested both her food and my question.

"If I have to," she finally said.

"That's good, Margo. Now do exactly as I say."

Chapter 26

Margo

Like a bear to honey, Aleena's plan worked seamlessly. First, I had to tag in Carla. *"Who do you trust the most in this town?"* Aleena had asked. My immediate response was Carla—the one person who would do anything for Aaron. Her task was simple: take the photo of Sally's car parked in front of Aaron's house two days before he died, slip it into an envelope addressed to Detective Gupta, and deliver it. She was to walk into the station at exactly 9:00 a.m., during the morning stand-up meeting when the entire staff would be in the conference room and the common area temporarily empty. Officer Sanchez's desk would be easy to spot—it was the only one with personal items, including a framed photo of him skiing. Carla would drop the envelope on his desk and walk out, her hoodie pulled up to obscure her face from the cameras. The goal, as Aleena explained, was to steer Officer Sanchez toward Sally. An envelope addressed to Detective Gupta, mysteriously left on his desk, was bound to catch his attention.

Carla completed the drop-off and headed straight to her car, where I sat in the passenger seat. She agreed to wait while she passed the baton. Aleena had instructed me to walk into the station and ask for Officer Sanchez at exactly 9:35 AM, just as he would be brewing his coffee and not yet back at his desk. The timing was crucial. He needed to discover the envelope right after our conversation. It would seem like a perfectly orchestrated sign from the universe, even though it was entirely fabricated by three very different women.

I decided to dress casually. The night before, I'd spent an hour debating my outfit while running through the plan. Although wealth brings its own privileges, I figured the closer I looked to Officer Sanchez's level, the more relatable I'd seem. I'd packed a simple black tee, jeans, and pumps for what I thought would be a couple of leisurely days—though this trip was stripping more from me than I'd expected. Still, it was the best I could pull together for my meeting with Officer Sanchez. As I walked into the station, the padding of the pumps hugged my heels. My fingers absentmindedly stroked Mom's butterfly brooch, as if it held a bit of fairy dust. A little magic was needed today.

I asked for Officer Sanchez and was guided to an interrogation room by an officer with a baby face.

Officer Sanchez appeared almost immediately, *as expected.* "Margaret," he said, sitting down across from me. "What can I do for you?"

He was eager. I could tell by the crease in his eyelids as he narrowed his gaze on me.

"I have information to share with you," I proclaimed.

He turned on the camera.

"Would you like some water or coffee?" he asked, suddenly hospitable.

"No, I'm fine."

My heart was pounding against my chest. "But first, I want immunity."

The words came out exactly as I'd practiced. I had stood in front of my faded mirror, repeating that sentence a hundred times before I could get the tone just right. I wanted to sound as crisp as spring water: no stutter, no hesitation, no misunderstanding.

He leaned back in his chair, surprised. "Margaret, I can't go around giving immunity to anyone who has *something* to say," he said coyly.

"I have information about a drug trafficking operation that would be vital to your investigation into Aaron Moore's death."

Aleena had prepped me on that line. I had to position it as intel big enough to grab his attention while directly tying it to his big-break case.

He crossed his arms and remained silent. I gave him all the time he needed to think, watching as he worked through the pros and cons of granting immunity to his number one suspect.

As Officer Sanchez sat there thinking, my mind wandered back to the conversation I'd had with Aleena. During our prep, I'd asked why we weren't also seeking immunity for information related to Richard's death. After all, I had evidence—my mom's letter, the flash drive. But Aleena had gently explained that neither was strong enough to hold up in court. The letter would likely be tossed due to my mother's unstable mental state, and the audio on the flash drive lacked the context needed to make it truly incriminating. With her warm smile, steady eyes, and sharp detective mind, she had laid out the strategy: give Sanchez just enough to build probable cause—enough to get a warrant for Sally's estate. If the police could search her property, we might finally uncover what "Fuchsia Summit" meant. And with any luck, that would lead to real, admissible evidence. *"Don't forget to tell him about the tricked lipsticks,"* she'd reminded me as I was leaving. *"He needs to walk into Sally's place knowing exactly what to look for."*

"We will grant you immunity," he whispered. At first, his voice was so low it didn't penetrate my thoughts. But then he repeated himself, loud and clear.

I nodded slowly, just as Aleena had directed.

She knew Sanchez would have more to say.

"Let me be clear, Margo. If your intel helps us build the case — whether it's the murder, the trafficking, or both — you'll have full immunity from prosecution related to the drug operation. That includes possession, distribution, conspiracy, and any related charges we might've pursued. But that's contingent on full cooperation and corroboration. No exceptions."

"I understand."

"Then, and only then, will you be immune to charges related to this investigation."

"I understand," I repeated.

"This has been stated on record," Officer Sanchez said officially. He leaned closer to the table. "Please proceed in sharing your information."

I took a deep breath. "Sally Beaurshop runs an underground fentanyl drug trafficking ring."

Aleena had instructed me to stop there. A clean, simple statement. The more I shared, the more my words could be used against me. *"It's important you say fentanyl specifically,"* she had emphasized, because of the elevated levels found in Aaron's autopsy.

Spoon-feed Sanchez.

"Do you have any proof of this?" he asked, expressionless.

"She uses tricked lipstick to transport her drugs."

I had asked Aleena if I should show him the lipstick hidden in my handbag. She gave me a firm no.

"I see," he said, clearly contemplating his next move. "Anything else?"

Yes. I have a fuckload of anything else.

"No, sir."

He paused, then said, "I will verify your information. At this time, you are immune from what we find in regard to Sally's drug operation."

I nodded steadily, shook his hand, and walked out of the station — hopefully for the last time.

Chapter 27

Eva

I've never believed in love stories. If anything, I'd be the first to show up at an anti-love protest. The entire framework of my life was built on the idea that love is transactional, consequential—a form of armament. Aubree always challenged that mindset, pointing to herself or bringing up my father and grandmother. *"Exceptions to the rule,"* I'd say, with the confidence of a girl raised in a cult. Maybe Andrew was an exception too. But lately, the balance was shifting. The foundation I'd built my fractured mind on was beginning to crack.

These past couple of days felt like a Nora Ephron movie. Boy meets girl. They connect instantly — too instantly. Boy falls for the damaged girl. But maybe this time, she changes too.

After Aaron's funeral and our impromptu coffee date, Andrew dropped me off at the Montpelier Inn with a kiss on the cheek. My mind split in two: one side hungry for his body—to use, abuse, and be abused—the only kind of intimacy I'd ever known. The other stirred with a feeble, unfamiliar feeling of excitement, safety, and fairytale wonder at what might be.

He refused to come to my room, despite the lust in his eyes. He didn't want to rush something that could be special. *"I'm forcing myself not to eat the marshmallow,"* he had said. At first, I thought it was an innuendo for a white girl's privates. But when my face twisted in confusion, he chuckled and explained a Stanford study on delayed gratification. Children were offered a choice: a small, immediate reward or a larger one if they waited. They were left alone with a marshmallow for fifteen minutes. The ones who held out were given an extra treat. *"I choose to wait, and also be rewarded with your heart,"* he concluded. I remember sticking out my tongue in disgust. *"Too sappy for my taste,"* I'd said, shoving his shoulder. But he just laughed and took my hand gently. *"Can I pick you up for lunch tomorrow?"* And I nodded, smitten.

We haven't left each other since.

"Wait did you see this?" Andrew's voice lingered as I slowly woke up in his arms.

His chest was broad against my head yet soft like a pillow, and his arm felt heavy around my waist. This must be what weighted blankets try to emulate. I'd never experienced this kind of affection before. I'd never cuddled into a blissful sleep, only to wake with the same warmth still hugging me. A thunder of emotions prickled in my head like distant lightning bolts. Is this real? Can I trust it? Is it even possible to fall in love this quickly? Will he break my heart? It would destroy me. But what if he doesn't? What if it's possible to find your match for life—someone who treats you well and loves you forever? What if vows do hold merit after all? What if the way I feel around him—natural, untethered, comfortable—means something? What if love really does exist in this saturated world of damaged people, linking us together like a golden life raft? If that's what I have with Andrew, then I'll get to experience love for what it truly is: the most precious of all currencies.

Andrew refused everything I offered on our first night together. I asked him to choke me, grip me, spank me, bite me—to unleash his animal instincts on me. He looked taken aback, even mortified—the way a girl might be when she first learns what rape means. A wave of shame flooded my veins. I was convinced he was disgusted by me. But then, in the same breath, his expression softened into something else: compassion. He held me tightly and didn't let go, despite my attempts to wriggle free. He held me until I cried. I sobbed in his arms for what felt like an eternity, until I fell asleep to the rhythm of his fingers stroking my hair.

By the second night, he took the lead. He caressed my body, kissed me slowly and tenderly. He took his time, drinking me in like water after a drought. He was intentional—careful, yet determined to help me break free from my own mental prison. His version of dirty talk came wrapped in reverence: *"I'm incredibly lucky to be with you. You're a diamond in the rough, and I intend to treat you as such."* Every fiber of my being wanted to push him away, to call him out on what I assumed was performative nonsense. But my heart stayed and drank his words like liquid gold.

That night, I had the best sex of my life. That night, I made love for the first time.

Making love was surreal. Although the physicality was the same as sex, being with Andrew unleashed a depth in me I never knew existed. It felt raw yet unsettling, true yet mystical. I had never been close to the gates of romance before, but Andrew managed to open the door and walk me in. Our souls intertwined as our bodies did, like an invisible bridge connecting two hearts—two melodies weaving into perfect harmony. Was this the feeling Grams tried to explain when she talked about faith? The conviction in something unseen but felt so fervently that everything else seemed trivial yet intentional. Had all my trauma, pain, desperation, fear, unworthiness, and mistakes become stepping stones to a greater purpose—a blessing… to Andrew? Or was this simply infatuation mixed with fantasy? A play my imagination put on to distract me from the darkness around me. Was it truly possible to fall in love with a man I had just met? But as Grams's rhetoric on faith would have it—*"It's true, God does exist"*—I was persuaded by the inner workings of my being to believe: It's true, soulmates do exist.

I became aware of an ache in my back and stretched my arms to relieve the tension. As I did, I looked out the window. He had rented a home, and it was gorgeous. Apparently, his parents were friends with the owners, and he'd always admired it. When he saw it on the StayHere app, he booked it immediately. Officer Sanchez didn't push Andrew to stay at the Montpelier Inn after learning of the arrangement. *"As long as you stay in Vermont,"* he had said. Floor-to-ceiling windows revealed a dense forest alive with singing birds, ancient trees, rustling leaves, and passing deer. The morning light poured in liberally, giving the illusion of a beach on a summer's day. I dropped back onto the white duvet and wrapped my arms around him, my bare chest pressing gently into his torso. He leaned in and kissed my forehead.

Then he shifted, wrapping his body around mine and whispering into my hair: "You are stunning, Eva Armstrong."

The phone slipped from the bed, hitting the floor with a soft bang.

He kissed me deeply, despite my morning breath, then reached down to retrieve the phone. I took the opportunity to squeeze his firm butt. He chuckled, turned the phone screen toward me, and clicked play on a video.

"Breaking News: Sally Beaurshop has been arrested in connection with the murder of Aaron Moore. Beaurshop, a prominent Boston art gallery mogul, was found with large quantities of opioids at her estate. She is also accused of trafficking fentanyl, allegedly using disguised lipsticks to distribute the drug among Beacon Hill's elite. Aaron Moore was discovered dead in his home several days ago from a fentanyl overdose. Sally Beaurshop was a longtime business partner and close friend of Aaron's late father, having been involved in Aaron's life since childhood. She will be held in custody in Vermont pending further investigation. Reporting for WBC News, Susie Lace."

Video footage showed Sally being arrested, her head bowed and footing steady. At the same time, images of hundreds of lipsticks sealed in evidence bags were displayed, scattered across a luxury bathroom floor. Some photos zoomed in on white powder contained inside the lipsticks.

"That's insane," I gasped.

"I can't believe we saw her a few days ago at Aaron's funeral," he huffed.

We were both quiet. Sally presented herself as a pseudo-family member of Aaron's, giving a eulogy and funding his mausoleum.

"Did you know her?" I asked.

"Growing up, I'd sometimes see her visit, but she mainly hung around Aaron's dad, always in business mode."

"Did she recognize you at the funeral?"

"No," he said. "I don't think she even tried."

We both stared at the ceiling for a beat.

"I can't believe it," he muttered. "I know Aaron and I haven't spoken since high school, and I despise him for what he did to me, but I never thought this would happen. He's dead—and a woman who claimed to love him killed him with the same poison she illegally trafficked."

"Phew," I said. I turned my body to face him, inches away, his brown eyes steadying my blues.

"You were with Aaron the night he died, right?" He asked, wincing at the thought.

"Yes," I sighed. "Do you really want me to repeat it to you?"

He had asked for a play-by-play, and I had told him exactly what I told the police—which wasn't much. A hazy memory is a witness's foe. I even confessed to Andrew that I had disclosed his relationship with Aaron to the cops, intel I got from Bee, when I was interrogated. *"Hey, it brought me to you, so I'm not complaining,"* he had said, also adding, *"It was time I faced my past anyway."*

"On second thought, I don't want you to repeat your night with Aaron," he admitted. "Sally must have done something to him while you were knocked out. You don't remember seeing anyone, right?"

I felt a bubble of frustration pop in my head. He already knew the answer to his question. I took a long inhale and allowed myself to calm down. There's a huge gap in my memory in which a man was murdered. I can understand the need for confirmation.

"Last I remember," I gulped as my chest tightened, "is sleeping with him."

His right eye twitched, and my heart sank.

"Then I woke up in the bed allotted to me as a StayHere guest, with his jacket on. I don't remember how I ended up on the other side of his house—or how I blacked out."

Shame befriended my cheeks.

He wrapped his arms around me and nudged my head against his chest.

"Don't blame yourself, Eva. If there's anyone to point fingers at, it's Sally Beaurshop."

I nodded as I breathed in his earthy aroma.

Before Andrew, I was a wanderer—aimlessly searching for satisfaction to meet my daily needs while my soul was left deserted to fend for itself. As Andrew shared his shadowed past and the choices that led him to a reclusive life, I saw a visceral similarity: he, too, had abandoned his weakened soul. But as we connected, our souls were quenched in one another after years of dehydration. Andrew completed me in a way I never thought possible. And though we may have been trauma-bonded, perhaps even infatuated with the fantasy of what could be, I couldn't shake the feeling of utter peace when I was with him. I felt fulfilled for the first time in my life. The purity of our bond was pristine—clear of pollution and deceitful intentions. It felt real, and I chose to have faith in that feeling. I chose to believe that a profound connection between two human beings was, in fact, possible. I chose to believe in soulmates. And I chose to believe I had found mine.

"I think I'm falling in love with you, Andrew Styversant," I murmured, lips pressed against his body.

He pulled me back and pushed a strand of hair out of my face.

"I'm *already* in love with you, Eva Armstrong."

As I searched his eyes, I couldn't help but realize how love truly is arcane at its core.

Love came to me in spits and slaps. My mom loved me with envy and self-loathing. My father loved me with eagerness and guilt. My grandmother loved me with opinion and tradition. My best friend loved me with empathy and hope. But now I see that Andrew loves me unequivocally. His love was so strong I could taste it—the antidote to burden, the spell that broke the curse, the light at the end of the tunnel.

I wrapped my legs around him, pulling him close. He inhaled sharply, a low moan slipping out as he took me in. I stroked the back of his hair—soft, curly, thick—while pressing my lips to his. His kiss was like clouds: gentle yet electric, his tongue meeting mine in a slow, delicious dance. My whole body hummed, tingling in all the right places. He kissed me just above my collarbone—the spot that made me groan—a pressure point of pure ecstasy.

"I want to be in your life for as long as you'll have me," he whispered in my ear as he slid inside me.

Chapter 28

Aleena

Turns out, Sally did not kill Aaron. I tossed in bed all night, the photograph of Sally on the night of Aaron's murder flashing in my head.

After I got the call from Margo yesterday confirming that the seeds had been successfully planted at the station, I began organizing everything I had. Rahul's home office was now fully dedicated to my investigation, complete with a lock to keep out wandering eyes—especially my son's. I had a great routine going: mornings spent educating Shaan, afternoons starring a one-woman show featuring a murder investigation while Shaan was with my parents. This was officially rogue territory, and I had every person of interest meticulously organized and col- or-coded by probability. Fiery red was reserved for Sally and she was the first person I dove into. Where had she been the night of Aaron's murder? We knew she'd been in Vermont 48 hours prior, but had she stayed—or gone elsewhere? I started with a simple internet search: Who was Sally Beaurshop to the rest of the world?

The phone rang, loud against the white walls. Captain Warshburg's name flashed on the screen. I cleared my throat and swiveled in my chair, my back to the investigation.

"Hello?"

"Aleena! What is this I hear about Shaan?"

My heart picked up speed.

"He's been struggling, Captain," I said, ready to begin what I had practiced. "I know this is abrupt, and I'm very sorry—but I need to devote time to my son before I lose him for good."

I heard him sigh.

"I vouch for Officer Sanchez, Captain." I continued as I rehearsed. "He's proven to be hands-on, quick on his feet, and knows this investigation as well as I do. Please give him a chance to step up while I figure out how to navigate Shaan."

I heard my voice crack at the end. Officer Sanchez was not up for the task. Although he showed promising qualities, he was impulsive and opinionated. He was easily blinded by his own perception and lacked a sixth sense for reading non-verbal cues. Margo was case in point.

After a minute of silence, the Captain spoke. "I trust you, Gupta. I'll have Officer Sanchez take point while you're gone. Please take all the time you need. As far as I know, you'll remain on paid time off for another month. I'll input your absence as bewilderment leave—but don't go around telling others about my kindness. The last thing I need is more people asking for favors, *capeesh*?"

"Thank you, sir."

"Give Shaan my love and good luck."

I felt horrible lying to the Captain. He was a good boss, and a great person. By effectively breaking his trust, I wasn't sure how I could ever earn it back if he found out. I closed my eyes and allowed the pressure in my temple to subside.

He will not find out.

I will solve this case and give glory to Sanchez, while simultaneously keeping Shaan on a better path and rebuilding my relationship with Rahul. I will then return to work and begin a new chapter—one better and brighter.

I swiveled back to face the desk and resumed researching Sally Beaurshop. She was an art aficionado, with galleries all over the East Coast and exhibitions on overlapping schedules. Her website was vague yet alluring. You didn't know if you'd get Picasso or a bowl of piping hot shit—but you wanted to find out. I scrolled until I found an exhibition that took place at the Beacon Hills Boutique Art Gallery the night of Aaron's murder. I clicked on it, and a picture album appeared. Photographs of people dressed in thousand-dollar fits were meandering through the open glass gallery. The place was buzzing, only catching a few faces at a time as heads turned toward the art pieces. As I clicked through the pictures, I didn't see anything of importance— until I did.

There was a photo of heads surrounding an abstract marble sculpture, and in the sea of people, Sally was captured leaning close to another person, whispering in their ear. Her hair was pinned, strands curled delicately along the sides. What caught my attention was her ruby red lipstick—stark against an otherwise bright backdrop. Sally wasn't in Vermont the night Aaron died. She was at her gallery exhibition, surrounded by at least three dozen people who could corroborate her alibi. It won't be long before Sanchez finds this.

Sally was also the type to hire someone to carry out a crime, just as she allegedly did in Richard's case. She was private, calculating, meticulous, and—most distinctively—paranoid. She would only trust someone within her own circle, someone she had trained and who had earned her trust, to kill Aaron. Sanchez should already have her phone records, but without hard evidence—which he won't find from a mastermind like her—we couldn't touch her security team. Unless, of course, I decode the audio tape between Sally and her bodyguard, whom Margo had confidently identified.

I had to figure out what Fuchsia Summit meant before it was too late.

It was time to restart and trace my steps back to the beginning. What happened to Aaron that night? The only person we know for certain who was near him was Eva Armstrong. Did we do a thorough background check on Eva? Is there any possibility she may be linked to Aaron—or even to Sally?

I began leafing through her files again. I remembered seeing no flight or DMV record of her ever coming to Vermont. The receipt from StayHere showed she booked Aaron's house the same day she arrived. She appeared to be in a rush to leave home. It was odd—booking a place the same day you leave, especially when a flight and a long drive are involved. Was she running from something back in Long Island? Was there more to her story than she let on?

I scavenged the internet. Facebook proved the most helpful. I traced her family line, cross-checking albums and timestamps. Eva had been an avid user since 2007, which gave me plenty to work with. I watched her face mature into those mesmerizing eyes, collecting glimpses from different chapters of her life. Her recent photos were bright and full of joy—many featuring another woman, her age, short with dark hair. Eva smiled the most when she was with her. There were also pictures with her father and grandmother, mostly taken at a small restaurant. But when it came to her mother, young Eva looked different—boyish, withdrawn, unhappy.

Next to her daughter, Amanda Armstrong looked radiant, almost as if she had siphoned the youth from Eva and injected it into herself. A photo from 2010 caught my attention. Captioned *Throwback Thursday*, it showed Amanda holding baby Eva in her arms. The backdrop made me pause. Tucked among towering trees and lush greenery, I zoomed in on the tip of a building— unmistakably the sculpture of Ceres, the Roman goddess of agriculture. As I adjusted the zoom, the color shifted—from green to a faint yellow. The yellow dome of our State Capitol peeked through the trees.

What was Amanda Armstrong doing in Vermont with infant Eva—the same daughter who, years later, would discover her host dead? Not just in the same state, but in the very same town.

I gave her a call. By the last ring, a breathless voice came through the line. I reminded her who I was and asked if we could meet for coffee. She didn't hesitate and agreed to see me in twenty minutes. I took a mental note of her eagerness. It may mean nothing. Or it may mean everything.

Chapter 29

Margo

Sally *fucking* made bail. I couldn't close my mouth when Officer Sanchez called me with the news. The emotional bombshell left me temporarily paralyzed.

"So what does this mean for my immunity?" I finally asked.

"Although she has alibis for Aaron's murder, she's still under investigation for her drug operation. Your immunity from any related charges remains intact, per your cooperation."

As the words came out of my mouth, they scratched and ached my dry throat. "But she'll be looking for me. I'm not safe."

He was silent for a moment. "Sally has no idea about your involvement with us. My advice to you is to keep your head down. If you find yourself in a situation where your life is being threatened, you can call me directly—and I will come to you."

Fucking great. If I was ever in actual danger, I bet Sanchez would stop for a donut on his way to me.

I thanked him and hung up the phone. He cared for me as much as he cared for a beetle crossing the sidewalk.

I strolled down to the lobby for a cheap cup of coffee. At the entrance, a silhouette stood against the glare of the outdoor light, holding me momentarily transfixed. But as the silhouette moved closer, Carla's face came into view. My first instinct was to duck and hide. But when I caught a glimpse of her longing eyes, searching for me like a lost puppy, I couldn't help but go to her.

"Hey, what are you doing here?" I asked, a smile plastered on my face.

"I wanted to come see you." Her expression remained gruff.

"Glad to see you. Thank you again for helping me drop the envelope at the station."

She nodded. Her baggy shirt was covered in mud, and her hair was tangled. She smelled of grass and body odor, and her eyes darted around suspiciously.

"Is everything okay?" I asked.

"Uhh—I've been a bit paranoid." She scratched her head aggressively.

"Why?"

"I keep thinking that now Sally's free, she somehow found out I took that photo of her car in front of Aaron's house— and that she's out to kill me. Maybe she even saw me when she came to see him." She sighed. "I miss Aaron so much. My home doesn't feel like home without him."

I guess a stalker's worst nightmare is for the person they're stalking to *poof*, vanish.

"Sally is too self-centered to notice anyone. You'll be fine," I lied, impressed by how convincing the words sounded.

"I'm going away for a while," she said, expressionless.

"Will you be safe?"

"Safety is my middle name." She finally smiled with her yellowing teeth. "Anyways, I wanted to say goodbye. But I'll call you when I'm settled."

"Please do."

God, please watch over her.

And with that, she was out the door—settling the tension between the eyebrows of the front desk representative.

I took a seat with a piping-hot cup of coffee and looked around. Was Carla right? Was she being followed? Did they have tabs on me too? Did Sally figure out I was the mole?

I took a sip and allowed the bitter heat to soothe my tense muscles. My ears perked toward a newscaster's low hum. The television mounted in the upper right corner of the wall displayed a picture of Sally, walking down a flight of steps. Below, a banner read:

SALLY BEAURSHOP MADE BAIL.

Her expression seemed docile, unattached. But I knew better. Behind her neutral guise, she held an anger only visible to those who've experienced her wrath. The elevated cheekbones and clenched jaw, the blinkless eyes and stiff fingers—she was on the hunt, and I sure wasn't going to be a frolicking deer.

A text message came in. It was from Aleena:

"Sally was at an exhibition in Beacon Hill the night of Aaron's murder. That's why she made bail. I'm working on decoding the Fuchsia Summit. We'll get her, Margo. One way or another, Sally's going away for a long time. In the meantime, keep yourself safe. I'll be in touch."

This wasn't looking good for me. Now that Sally had made bail, she was free to tighten up her claims and carry out her plan by framing me as the mastermind of her operation. She would find out I had immunity when I wasn't arrested, and then she would know I was the one who snitched. By the time Aleena could tiptoe around her own investigation to dig up more on the recording between Sally and Mustache Man, I'd be long dead, floating down a river somewhere.

My heart started picking up at a concerning pace, and sweat beads rolled down my neck. The thought slithered in before I could block it — the warm numbness of Tranquility Hour melting every edge, the hypnotic spin of LaVida Online Casino promising just one more win. My mouth watered at the memory of the rush, the illusion of control. I shook my head hard, unwilling to succumb. I had to keep fighting.

My entire life, I fought. With every dead end, I managed to find a rat's hole and squeeze through to the other side. I owed it to myself—and to my mother—to at least fight until the very end. I wasn't going to let this bitch control my life any longer. I was done microdosing on lethal drugs. I was done self-deprecating through gambling. I was done withering away.

It was time I played my queen in this fucked-up game of chess.

I took my cup of coffee and fetched a danish from the open breakfast buffet before making my way back to my room.

I dialed Sally.

"Let me call you back." With that, she hung up the phone. Her voice was direct and icy.

Was she already on to me?

My phone rang.

"I needed a secure line," she said.

"How are you doing? I can't believe what I've seen on TV," I said, motioning a gasp.

"Somehow they were able to get a warrant for my home," she paused, level-headed. "Do you know anything about this, Margo?"

My stomach shouted with an acute ache. My body was crumbling under the stress.

"Absolutely not. If you go down, I go down with you—everything is under my name," I said, pausing to close my eyes and steady myself. "I would never be so stupid as to double-cross you, Sally."

Logic and pride—Sally's greatest weakness—were my only weapons. I wished upon my lucky stars that they would be convincing enough.

"*Ahh*, I know, Margo. You're my little sidekick. Whatever I tell you, you do."

Heat rose in my throat like bile, but I forced it down. "And with pleasure. You gave me a new life, and I'm forever indebted to you," I said through gritted teeth.

More like shackled to your rotten soul.

She snorted through her nose, a swift breath followed by a hiccup. Her genuine laugh. "Debt is my biggest asset. The ones indebted to me always prove to be the most loyal." I heard her shuffle. "I do have one person who hasn't been indebted to me for a while now, and I believe their loyalty has faltered."

Before I could inquire more about her eerie comment, she sighed in relief and exclaimed, "Anyways! You have nothing to worry about, dear. These dumbasses who call themselves law enforcement have no substantial evidence on me—just frivolous charges. And best believe, I will make sure it stays that way."

I sank to the floor. What was I thinking? Sally was indestructible. She had everyone wrapped around her dainty finger, and I was dumb enough to try to play God in her world. My heart slowed; blood stalled in my veins while my organs screamed. I dug my nails into my stomach and focused on the bathroom light. *Steady, steady…*

"Margo, are you still there?"

"Yes, sorry. The service in my room is a bit spotty."

"So move."

"Yes, I'm good now. Sally, are you safe? Is there anything I can do?"

"No, no. I'm well taken care of."

I could see the smirk, that crooked smile. She prided herself on being plugged in.

"Oh, that reminds me, Margaret." She cleared her throat. My stomach dropped deeper into my carcass. She only called me Margaret when she was threatening or manipulating me. "As you can imagine, my bail was set at an absurd amount. These fuckers are always leeching off the rich." She sighed, and my skin crawled. "I need that 1.2 million dollars I transferred to you."

It all happened so fast. As soon as I registered that I'd already given a million of the 1.2 million dollars to the loan shark Sergio, my eyes went blurry and my mind went blank. The bathroom light faded into darkness until I was gone.

Chapter 30

Aleena

Shaan was hard at work. Math had always demanded intense mental exertion from him. He could concentrate so deeply that even a stomping rhino couldn't break his focus. I used to think he'd hate the subject, but when he answered correctly, he wore an unmatched look of accomplishment. He had his adoptive father's purity for life—a belief in hard, genuine work leading to positive outcomes and a sense of fulfillment.

As I observed Shaan erase, scratch his head, and try once again on a fraction problem, I couldn't help but be washed with solace. He was a bright child with the right intentions. I've interrogated my fair share of sociopaths and psychopaths, and they all had certain characteristics in common. They worked from a place of hate, and they reacted from that very place. My boy had no hate in his heart. Anger was simply a tool he used to cope with uncomfortable situations. All Rahul and I had to do was introduce other coping mechanisms into his mental toolbox.

A tear slid down my face as I realized my son was more like Rahul than Aaron. For the longest time, I'd been convinced Shaan was just an angry kid—that he'd inherited Aaron's temperament, etched permanently into his genetics. But homeschooling taught me something important: nurture is a powerful force in shaping a child. And Shaan was in good hands.

I love my son deeply. As a mother, I'd do anything to protect him, despite my own maze of baggage. Every child deserves unconditional love, and my heart panged at the thought of Eva and what she'd shared with me at the café. At first, she was a bit dismissive. Between sips of coffee, she explained how her mother wasn't nurturing or compassionate. I nodded—both in understanding and relatability. My own mother hadn't possessed much of those qualities either, and over time, a stone wall had been built around both our hearts.

But as I pressed further about Amanda Armstrong, the tight wiring around Eva's rhetoric began to unravel. I remember the exact moment I had an epiphany: as she spoke of her mother, I thought of my own. My perspective shifted, and a wave of unexpected appreciation washed over me. Compared to Eva, I was lucky. Amanda Armstrong was a terrible woman—one who abused her daughter for years, grinding her down until she was no longer a vibrant child, but a shell of a girl, and eventually, a broken woman.

Eva had no recollection of her trip to Vermont as a child. I had printed the picture I found on Facebook and watched as she stared at her young mother with anguish. Part of me wanted to take it away and hold her, but another part knew this was the right thing to do. I'd done this with crime victims before—it can be cathartic to see an abuser reduced to a two-dimensional image, powerless to ever approach again. I've seen it strip away fear and replace it with the quiet strength of knowing how far they've come. That's exactly what I saw in Eva as she processed her past: her mother was dead, her abuser gone forever.

Amanda's visit was proven to be a dead end. I couldn't link her to Aaron or Sally. There was also no evidence of Amanda in Vermont since. Eva had mentioned her mother's sexcapades, and how she clung to one man after another—likely her reason for being in the Green Mountain State, further committing adultery on Eva's father.

She did mention something that piqued my interest. I asked her how she was holding up in Vermont since Aaron's death, and she told me about her newfound friendship with Bee. She went on to speak about Bee, her father, and their compost business. I told Eva that Bee must have grown on her, because last I remember, Eva was spilling the beans during her interrogation about Aaron's infidelity with Andrew. I could have sworn I saw her smile, with rosy cheeks, as she remarked that a couple of people had grown on her during her time in Vermont.

I asked if she thought Bee and her father might have had any involvement in Aaron's death, and she shook her head frantically. *"No, no, no. They may be quirky, but they would never kill another person. Their whole livelihood is based on conserving the planet. I bet they wouldn't even hurt a fly."* I nodded in agreement but made a mental note to look into them. Although it seemed like Eva had grown close to the Wrights, she didn't know them well enough to respond so confidently. Was she protecting them, or was she being sincere? Sometimes, the people you least expect are the ones who do the most harm.

I HAD SEEN THE NEWS ABOUT SALLY'S BAIL BUT TURNED IT OFF AS soon as Shaan made his way to our "classroom" earlier that morning. Margo was in danger, and implicating Sally in the murder was the only way to ensure she'd be arrested without bail. Anxiety heated my forehead at the thought of running out of time. I was moving as fast as I could, yet the finish line kept slipping further away. I had to decode what the Fuchsia Summit was code for—today.

After I dropped off Shaan for a baking afternoon with Mom, I dove right into work. I spent the rest of the afternoon leafing through all the evidence I had. I replayed the tape Karen Vessel had given her daughter over and over again, searching for any sign that could point me in a specific direction. But I didn't have enough to work with. I had to get my hands on the evidence they seized from Sally's estate. I held one piece of the puzzle, while our homicide unit held the other. I swallowed a gulp of lemon water as I came to terms with my next steps. I couldn't move forward without Officer Sanchez's help. His only condition for protecting my reputation was that I stay away from the investigation— and yet, I was about to saunter back to the station with a lead.

I thought of Margo—her scared eyes and shaky hands. I thought of her mother, wasted away in a mental hospital. I thought of Rahul, a husband who coped for years with a cheating wife. I thought of Shaan, his precious innocence at risk with danger all around him. I thought of my parents, immigrants who built a life from scraps. I thought of Aaron, a damaged man who used his pain to spew hate—now buried beneath the earth. I thought of Eva, a bystander to a horrific crime, a beautiful woman with a vandalized past. And I thought of myself—someone who had long operated from fear and low self-esteem, finally turning the table and trying to be better.

I had to be better.

I swallowed my pride as I finished my lemon water. If I lost my job, at least I could say I gave it my all. Now that I had come clean to Rahul, we were a team. I no longer had to skirt around my family because of my past decisions. If I were fired for my involvement with Aaron, I wouldn't have to hide it from Rahul anymore. If shit hit the fan with my career, at least I wouldn't be riding the wave alone. I grabbed the flash drive and drove straight to the station. If I looked back, even for a second, I'd lose my nerve.

It wasn't until I stepped out of the car that I noticed what I was wearing: gray sweatpants and a navy blue sweatshirt with a coffee stain. The whole station was about to see their boss looking like a disheveled woman. If my reputation was already on the line, I might as well look the part. I shook my head and let out a low growl. Just a few days ago, I was wearing a perfectly tailored pantsuit, commanding respect as the lead detective. Now, I was a discarded employee—on the mend, going rogue in the two most comfortable pieces of clothing I owned, headed to convince my own subordinate to work on the very case I once led. Life had a cruel sense of irony, always twisting the knife while simultaneously slapping me in the face.

To my surprise, the station was locked. Luckily, Sanchez had forgotten to confiscate my key. I checked my phone; it was past 5 PM. In this town, work-life balance apparently took precedence over catching a potential killer. I texted Rahul a quick rundown of my plan just in case I got home late. He replied instantly, likely a voice message while on his way to my parents' house to pick up Shaan, wishing me good luck.

The lights were off, except for a fluorescent beam above Sanchez's desk. I heard a flush from the bathroom and decided to stay put by the entrance in case I had to exit immediately. Sanchez came out, still tucking his shirt into his pants, when he saw me. He faced me directly, his eyes bulging.

"Hey, it's me." My voice echoed.

He looked stunned, and for a moment I expected him to draw his gun and shoot me.

"It's me, Aleena," I repeated.

Suddenly, his stupefied expression melted. He waved me over with relief.

"*Ah*! All I saw at first was your shadow." He sighed with relief. "Thank God. I need your help, Detective Gupta. I'm way in over my head." His tone shifted—humility sounded like it belonged to a different version of him. He was immediately more likeable.

"Wow, I thought you were going to kick me out," I said, pulling my chair up to his desk.

"Well, you're not supposed to be here," he admitted, "but at this point, what you did pales in comparison to the behemoth we're dealing with."

His desk was buried in paperwork. He'd even had to displace his framed skiing photo. As he sat down, he seemed to shrink, buried under the piles of files.

"Is this from Sally's estate?" I asked, scanning some of the documents.

"Yeah. We didn't even get a chance to go through everything before she made bail." He moved a box of files aside and faced me. "But we did get something from the interrogation when Sally was arrested. She was mostly tight-lipped with her lawyer, dodging most questions. But he did allow her to explain why she was at Aaron's house two days before his death."

I fixed my sweatshirt and pulled my hair into a tight ponytail, eyes locked on his.

"She said she's been trying to recruit Aaron to take over what his father used to do for her company. Offering him a partner role in her gallery firm, hoping to use his expertise to expand to more locations."

I rolled my eyes and he chuckled. "Yeah, we both know what she really wanted was his involvement in her drug operation. But apparently Aaron wasn't interested, and her showing up at his house was a desperate attempt to convince him."

If that were true, his death just 48 hours later must have been a serious blow to her plans. She was the type to get what she wanted and if she wanted Aaron on her team, she needed him alive and well.

"Do you believe her?" I asked.

"It's hard to trust a psychopath, but her phone records show multiple calls with Aaron over the past few months."

"Listen, I have something that will help," I said, ruffling through my sweatshirt pockets.

I shared the recording and told him I received it anonymously. I wasn't sure if I could trust him yet, especially if he was still gunning for Margo. To my surprise, he didn't press me any further. He listened to the recording twice before commenting.

"*What the fuck* is Fuchsia Summit?" he asked.

"That's exactly why I came to you. I believe the answer is here," I said, pointing at the mountain of files on his desk.

"Even if we find something, Sally has a bulletproof alibi for Aaron's murder." He wiped a glaze of sweat off his forehead. "And now that she's made bail, she'll have an airtight case—especially since…" He paused for a moment and shifted in his seat, clearly contemplating. "Especially since everything fraudulent is under Margaret Vessel's name."

Although I already knew all of this, I wondered if he trusted me enough to tell me Margo had immunity.

I decided to poke the bear. "Why don't we go after Margaret, if everything is under her name?"

He rubbed the back of his neck and took a breath. "She has immunity with regards to Sally's drug operation," he admitted, "because she's the one who gave us what we needed to get a warrant for Sally's estate."

Before I could respond, he added, "But I still think she murdered Aaron. I just can't pin her enough to arrest her."

If I hadn't been looking at him, I wouldn't have noticed his mouth move—and if I hadn't been paying attention, I wouldn't have read his lips as he mouthed: *"That fucking bitch."*

"What do you have against Margaret?" I blurted, my head hot with anger.

"She's impulsive. A gold digger. She destroyed the Moore family—first with Richard, then with Aaron—just so she could gamble their fortune away." He jammed his right hand on the table with a deafening *clank!*

"Woah, Sanchez… are you okay?" I mustered, my heart jumping a beat.

"It's just—" he was speaking between breaths, "she reminds me of my mother. She made our lives a living hell with her gambling addiction. At one point, my dad was working four jobs just so we could have canned beans and rice for dinner!"

Sanchez was my blind spot. As good as I was at reading victims and suspects, I missed the mark in reading my own teammate. I hadn't paid much mind when he was transferred from New Mexico or when he spoke of his past with quiet disdain. But hearing this now, I felt a pang of empathy I hadn't allowed myself before. His past wasn't just background noise—it was the fire that forged his relentless drive. Despite everything, he was the only one in the entire department working himself to the bone to solve this case. He was also the one who didn't report me for misconduct when most would have. As we sat side by side in an empty office, I realized we shared more than just a job—we shared a resilience born from hardship and a commitment to seeing this through, no matter the cost.

"Eric, I'm so sorry," I finally said. "I can understand how tempting it is to associate someone's behavior with someone else who has hurt you. But Margaret is not your mother—and the sooner you realize that, the sooner you'll look at this whole case with a clearer perspective."

"You don't think she killed Aaron?"

"I don't."

He sighed, and I watched as his fingers stopped trembling.

"What if Sally hired someone else to kill Aaron?" I asked.

"It would make sense, given her alleged tendencies based on the audio recording."

"Did you get any information on her security team?"

I couldn't tell him I knew who the man in the audio was without compromising Margo. But if I could see what he looked like, maybe I could identify him from Margo's description of his distinctly animated mustache.

Sanchez quickly got to his feet and shuffled over to a box on the floor. "As a matter of fact…" he said, pulling out a file and moving to my desk. There, he laid out five different photographs. "Alfanso Conti, head of security. Ashton Keller. Ramona Leighton. Samuel Ink. Foster Geller."

He pointed at each photo as he said their names, and Alfanso stood out like a sore thumb. He must be the man Margo was referring to. He had a thick mustache, dark brown hair, and pale skin. He and Ashton were both large men, especially when compared to the dainty frame of Ramona, who stood beside them. Her team looked innocuous at best, conspicuous at worst. Sally was smart—she knew how to pick people who could either blend in or stand out, depending on her needs.

"Wait a second," I said, narrowing my eyes at the photos in front of me.

They all looked familiar. I pulled out my phone and opened the tab I had saved from Sally's gallery exhibition on the night of Aaron's death. After a few minutes of meticulous scanning, I found every single one of them in the images. Alfanso and Ashton were stationed at the entrance, standing guard. Ramona and Foster were disguised as caterers and Samuel appeared to be acting as the floor manager. Her team was versatile—jack-of-all-scheming-trades.

"Shit," I said, louder than I meant to.

Sanchez jolted upright at his desk, startled mid-read on some file.

"Her entire team was at the exhibition the night of Aaron's murder. None of them could have killed him. And Sally isn't the type to outsource something as risky as murder."

He suddenly looked depleted, as if every bit of energy had drained from him. "Honestly, Aleena… at this point, Aaron may have died of an accidental overdose."

The Aaron I knew would have never taken those drugs willingly.

"Listen, Sanchez, we need to play this right. If we jump the gun, we could lose everything. I think we should find out what Fuchsia Summit is code for first—then who knows, maybe it'll help us figure out what happened to Aaron."

"I guess that's fair," he murmured.

And with that, we began mapping out all the evidence collected from Sally's estate. Three hours and some Chinese take-out later, the floor was covered in papers and color-coded tabs. Much of what we found implicated Margo in the drug operation—except for one specific folder buried within a vast hard drive. We stumbled upon it through an email thread between Sally's assistant and a floral company, in which the color *fuchsia* was mentioned. The exchange was about fuchsia florals for an exhibition, but it pointed us to a design folder that led to an entire database of information. One subfolder was labeled *On-boarding* and inside was a single password-protected document titled *Guide*. Why was a password-protected file buried in an otherwise mundane database?

"On it," Sanchez exclaimed before I could even ask.

Thirty minutes later, Jacob—our young cybersecurity genius with a long beard and an affinity for forest expeditions—was at the office, working on decrypting the password.

"Sorry to have called you in this late," Sanchez said.

"Honestly, this is why I got into this line of work. Finally, something exciting!" He let out a soundless chortle before diving back into his code.

What we discovered was the holy grail. After Jacob hacked the password, we were introduced to a repository of code words. It appeared to be an appendix, a cheat sheet one would memorize during onboarding onto Sally's team.

Blue Kins = Surround Sally
Yellow Conference = Get Sally out
Pink Floss = No deal
Fuchsia Summit = Kill

I jumped out of my chair. I couldn't believe we actually decoded the audio! Sanchez followed suit, and the next thing I knew, we were hugging in excitement. His shoulders were leaner than I'd expected beneath his loose-fitting uniform. He smelled of cotton, coffee, and tobacco.

"So Sally put a hit on Richard Moore," he said, settling back into his chair.

"It won't take a genius to match her voice from the recording—and with this database, I believe we can get a judge to deny her bail!"

"It's odd, isn't it?" Sanchez remarked. "In the process of trying to find Aaron's killer—a victim from days ago—we managed to find his father's killer, a victim from ten years ago." He paused and exhaled slowly. "Yet we still don't know who killed Aaron."

I nodded, feeling a pinch of disappointment. Why couldn't I figure out what happened to Aaron? If anyone could, it should be me. I had the advantage—both as a professional detective and as his ex-girlfriend.

"Maybe there was no killer," Sanchez said with a sigh of exhaustion. "Aaron overdosed, smacked his head on the counter, and died."

Perhaps it was the opposite of what I thought—maybe I was at a disadvantage all along. Since his death, Aaron's true character has been revealed, and it's nothing like the story he so carefully constructed. I had been enthralled by his narrative—and by my own fantasy—that I ignored, or even rationalized away, all the signs, even the blatant ones, like the bloodied lip he gave me after finding out I was pregnant. He hurt people and left them to bleed. The Aaron I fell in love with never really existed.

Maybe karma finally caught up with him. Maybe he chose to let go of reality and succumb to Sally's fentanyl, never realizing he was letting go forever.

Yet… I couldn't shake the feeling that he was murdered.

Chapter 31

Eva

The clouds hung low, as though the mountains were wearing top hats. We drove past one, then another, winding up the ravine. This time, I insisted on driving my rental Corolla. I had grown comfortable in this borrowed car—snacks stuffed in the glove compartment, two coats laid out on the back seat (one for rain, the other for chilly nights), and my travel backpack beside them, packed with essentials I'd needed during my stay with Andrew. With a steamy cup of coffee in his lap and a smile on his face, I drove nervously, tapping my fingers against the steering wheel. *He won't like this. He won't like this one bit.* What if he breaks up with me because of it? My heart began to pound at the thought of Andrew leaving me over something I had no business doing. Anxiety prickled at my fingertips, and in a frantic attempt to ease the tension, I jammed the radio button and a loud voice boomed:

"Breaking news: Sally Beaurshop has just made bail—only to be arrested once again. Today, she was detained in connection with a cold case. Our sources confirm that Sally ordered a hit on Richard Moore, her former business partner and the father of the recently deceased Aaron Moore. Police are still actively investigating Aaron Moore's death. Shocking revelations for the otherwise peaceful town of Montpelier. This is Shauna Ryder reporting for *What's Happening, Vermont?* Stay tuned after this short break."

"Holy shit," Andrew said, his voice echoing off the metal of the car.

I sat frozen, my mind racing. Was this finally over? Could I go home? Would Andrew come with me?

"How terrible," I finally managed to say, the words hollow in my throat.

"I hope this woman goes away for a long time," he muttered, sipping his coffee.

Shauna Ryder's voice blasted through the speakers once more.

"We interrupt our break with another update in the Sally Beaurshop case. Sources confirm that her head of security, Alfanso Conti, has been arrested and detained in Beacon Hill, Boston. He's facing charges for conspiring with Sally and orchestrating Richard Moore's death by tampering with his brake lines. Is there a curse haunting the Moore family? With Aaron Moore found dead just days ago, the question remains: was it an accident—or premeditated? Did Sally put a hit on Aaron too? Stay tuned as this case unfolds, only on *What's Happening, Vermont?*"

I nearly missed my turn. Andrew didn't seem to notice how far into the mountains we'd driven. Cottages were spaced out by acres—privacy here was currency. It would be easy to disappear in a place like this. He was still lost in thought, his face unreadable as he turned the names Sally, Richard, and Aaron over in his mind. He didn't even glance up when the old Wright Composting sign came into view, glaring against a ruby-red backdrop.

"Babe?" I broke the silence, my voice pulling him from his trance.

"Hmm?"

"We've arrived."

He looked around, taking in the oak fence and red brick house.

"Where are we?" he asked, his brows furrowed.

"Please don't be mad, but... I brought you to see Bee Wright."

He glared at me with utter shock and the next thing I knew, he was outside the car, pacing.

I stepped out gently, walking around to face him.

"Does she know I'm here?" His voice wasn't loud, but I caught the rising panic in its undertone.

"Yes."

"Why did you bring me here?" He hissed.

This was the closest I'd seen him come to anger. His jaw was tight, both hands clenched into rock-hard fists. But after a beat, his shoulders dropped as he locked eyes with me. He wanted answers before he reacted. The first time I saw someone suppress rising anger to seek understanding and validate their emotional response was my father. I'd been stunned, as if I'd witnessed a wizard at work. I drew in a quick breath of gratitude that Andrew possessed that same kind of magic.

"What happened between you two... it happened a long time ago." I said.

I paused, breathing past the knot in my throat. "Bee is my friend. And you are—" My heart skipped as the words fought their way forward. "You are the love of my life."

His eyelids fell, and the sharp edges of his anger softened. "She hates me, Eva," he said, just above a whisper—his voice low as the wind.

"She's open to speaking with you," I managed, just before the front door swung open. Bee stood on the steps, arms crossed, in a floral pink dress.

"She doesn't look like she wants to speak to me."

"After getting to know both of you," I said gently, "I believe you were both victims of Aaron. And if anyone can understand the state of mind you were in... it's her." I stepped a little closer. "Remember when you told me it was time to face your past?"

He shrugged, unsure, his weight shifting on the gravel.

"Babe," I said softly, "it's time to find closure. It's time to move on."

His big brown eyes met mine—sheening now with something raw and human. "I'm ashamed, Eva!" he shouted suddenly.

I flinched, more from the emotion than the volume. I wondered if Bee heard his voice carrying over the growing grass like a song only the broken can hum.

He stood still for a long moment. Then, finally, he walked to me. He kissed my forehead, lips trembling. "You're right. I need closure," he whispered into my hair.

And together, hand in hand, we walked toward Bee.

The anguish on Bee's face was unmistakable. For a woman usually so cheery, she now looked bitter—disdained, even. Her self-worth, once firm and grounded, had been shaken by Andrew. And now, a decade later, here he stood in front of her.

"I've been preparing to see you since Eva told me," she said, her words carefully controlled, like she was fighting the urge to cry or yell.

"Hi, Bee," Andrew offered with a small wave, his cheeks flushed.

"Why don't we go inside?" I said, gesturing toward the door.

Bee shot me a look—stern, unreadable. "Only if that's okay with you," I added quickly.

I felt off-balance, like I was standing in heavy dew between two opposing magnets—drawn equally to both, suspended in the tension. The pull was strong and even. I took a steadying breath as they both turned their eyes to me, waiting. I wasn't here to take sides or pass judgment. I was the bridge—a mending bridge between two people I'd grown to care for, for the first time since Aubree.

Bee surrendered her post and stepped aside, letting us into her humble abode. The house smelled of fresh rosemary and roasting potatoes. As I slipped off my jacket, a surprising warmth settled over me. Despite Mr. Wright's erratic behavior and uncomfortable comments, Bee had quietly found her way into my heart. There was something about her—an aura of sorts—that was soft yet steady, planting a sense of coziness all around her.

"I'm making a casserole for us," she said, glancing at me.

I nodded in appreciation and led us to the dining table. As I sat, I couldn't help but notice how immaculate everything looked. Bee must have been up for hours, cleaning, cooking, and preparing. Her nerves had probably vacuumed the house from top to bottom.

"Is Mr. Wright here?" I asked gently.

"No. He's gone to Marshfield to fish." She blew a wild strand of blond hair off her face, which had broken free from her tight ponytail.

Andrew cleared his throat. It boomed through the small dining room like a stampede of elephants.

Talk about the elephant in the room.

"Right," Bee said, crossing her arms.

"Listen," I began, turning slightly so I faced the center of the table—positioned between them, both literally and emotionally. "In this short time, despite the circumstances, I've come to feel incredibly lucky to have gotten close to both of you." My eyes rested on a painting of a murky green creek hanging on the wall across from me. "You're both good people… who happened to be in a bad situation."

"I wouldn't consider Aaron cheating on me with Andrew a bad situation," Bee interjected, her voice rising like a struck chord. "I'd consider it a human error."

I tilted my head slightly, just enough to catch Andrew in my peripheral vision. His eyes were cast downward, his shoulders hunched as if shame had physically reshaped him. "You got this, honey," I whispered, barely audible, yet praying it echoed in his heart loud enough to give him the courage he needed.

After a beat of silence, he spoke. "I want to start by saying how deeply sorry I am."

Andrew's voice was unrecognizable, like a mouse trapped inside a lion's body.

"I'm sure you are," Bee snapped.

"The guilt's been gnawing at me for years," he continued, his voice trembling. "Please, Bee... I never intended to hurt you."

"Well, you did."

"Aaron was—he was—a very convincing person." He hesitated, struggling to string the words together. "He kept pushing this idea of us... being romantic. And I wish—" Andrew sniffled as a tear slid down his cheek. "I wish I'd been brave enough to stop him."

He stood abruptly and began pacing, confined to the few feet of space between the dining table and kitchen counter. "I never wanted more than friendship. I never wanted to be with him. Or with any man... not in that way." He ran his hand through his hair, agitated. "Even though I never explicitly had the courage to stop Aaron, I also never explicitly consented either."

He stopped and turned toward us, eyes hollow. "Part of me wants to accept that I was sexually abused." His voice cracked. "But another part of me floods with self-loathing because I never stopped it." He looked down at the floor as though searching for answers in the woodgrain. "That back and forth... it ruined me."

My heart ached as I watched him pour out the darkness he'd clung to for years. I was reminded of my mother and how she controlled me. Though I never objected to her treatment, that didn't make it any less abusive. I was never given the grace to decide what was best for me. I was never given the option to say no because I was held in a chokehold by the one person I thought I loved—who I believed had the best intentions for me. But the unbearable shock of how she treated her own child—so cold, so calculated—was incomprehensible. My body couldn't respond; it folded in on itself, muting me. *I was just a kid.*

"I was just a kid," Andrew said aloud, reflecting my thoughts like a whispered secret shared between wounded souls.

A full minute passed in silence, heavy and thick with revelation.

"I didn't know," Bee finally said.

She rose and approached him slowly. Andrew flinched, instinctively taking a step back. But she reached for his shoulder and steadied him, then pulled him into a hug. As she rested her head on his chest, she whispered, "Although... may he rest in peace, Aaron was a real piece of shit."

Andrew snorted, and Bee let out a wheezy laugh. I held the moment close, pressing it into the folds of my memory—a snapshot to revisit whenever the world felt bleak. Watching them—two fractured souls finding peace in each other's presence—was a balm for my own sore heart. My trip to Vermont had been a whirlwind, but now, in the stillness after the storm, a quiet truth settled in: the chaos had delivered me to two people I'd carry with me for the rest of my life. Strangers just days ago, now divinely bonded, as though our pasts were only the opening act to the real show of our lives together. Aaron may have shattered lives, but in his absence, healing had found its way in. His death, cruel as it was, had stitched shut wounds he once left gaping.

"Well, I'll finally sleep well tonight!" Bee exclaimed, a brightness returning to her cheeks.

"Same," Andrew said, giving her one last squeeze before gently releasing her small frame.

Bee glanced at her watch, then at her phone. She opened an app and began showing us the progression of her sleep over the past year. She explained that she started tracking sleep because her father had been experiencing night terrors—watching, every night, as his wife was consumed by the fire that burned down their red brick home. Bee, who leaned on science for answers, took a deep dive into the study of circadian rhythms and sleep therapy. She was delighted to see progress in her father's sleep over the past couple of months as they spent more quality time together.

Bee, on the other hand, hadn't had a night of quiescent sleep since Aaron's death. She would toss and turn, mind replaying her own gullibility—how she'd believed his lies, how she'd taken his hush money under the guise of saving her father's business. When sleep finally came, it betrayed her. A voice, low and mocking, would slither through the dark, telling her she'd done it to protect the man who had humiliated her. Then the darkness would part, revealing Aaron and Andrew in bed together, their laughter sharp and cruel. Aaron would watch her while touching Andrew, whispering something in his ear that made them both smirk, as if her pain were foreplay. The voice would swell, the laughter turning jagged, until she woke with a start—pulse racing, body locked in place. According to her research, unre-solved feelings often force the sleeping mind to process trauma, and she was living proof of the prolonged agony that comes with a lack of closure.

"Until today," she concluded wistfully.

"That's terrible," Andrew said, taking her hand in his.

I, however, was focused on a different part of her story.

"You've been tracking your and your father's sleep every day for the past year?" I asked.

"Yes, every day," she replied, with a hint of pride.

"Bee, take this tracker to the station—you might have just found the alibi you and your father need for Aaron's death."

Chapter 32

Margo

I must have been driving for an hour and a half when God presented Himself through the voice of Shauna Ryder.

"We interrupt our smooth jazz hour with another breaking news update on Sally Beaurshop. It's been confirmed that she and her head of security are currently being held without bail. I repeat—without bail! Authorities say Sally was arrested in connection with the murder of Richard Moore, business partner and father of the recently deceased Aaron Moore, as well as on allegations of running a fentanyl operation in Boston's thriving district. She had previously secured bail due to an alibi in Aaron's death and legal maneuvering on prior drug charges. But now, the once-untouchable Sally may have lost her only leverage for freedom, facing this latest, high-profile accusation. What will become of Sally Beaurshop? Stay tuned as we follow every development. This is Shauna Ryder for *What's Happening, Vermont?*"

I couldn't believe it—Sally and her right-hand man had been apprehended, and likely for good. With her still facing charges for running an entire drug operation, my immunity from anything tied to it remained intact. I no longer had to fear my own name; Margaret Vessel didn't belong to her anymore. A jolt of adrenaline shot through me, prickling my limbs, and I pushed the car to 80 on the empty freeway, smooth jazz blaring at full volume. The wind from the open windows slapped my face like a thousand cold snowflakes, carving a new sense of self into me. I was free. Could I finally begin a life unshackled from the crushing weight of my past?

Sally's text no longer burned in my pocket. After fainting from the realization that I couldn't return her money, I came to on the hotel room floor, my skin slick with sweat, a small pool of drool beside me. The sun hung low on the horizon, casting a golden haze across the room. I had blacked out mid-conversation—my body folding under the avalanche of fear and pressure. A million dollars I couldn't give back, and the consequences were unthinkable. I had no choice. I had to run. I packed everything I owned, called for a rental car, checked out of the hotel, and took a taxi to the pickup location. Now, I was behind the wheel, putting miles between us.

It wasn't until I was southbound on I-89, idling at a light, that I finally felt ready to check my phone. Sally's message had been waiting for hours.

"Margo, your service is shit. Get somewhere you can wire me the money. Don't fuck up—or else…"

She had the audacity to type out an ellipsis.

During the first hour on the freeway, I watched as the sun peeked from behind a forest of pine trees like a shy child, casting an extravagant display of pink cotton candy clouds and a yellow sky. At the same time, I kept checking the rearview mirror for any cars that might be tailing me. I was officially running from Sally. I had voluntarily taken the target and placed it on my own back. With the remaining $200,000 in my bank account, I was driving into the sunset, praying for the best.

The rest of the drive—after Shauna Ryder shared the good news—was a blackened breeze. Sally must have gotten arrested shortly after her threatening text message to me.

The night shadows didn't scare me anymore. The solitude wasn't depressing anymore. The newfound prospect of a better life had birthed itself in my heart. But before I could repaint my story, I had to make a pit stop.

I found myself at a gas station on Main Street in Concord, Massachusetts. The town bewitched me. Quaint mom-and-pop shops lined the streets, and bedazzled string lights twinkled above cobblestone sidewalks and the warm-toned sandalwood square. Although I hadn't yet reached my final destination, my heart fluttered at the charm of this place—a town Mom used to describe in bedtime stories, back when we lay curled up in our creaky, gunshot-riddled, and foul-smelling apartment. As gas flowed into the white Chevrolet Spark, I rummaged through my suitcase for the letter from McLanes Psychiatric Hospital. It held the location of Mom's burial: Sudbury Cemetery. Just one more town over, and I would finally pay my respects to the one person I loved with all my heart.

An icy air had settled over the night sky as I walked through the cemetery gates. I shivered despite my ivory fuzzy jacket, navigating the terrain dotted with gravestones planted upright on the otherwise flat land. An owl screeched in the distance, and whistles from nearby trees echoed like ghosts trapped in purgatory. The cemetery was vacant, except for a family of four paying their respects at a tombstone too far away to make out. Finally, I found Karen Vessel's resting place. The hospital had chosen a gray headstone, engraved with its logo—a golden eagle carrying an eaglet—in the bottom right corner. It matched the emblem stamped on the letter I held in my hands. As I surveyed Mom's phantom neighbors, I noticed three long rows dedicated to patients from the hospital. Their common room may have been filled with children's games and softly humming televisions, but this was where those lost souls found peace—resting in their eternal common room. Mom was finally inducted past the gates of life. I bent down to read what was inscribed on her gravestone:

In loving memory of Karen Vessel
A mother and a daughter
A lover of all things, especially butterflies
1959–2024

I slumped on the cold, wet grass, settling into an area of fresh mud. As my nose and hands dropped in temperature, my cheeks and stomach ached with agony. If only the world saw Karen the way I did. She truly was a lover of all things, mesmerized by God's miraculous brushstrokes. Even the most mundane gave Mom a sense of untethered joy.

I got back up and touched her grave. To my surprise, the gravestone was warmer than expected, as if she were reaching out to touch my hand in return. From my breast pocket, I took a single red rose—one I had preserved for years, ever since the first night Richard hit me. I'd wrapped it in a paper towel and pressed it between the pages of the largest book I owned: the Bible. When I finally opened it years later, the rose was still there, flawless as ever. Even in its afterlife, it held its curves and beauty—the same way I remembered Mom, as if her spirit hovered beside me.

I carried that Bible everywhere I traveled. It lived at the bottom of my suitcase, untouched, resting in the dark. I'd grown so used to bringing it along that I barely noticed it anymore—until I found it again in that musty hotel room in Vermont. With a heavy heart, I cracked it open and read the scripture where the rose's center had rested: *"Love bears all things, believes all things, hopes all things, endures all things."* I gasped. It was the most accurate description of my mother I had ever read—one who bore, believed, hoped, and endured.

With hot tears streaming down my raw, icy cheeks, I whispered, "I love you, Mom. I know you're sitting at God's feet now, learning the infinity of His wisdom—finally at peace and delighting in the woman you were, and the eternal life ahead of you. From this day forward, I vow to live differently, to see the world through the same love and grandeur you always did. I promise to cherish and use the rest of my time on this earth for my own healing and growth—just the way you always wanted me to. Rest in peace, Karen."

It hurt to sniffle. I touched my nose to find solid stone. I was forced to move my legs and clutch my arms. I took a final glance at Mom's grave and felt an overwhelming warmth of surrender. As the scarlet rose lay upon her gravestone, accepting its new home with my mother, I also began to accept my new home— one far away from what used to be.

I headed back to Concord, Massachusetts.

I managed to check into a bed and breakfast right in the heart of Main Street. As the wind picked up, whipping through the old trees and rattling the aging building, I felt grateful for the spare room. The house, built in the mid-1800s and recently refurbished, smelled faintly of wood polish and dandelions—a quiet, cozy scent that settled over me. I'd never truly felt at home before. Though I grew up in Roxden, the violence there never let me settle. Beacon Hill was utopia by sight, but it hid its brutality behind closed doors. Here, though, something felt different. It tingled deep in my gut, as if my soul was somersaulting. That night, I finally rested—truly rested—for the first time in years.

I woke up with the sun high in the sky, as though it was ready to play. The rustling leaves and soft murmur of passing pedestrians greeted me. My window looked out onto Main Street, lined with historic buildings turned local shops, bike trails, and stretches of green fields. Sunlight flooded the room, energizing me with its warmth. I couldn't wait to step outside.

The shops buzzed with life—people coming and going, smiles brightening their faces, hot drinks warming their hands.

I'd grown used to strangers being just that: strangers, eyes down, no accidental kindness, no conversation. But here, people of all ages waved as I walked by, saluted as I passed, and greeted me warmly. At first, I felt wary of the attention, but soon I found myself returning their smiles, salutes, and greetings. One particular salute was for an older woman with a salt-and-pepper perm and healthy curves. She smiled back, her blue eyes crinkling behind a dentured grin. Her charcoal apron was painted with delicate lavenders and the words *Dolly's Flower Shop* scripted across the front.

I stepped back to take in the shop more fully. Though small and nestled between two antique stores, the spot was beautiful—bursts of lilacs spilled over a built-in white picket fence, while magenta rhododendron and azalea shrubs were carefully arranged at each corner. Off-white planters overflowed with greenery, framing a blazing white neon sign that proudly spelled out the flower shop's name. Just behind the shrubs in the back corner, I spotted the ruby-red, vertically growing flowers I recognized.

"Excuse me?" I asked.

The woman looked at me with the same kind eyes.

"Yes, darling, how may I help you?" Her voice was soft like butter.

"Are those hollyhocks?" I pointed at the ruby-red flowers at the far end of the store, leaning against the brick wall.

"It sure is! Good eye, darling." She took a step closer and watched me as though she were trying to read my mind. "You sure know your flowers. I'm Dolly, and this is my flower shop. Nice to meet you." She extended her hand, and I shook it gently.

"Hello, Dolly. You have a beautiful shop. I'm Margaret, but call me Margo. Pleasure meeting you! And I wouldn't say I know flowers, but I do know my hollyhocks. They used to blossom around the apartment I grew up in."

Something about her inviting gaze made me want to keep sharing. "My mother and I used to watch for butterflies, and when they landed on hollyhocks, we used to dance with joy."

"What a beautiful memory!" She flung her hands up as her eyes widened with excitement.

I appreciated how animated she was—it docked years off her.

"My mom recently passed, but the memory remains alive, especially after spotting those hollyhocks." I said.

She nodded and glanced behind her at the shop. "I know I'm pushing my luck here, but I like you, darling, and my intuition has never failed me." She pointed to the glass window, where a small *Help Wanted* sign was stuck. "Are you looking for a job?"

I looked around, taking inventory of my surroundings. I still couldn't fathom how I had managed to escape the impossible and arrive at this very moment—whole, unbroken, ready. If I were to start over, I couldn't imagine a better place or a better chance.

"I guess I am now," I said.

Thank you, God, for giving me a second chance.

Chapter 33

Aleena

I was invited back to the station. Once we had the Fuchsia Summit decoded, everything tumbled into place. Sally was now detained without bail, along with Alfanso Conti. Although it was satisfying to catch Sally, it still felt incomplete. Aaron's death remained undetermined, and Margo was nowhere to be found, despite my multiple text messages and phone calls.

"I still think Margo murdered Aaron. I just can't pin her enough to arrest her."

Sanchez's voice rang in my ear as I began to conceptualize an alternative scenario—one outside my radar. What if, once Margo got immunity, she decided to run off to avoid being caught for Aaron's murder? Even as I thought it, I couldn't help but grimace. The Margo I met wasn't a killer. Maybe undirected and impulsive, but not a killer. Her heart remained pure, and someone with a pure heart couldn't pierce another's forever. But what if I was wrong? What if bad blood ran deeper between Margo and Aaron than I had thought? What if Margo was pushed to her limits and took matters into her own hands? What if her impetuous tendencies ended another person's life and the guilt from it all drove her away?

I had to get a hold of her.

I ruminated on these questions as Shaan finished up his last assignment. In a short period of time, I noticed a stark improvement in Shaan's discernment of his emotions. We were doing more exercises around reacting with empathy, and he was channeling the other person's perspective well when faced with hypothetical scenarios that aroused his anger.

"He's dealing with his own challenges; it has nothing to do with me." He said it of his own accord, unprovoked by my simulations but placed in a real-life situation by Thomas, when we passed him and his mother at the grocery store. Thomas pointed at Shaan and laughed at him for getting expelled, while Candace remained icy, her glare sharp enough to stab. But Shaan's reaction was different—he met Thomas's taunts not with anger, but with a quiet pity, almost as if he understood the pain behind the cruelty. It wasn't weakness; it was strength—the kind that comes from knowing when to hold your ground and when to rise above. He didn't let the insult define him. Instead, he kept walking by my side, calmly fascinated by the unique, exclusive-to-Vermont Ben & Jerry's flavors—an emotional control that spoke volumes about how he'd come.

Spending quality time with Shaan—as both a mother and an educator—proved more fruitful than Rahul or I had expected. Shaan wasn't distracted by other boys' baggage; he was able to tune into his own frequency of authenticity. To my surprise, I wasn't elated to be called back to the station. As I dropped Shaan off at Mom and Dad's for a lesson on money management (Dad's favorite), a pinching ache bubbled in my chest. The thought of going back to work full-time and sending Shaan to another educator, another system of growth and development, another pool of people from unknown walks of life influencing my child felt overwhelming.

When I entered the station, the place was packed with uniforms. The whole department had been called in on this one. Despite our police force being as small as it was, I could feel the camaraderie and my *raison d'être* for being in this industry.

As I watched Captain Warshburg share a cheap cup of coffee with a cadet and Officer Sanchez gather his files with a new pep in his step, I couldn't help but give a symbolic high-five to my younger self—the little Aleena who dreamt of being a detective. I often forget about my progress in life, how far I've come, and how much I've achieved. I made it as a detective and helped crack not only a large underground drug operation but also a cold case, finally bringing peace to my ex-boyfriend's father. Despite the personal hiccups with Aaron's case, I proved to be a good detective. I took a slow inhale, finally commemorating my professional attainments as I approached Eric.

"Congratulations, Officer Sanchez," I boasted, while extending my hand for a shake.

He took my hand with a grin. "Couldn't have done it without you, Detective Gupta."

"Hey! Did you ever hone in on Bernadette Wright and her father?" I asked.

"I kid you not, Bernadette pranced into the station and asked for the lead on Aaron's case." He looked around and nodded at Cadet Stevens, who had caught eyes with him. "So, Bernadette has been tracking her and her father's sleep for a year now, and they were sound asleep the night of Aaron's murder."

I didn't know much about the technology behind tracking sleep, but I did know about watches. "Eric, they could've easily had someone else wear their watches that night."

"Right, that's what I thought too. But she insisted it was impossible with their watches. They must've paid a pretty penny for them, because apparently they're high-end models that only work for the registered owner. The sensors track body temperature patterns and subtle biometric data unique to each person. No two people regulate heat exactly the same, so it's nearly impossible to fake." He nodded with a baffled smile, mirroring my reaction. "I know! I even went a step further and tested it," he continued. "I wore her watch for almost a minute before it threw an error."

Technology was an awe-striking concept. For one, our state-of-the-art computers still froze as frequently—if not more often—than they used to, but a watch could detect its owner like a service dog.

"So they didn't kill Aaron," I said.

He nodded and shrugged. "If he was murdered, I still think Margo did it." He put his hands up in mock surrender. "I know you don't, but all our main suspects have ironclad alibis—except her." He sighed and dropped his head. "Alas, she has immunity for the only evidence I've got against her."

And with that, he strolled off to shake hands with the Captain, who had made his way to the catered pastries.

Sanchez had a point. It was never confirmed that Margo was actually in Boston the night Aaron died. She didn't have anyone who could attest to her being at home. When we cross-checked with her house manager, Shannon, we learned she was in North Carolina, visiting her sick father that weekend, leaving Margo to her own devices. Margo was elusive and erratic, like a street cat. Given her history with the Moore family, I understood where Sanchez was coming from. But he had made up his mind about her long before we vetted everyone else—and with his fractured relationship with his mother, whom Margo reminded him of, his accusation felt premeditated. It also didn't help that my gut told me Margo didn't kill her stepson.

My thoughts were interrupted when the Captain made his way to the front of the station with a cheery smile.

"Attention! I'd like to share a few updates."

The whole force quieted at once—a side effect of our grueling training.

"First off, let's put our hands together for Detective Gupta and Officer Sanchez. They single-handedly broke ground on a drug pin operation and solved a cold case homicide."

Thunderous applause erupted as I gave a nod to Sanchez from across the room.

The Captain cleared his throat and clapped his hands, and we all stopped abruptly to pay attention. "In related news, I've just been notified that Sally pleaded guilty to all charges—"

The room exploded again with whistles and claps. I felt a smile crease my cheeks. I couldn't believe it! She must have taken a plea deal without going to trial.

"Attention!" the Captain's voice roared, and silence spread through the station like a plague. "Sally and her head of security decided not to risk going to trial and took a plea deal. They've all been sentenced to life in prison with the possibility of parole after 20 years. The news goes public first thing tomorrow."

This time, we waited before reacting. We stared at him as he bent his knees like a cannon about to fire and yelled, "We did it, everyone! We locked up some BAD PEOPLE for a VERY, VERY LONG TIME!"

I joined in this time. Excitement surged through my body in small jumps, woots, and claps.

"The Beacon Hill team owes us big time!" Cadet Stevens bellowed, nudging another cadet. It was the first time I'd heard him sound like a grown man and not a timid rookie.

The cheer in the room began to trail off like the end of a song as Officer Sanchez took position beside the Captain.

"Attention," the Captain said, even-keeled. "I brought Officer Sanchez up here because he has shown excellent foresight, hard work, and intelligence." He turned to a proud, stoic face. "Officer Sanchez, I am honored to promote you to Sergeant Eric Sanchez of the Montpelier Police Department, District 8. You have proven to be an excellent example to our future officers as their new lead trainer."

I was the first to clap.

The Captain proceeded to add another stripe to his uniform as the whole department harmonized in applause.

Cadet Stevens's face dropped at the thought of an upgrad-ed disciplinary training program under a tyrant like Sanchez. I nudged him, my smile as wide as I could manage. "Good luck, Cadet!"

He thanked me, flushed and with buggy eyes. I couldn't help but snicker.

"Excuse me," Eric's voice boomed. "I would like to thank the entire police department for helping put Sally behind bars. It was truly a team effort." He scanned the room until his eyes met mine and nodded earnestly. "Although we helped Massa-chusetts find their criminal, our in-house case remains open—the death of Aaron Moore."

Aaron Moore. A name that used to stir a flight of butterflies in my stomach every time I heard it; a name that would launch a stream of aching memories, trapping me and dragging me deeper into his quicksand; a name I had grown so used to keep-ing at the forefront of my mind. Even with his often sporad-ic and abusive tendencies, I was wrapped around his finger—blinded by it all, inebriated by his toxicity. But as I heard Officer Sanchez proclaim him, I felt no butterflies, no memories, and certainly no love-stricken delusions.

I had worn blinders about him for far too long. If there's one thing his death has taught me, it's how cunning, manipulative, selfish, and downright evil he could be. So, it didn't bother me when Sanchez declared:

"I will be closing Aaron Moore's case today as an overdose. There is no substantial evidence of murder, and with the rising cases of drug abuse, it's more probable that he fell and hit his head on the kitchen counter as he reacted to the fentanyl."

I bowed my head as the Captain called for a moment of silence to honor a lost soul. Nobody will ever truly know what happened to Aaron, but may he rest in peace—and may the lives of all he hurt begin to heal, just as I have.

I wondered if Eric would continue pursuing Margo on his own time. Just like me, Sanchez was relentless when something got stuck in his head. Or now that he's been promoted, would he shift his attention and focus on being the best Sergeant in the Green Mountain State? With Margo not answering me, I was unable to help her — and if Sanchez were to pursue her, she would need to cooperate to avoid giving him a reason to detain her. I crossed my middle finger over my index behind my back, like I used to before receiving my report card. Straight A's, please. Margo, contact me back, *please*!

The station was buzzing once again with congratulatory rounds. Coffee had turned into beer, and small talk had turned into stories. Cadets were approaching Eric like he had just won an Oscar, praising him in hopes of gaining brownie points before their grueling Monday rolled around.

I decided to go visit my old friend, my confidant, and my prized possession as a detective: my desk. I slid my fingertips across its linoleum surface. It prickled under my fingertips, cold and smooth. Three gel pens were lined up perfectly, with a black-screened computer towering over them. Stark pink, yellow, and blue post-its were stacked in the far-right corner of the desk, next to my detective badge. I had forgotten about a yellow note with the neat cursive of my own handwriting, placed right beside the pens. I bent my neck to get a closer look and read:

Trust your instincts.

I stared at my handwriting and took a deep breath. The feeling was overwhelming now. It was time—I had to trust my instincts. Maybe it was being away from my desk and swept into a new routine, or maybe it was just the natural progression of life. Either way, I knew what I had to do. It was time to speak to the Captain.

I found him in his office, laughing on a call.

"Oh, sorry. I'll come ba—" I whispered.

"Let me call you back." He hung up the phone and signaled me in.

"Don't be silly, Gupta. I always have time for you." His gray beard shuffled as he repositioned himself in his chair.

I took a seat but quickly stood up, scratched my head, and sat back down again.

"What's going on, Aleena?" His thick eyebrows furrowed. "How's Shaan holding up?"

"This is actually why I'm here."

"Listen, Aleena, Eric told me he wouldn't have been able to solve the case without your discovery of the coded message." He swept a hand across his balding head. "Thank you, Detective Gupta."

Was I making a mistake? I could simply say my thanks and waltz out of the office.

But my thighs suddenly felt heavy as I slumped into the chair, unable to move. All my life, I had worked tirelessly to prove to myself that I could build the career I dreamed of. I maneuvered through the trenches of disapproving parents, crippling self-doubt, and fractured relationships—all for the simple satisfaction of lining up three gel pens on a linoleum desk, beneath a detective badge that bore my name. My self-worth had become so tightly bound to professional success that I lost sight of everything else, including the people I loved most.

"Captain, I'd like to resign."

The cheerful chatter from outside the door was the only sound interrupting his dropped jaw and my clenched chest.

"You what? — Why?"

I'd never heard this man stutter before.

"I've come to realize that my worth has nothing to do with me anymore. It has everything to do with what I give."

"To Shaan," he said, bowing his head.

"I owe it to my son to give him a true chance at love, life, and identity." I tucked a strand of hair behind my ear. "I owe it to my Shaan to be the mother I've always wanted to be."

His eyes softened with a mix of sympathy and sorrow.

"I believe the greatest gift is motherhood, Aleena — a gift my wife never got to unwrap." He kept his head down, lost in thought. "It truly is a blessing to have a child, and I'm the last person who would ever take that away from you."

As he stood up, heavy on his feet, I believed our time together had come to an end. He would shake my hand, and I would walk out of the station once and for all, bidding farewell to my career.

Instead, he crossed his arms.

"I have a proposition for you, Aleena," he said, his tone austere.

I looked at him with doe eyes, eager to hear.

"What if I give you a one-year paid sabbatical, so you can finish this school year with Shaan and get the time you need to figure out your next steps? If coming back isn't in your cards a year from now, then so be it. At least you'll have the option."

"I cannot ask that of you!" I gasped. It's one thing to get some time off to mend Shaan's expulsion — it's another to have a full year.

"You're not asking, I'm offering. Aleena, you've been an asset to our department from the moment you stepped in as a cadet. You've proven to be bright and perceptive, skilled and determined, astute and clever — and most impressively, you possess emotional intelligence in a way I've never seen before. You've taken horrible people off the streets for years. Spending one with your family is the least you deserve."

By this point, he had gotten around his desk.

I stood up and fell into his arms. As he hugged me, I was immediately engulfed by his thick frame, suddenly a little girl again, wrapped in the arms of a guardian angel. He patted my back while I cried against his shoulder.

For so long, I had yearned for approval, for acknowledgement, for validation. I may not have gotten it in the places I once expected, but I was grateful to have found it in Captain Warshburg.

"Take a beat and wipe your tears, Detective. If these cadets see you like this, they'll eat you alive," he said with a grin.

The Captain strode out of his office as I collected myself. I took a breath and focused on my surroundings. His office was a reflection of his personality: calm, orderly, and deeply personal. I breathed in his signature scent of sandalwood, cigar smoke, and sycamore figs. My eyes wandered to his grandfather's rifle, still proudly displayed on the wall above the chestnut desk. On the desk sat only a framed photo of his wife and a computer. His files were stacked neatly on a corner table beside a terracotta reading chair. Brown slippers rested at the foot of the chair, with an electric yellow kettle and a matching mug placed on a small side table across the room.

"Whatever you do, make yourself as comfortable as you can in any situation." That had been the Captain's first piece of advice to me when I was a cadet. Despite his decades of service, he always prioritized peace of mind. Whatever was within his control, no matter how small, he treated with care and intention.

So, it felt right to sit in his reading chair and take it all in. Blessings often come from unexpected places, and Captain Steven Warshburg was one of them. My heart ached at the thought of having lied to him about why I gave the case to Sanchez. One day, when the dust settles, I'll tell him everything—maybe over a bottle of whiskey in a quiet, worn-down pub.

The rest of the evening blurred into stories from the Captain, told over endless rounds of booze and softened edges. I switched to water midway through his emotional retelling of a shootout in Detroit. By the time he finished sharing his winding journey to Montpelier in search of a quieter "retirement," I had flushed the alcohol from my system.

A wave of drowsiness hit me hard. By the fifth yawn, I saluted the team and pulled Sanchez aside to let him know I'd be taking a sabbatical. He hugged me, then shook my hand with professional restraint—a quiet "see you later." I considered asking about his plans to pursue Margo but decided against it. Better to keep her far from his thoughts, hoping he might let the case fade for good. Instead, I patted his back and congratulated him on making Sergeant.

I managed to park in the driveway with only one thing on my mind: curling into Rahul's chest and falling asleep on our Tempur-Pedic bed. Beer had always cost me a few yawns, but now the weight of age added its own toll. I grimaced, feet dragging up the porch, already half-asleep when my hip vibrated.

It was a text message from Margo.

Chapter 34

Eva

The news came flooding in. Andrew lay beside me, the sun speckling his dark chest hair, bronzing it. I was jolted by his sudden gasp and the bed shaking beneath me. He brushed his palm across my cheek, kissed my forehead, and when he saw my eyelids flutter open, he turned back to the TV mounted on the wall and raised the volume.

The newscaster's crisp voice now bounced off the walls. I propped myself against the headboard, searching for an explanation for the abrupt awakening.

"We are back on Fox News as we bring you the latest update on Sally Beaurshop—"

"You won't believe this," Andrew nearly shrieked as he grabbed my hand.

"Sally Beaurshop, an elite socialite of the Boston area, was detained in Vermont for the death of her former business partner, Richard Moore—a previous cold case—and for leading an underground opioid operation. She specialized in a powdered blend she called Tranquility Hour, a designer drug laced with trace amounts of fentanyl, engineered for microdosing. It catered to wealthy clients chasing a controlled high, part of a growing trend among the elite. Although still speculative, it is rumored that the same Tranquility Hour is what killed Richard's son, Aaron Moore, less than two weeks ago. —"

"Wow, the national news picked up this story," I said, bewildered, unsure why this would make Andrew so excited.

"Yes, but—listen—" His eyes were transfixed on the TV.

"We have just been informed that Sally and her head of security, Alfanso Conti, have pleaded guilty on all counts. I repeat—all counts! They've been sentenced to life in prison, with the potential for parole in 20 years."

I couldn't believe it. No swarming lawyers, no lengthy trials, and no scheming loopholes.

The blonde newscaster with impeccable makeup continued, "They were advised to accept a plea deal rather than risk going to trial, where they faced the possibility of a harsher sentence—including life imprisonment without parole."

My jaw hung open, and my eyes stung from the effort of not blinking, afraid I'd miss a single detail.

"Here is the press conference from Captain Warshburg of Montpelier District 8 with more: 'Our team has worked relentlessly to apprehend Sally Beaurshop and dismantle her entire underground drug operation. Initially, evidence pointed to Richard Moore's fatal car crash as a tragic accident. However, as we uncovered more of Sally's corruption, we discovered credible evidence that she orchestrated a hit on her former business partner and close friend. The tragedy doesn't end there—and this is where our district became involved. On September 23rd, Aaron Moore, Richard's son, was found dead in his home in Montpelier, Vermont. Due to insufficient evidence of foul play and an autopsy confirming elevated levels of opioids, we have concluded that Aaron Moore died of an overdose. We mourn the loss of the Moore family, and the countless others who have fallen victim to drugs. Our department remains steadfast in the fight against narcotics. May God bless the victims, their families, and the United States of America.'"

His entire demeanor resembled that of a Southern grandfather who put God first and family second. He had kind eyes and a hefty build, but his tenure showed in the way he spoke. The authority in his voice was evident, and his words were convincing.

"God bless America indeed!" Andrew shouted, wrapping his arms around me. He leaned in and kissed my forehead slowly. His soft touch sent a wave of desire down my spine.

We made love that morning, unshackled from the looming weight of unresolved death. I couldn't believe how much I loved him. How could it happen this fast? But it wasn't fast, not really. It felt overdue, as if our souls had been trying to find each other for ages but were constantly detoured by poor timing, misguided choices, and fragile hearts. What began as a hesitant attraction had already grown into something much deeper. It wasn't just passion, not the kind of summer fling that burns out with time. This felt infinite. Our languages, our silences, our rhythms—they translated into one seamless expression. We were connected. And I couldn't bring myself to move forward in this life without him

As he hummed while making breakfast, I sat on the barstool in my lilac robe, overtaken by consternation.

"Where do we go from here?" I whispered.

He gradually halted his humming and turned around. He looked at me with a blank expression.

I was unsure if he heard me until he said, "My life is—" he began.

But we were interrupted by my ringtone. I hurried off to grab my phone from the bedroom, hiding the tears in my eyes. I wasn't ready to depart from him. His life was miles away from mine—a mile too far for my heart to endure.

I cleared my throat and forced a smile before answering.

"Hello?"

"Yes, may I speak to Eva Armstrong?"

"This is she."

The voice was unrecognizable—an elderly woman with a robotic timbre.

"Yes, this is Marjorie with the Police Department of Montpelier District 8. I am calling to inform you that you are no longer requested to remain in Vermont for Case 8785930: Aaron Moore."

"Uh—thank you."

"Have a nice day. Goodbye."

I was officially free to go. Nothing was holding me back in a town of refurbished hotels and nostalgic StayHere homes. I could leave Vermont and never look back, storing this experience as a memory of an emotional roller coaster—one that carried me through the highs of untapped love and the lows of grief, one that twisted and turned through the aftermath of death and the solace of immutable connections.

One of which had just dinged my phone.

"Eva!!! I can't believe it! Did you hear? Aaron's case is closed as an overdose! We are no longer captive LOL! Want to grab a bite at the first spot we had lunch? How does noon sound?"

I texted Bee back immediately, suffocated by the upcoming conversation awaiting in the kitchen.

"Yes, please!"

I turned to plug my phone into the charger and mustered up whatever strength I had to carry myself out of the bedroom, when I saw Andrew leaning against the doorsill, arms crossed.

"Who was it?" he asked.

"The police department. They called to—"

"Yeah, I just got a call too."

"Right. The case is officially over," I said glumly.

"Why so sad?"

He uncrossed his arms and took a step toward me.

I took one back, using all my might to keep my eyes dry. "Andrew, what does this mean for us? I can't keep living here. My home is Long Island."

"I know," he said as he took another step, cautiously this time. "Eva, listen to me."

He took hold of my hand and delicately sandwiched it between his. "You have changed me. For so long, my struggles defined my identity: the coward, the victim, the bad friend, the quitter, the ruiner. My entire adulthood was shaped around the scraps left in my life. I became a loner, because if I could isolate myself, then I'd be less likely to hurt another person again."

I placed my free hand on his forearm and squeezed it.

"But since I've met you, the pillars holding my debilitated self-worth came crashing down. With you, I've been able to re-invent myself as the man I always wanted to be. You've been a conduit to discovering my genuine self. You make me feel whole, and my life is—"

My heart was beating out of my chest, leaving me with soft chokes.

"My life is wherever you are."

His words traveled to my ears and harmonized in my heart.

"We'll have to make a stop in New Haven and grab Roxy," he said, already mentally working through the logistics of moving to Long Island.

"Roxy is actually what I wanted," I chuckled between tears.

"Oh yeah?" He leaned closer, mischievous. "You used me to get to my dog?"

"What can I say? A girl's gotta do what she needs to do." I giggled and took a step back—next thing I knew, he swung me over his shoulder.

"Take it back or I'll fart!" he howled.

I dug my nose into his left butt cheek and exaggerated a sniff. "I dare you," I said as he toppled me onto the bed.

My stomach growled. "What was it you were cooking up in the kitchen?" I lifted my finger and placed it on my dimple in an endearing way.

He sat on the edge of the bed and took me in his arms.

"Eva, are you sure you want this? For me to move in with you?"

The chirping birds and swift bristles of leaves suddenly went quiet, awaiting my response. Was I sure? I searched the repository of people I knew, I searched and searched through names in my brain and couldn't find one person to relate to. I couldn't use anyone else's experience as a reference, nor could I use my own. This was uncharted territory. So my mind went to the next thing I knew best: math. Although being an accountant hadn't trained me in love, it had trained me in probability. And the probability of us working out was low—very low. Two people who had madly fallen in love in just a couple of days, bonded by the death of another man, forced to learn each other's sore spots before even going on a proper date. But data couldn't compute the metaphysical bond we've created, the emotional gravity pulling us close, the profound connection beneath it all. The data wasn't me. It wasn't us.

As I gazed into his eyes, I wrapped my arms around his neck and whispered in his ear, "I'm sure."

We finished making breakfast between kisses. I couldn't believe this was real. My mind was trained to expect doom around every corner, yet despite my weariness and circumstances, Andrew understood me. We talked endlessly about what to expect in Long Island—what my life had been like there and what he would be walking into. He listened graciously and accepted this new chapter wholeheartedly.

We started planning our next home after my lease ends in two months: a one-bedroom for his consultancy business and one for my accounting work, near a massive dog park for Roxy, and close enough to Dad so he wouldn't miss me too much. As I twirled my hair, imagining our quaint apartment overlooking the Great South Bay, I decided to keep Andrew a surprise.

If anyone back home could get behind our wild yet deeply human and graciously loving plan, they'd have to meet him in person—probe, observe, annotate, and reflect on him before even the slightest chance of acceptance.

I went to meet Bee for lunch as Andrew worked on getting everything ready for his big move. I broke the news to her as soon as we sat down, unable to contain myself.

She yelped up her seat. "That's insane and amazing!"

The clusters of tables turned towards us. The place was buzzing with dozens of eyeballs looking at Bee and then at me. I lowered my head, wary of the attention.

"Insane for sure! I still can't believe he wants to move to Long Island," I murmured, forcing her to sit back down so she could hear me.

She met my gaze and said, with a heavy twitch in her voice, "Love is precious gold, Eva. If you find it, hold it dear."

My heart ached. Through her eyes, I saw her soul, longing for the treasure of love. I hated that she still carried the weight of a lasting heartbreak.

"Bee, would you like to come visit us in Long Island?"

"I was planning on it anyway," she simpered.

I took her hand and cupped it in mine. "You've become one of my closest friends in such a short time. I can't believe how you made your way into my heart and claimed a permanent spot."

She nodded, about to fire back her own compliments, but I hurried on. "If you could do that with me—someone naturally skeptical and not open to making friends—you could steal a man's heart in a second."

I raised my hand to stop her as she opened her mouth again. "You've turned out to be an incredible woman despite everything. Please never change, and be open to new relationships—if your dad lets you, that is." I smirked.

"He ain't the boss of me!" she laughed, and her vibrance brightened the overcast sky.

But she quickly looked down at her twiddling thumbs and took a wavering breath. "That means the world to me, Eva. I'm thankful to have made a friend like you—even in the most absurd of situations."

Her eyes flicked toward an approaching waiter as she leaned forward, her torso resting on the edge of the table, her face just inches from mine.

"You have one hundred percent of my blessing with Andrew. Thank you for reconnecting us. It gave me the closure I needed, and I was delighted to see how amiable he turned out to be."

I matched her closeness, reached out, and gently took her by the shoulder. Pulling her in, I wrapped my arms around her in a warm hug—feeling the quiet relief and gratitude that hung between us.

Like our first time, we ordered a Farmer's egg white omelet and a nitro brew but unlike the first time, we dined with a side of different emotions. We laughed at all the quirky characters in our newfound sisterhood—from her father to mine, her family business to mine, and the crazy circumstances that brought us together. My trip to Vermont was not in vain, and I had Bee to thank for a big chunk of it.

As we descended the steps, full and overly caffeinated, I hugged her tightly despite the bustling pedestrians on the sidewalk. Her champagne-strawberry perfume wafted up, slightly burning my nostrils. I took it in a moment longer, hoping to store her scent as collateral for when I'd miss her. She promised to come down to Long Island once we moved into our new place—maybe even bring Mr. Wright so he could meet Mr. Armstrong. Our fathers would either become best friends or worst enemies. We banked on the friendship but wouldn't mind the mindless entertainment from the drama between two stubborn, self-accomplished Baby Boomer men.

With a final goodbye, I got in my car and drove to the Montpelier Inn, ready to check out for good.

Chapter 35

Aleena

(1 year later)

"Concord was sooooo fun!"

Shaan was beaming as Rahul helped him drag a pure brass antique telescope up the stairs to his room. The coloration had worn out, leaving a rustic print Shaan couldn't take his eyes off.

"It's safe to say Shaan enjoyed visiting Margo," I said to Rahul as he made his way downstairs, satiated by a happy kid.

"It's also safe to say Margo is officially Shaan's favorite auntie," Rahul said, amused, as he wrapped his arms around my waist.

"She shouldn't have paid an absurd amount for a semi-functional telescope." I heard my mom's voice in my head as I said it.

"She paid her entrance fee to Shaan's heart," Rahul said, nuzzling his nose into my neck.

"I can't believe it's been a year. It was nice seeing her settle in so well—now managing a floral shop and making a home in a cozy studio apartment. I admire how she liquidated her late husband's fortune and donated it to organizations advancing mental health care. I'm sure her mother would be so proud." I sighed, feeling a soft flutter in my chest. "Though she doesn't live in a mansion anymore, she seems truly at peace."

"Money doesn't buy happiness," Rahul recited.

I couldn't help but laugh at his boyish interception of wisdom as I turned around to face him.

His eyebrows suddenly furrowed. "I know a part of you still thinks Aaron was murdered." His tone was inquisitive, but his posture was unnerving as he took a step back and crossed his arms.

"*Ah!* No, I mean—it's been so long now, and no additional evidence—as far as I know—has come to light."

"But you've also been on sabbatical this whole time. Maybe there have been updates."

"I highly doubt it," I scuffled. "Sanchez would have told me. He emails me a weekly report on everything Montpelier District 8."

He took a sharp breath, hesitant. "Do you think it might have been Margo?" he whispered, wincing slightly, unsure if he had jurisdiction over this conversation.

"My intuition has said no from the beginning. But could it be possible?" I involuntarily mirrored his expression. "Yes."

"Is Shaan's new favorite auntie a murderer?" He tried to ask with a touch of humor, but fear creased his eyelids.

"Margo would never hurt Shaan." Without a shadow of a doubt, I knew that to be true. "But the investigation was far from clear-cut—especially for me," I continued.

"She wouldn't hurt Shaan, but she may have hurt Aaron?" he reiterated.

Our visit to Concord felt like Margo and I had been childhood best friends. Even though reality told a different story, my mind and heart came together to experience it as something real, with a genuine bond and a shared origin. We were incredibly compatible, despite our opposite tendencies. Where I planned and thought ten steps ahead, she thrived on spontaneity. She made me laugh like no other friend had. There was an innocence in the way she saw the world—and herself—that I admired. It softened me, loosening the tightness around my high-strung mind. Could she have masked murdering someone so convincingly that not a single crack had shown in the past year?

"I recently took inventory of my track record in my career, and I was reminded of the key to my success. Time and time again, I won cases because I trusted my instincts above all."

Rahul nodded earnestly. "So what do your instincts say now?"

I paused.

I tossed and turned for months after the night Aaron's case closed as an overdose. His voice would creep up in the middle of the night when insomnia took hold of me.

"Drugs are reserved for repugnant people."

He despised weakness in character. He looked down and spat on people who fell into hard drugs—especially the ones with shopping carts for homes. I had been blinded by his inability for humanity, and instead admired his convictions. But since his death, Aaron's character had been turned inside out and revealed to be rotten at its core. Still, he clung to his principles with religious fervor. And as much as I wanted to doubt even that last speck of him, insomnia wouldn't let me cross that line.

But do I think Margo killed him? After a whole year of rehabilitation, Margo didn't go back to money or status. She found peace in a lifestyle away from what the Moore family leveraged over her. She may have been a misguided wishful thinker, but she always held a steadfast heart for good. She may have made decisions with corrupt consequences, but they were intended for the betterment of herself and her mother. Even when she spiraled into self-doubt, she kept trying to be better. Now that she was finally unattached to the tug and pull of terrible people, she found joy in the small instead of chasing the grand. Along the way, she also wove herself into our family—a door I have a long habit of bolting shut to anyone of questionable nature.

"My instincts tell me that Margo did not kill Aaron," I finally said.

Rahul, patient as ever, didn't move an inch until those words came out of my mouth.

"Then trust it."

I reached for him and kissed him. After I confessed about Shaan's biological father, although he already knew, it shifted our relationship. The shackles around our ankles, pulling us down toward the pit of desperation, were finally released. We were better than ever. I could see Rahul for who he was, not as a shadow of my broken love story with Aaron. Every day since, I've worked to make up for years of neglect for the man I'm so blessed to have at my side. If my story were transcribed into a children's book, Aaron would be the ruthless hunter, and Rahul the northern star, the navigator to a healthy, loving relationship.

Rahul kissed my forehead and whispered, "Are you ready to break the news to Shaan today?"

Another good decision spurred by our newfound marriage was the confidence to tell Shaan the truth about his biological father. Risky as it may have been, Shaan's experience after Aaron's funeral gave him the closure he wouldn't know he needed until years later. It closed off an opportunity for the devil to travel a tunnel of mistrust, sadness, and even contempt over an empty stamp on half of his identity. To our surprise, he began to show heightened affection toward Rahul, as though he realized that, if life had been slightly different, Rahul would never have been his father. He exuded gratitude in the most anointed and beautiful way.

Gratitude was not the only characteristic Shaan was embracing. It was astonishing how he had changed and molded into a whole different boy than he was a year ago. His easily triggered, short-tempered, defensive "him-against-the-world" rhetoric underwent a dramatic shift. It was clear that home-schooling was keeping the monsters at bay while awakening the virtuous soldiers in his heart. At home, Shaan and I were a team, assiduously fine-tuning his erudition and giving him the space he needed to learn. Part of our teamwork was understanding where Shaan thrived. And just like his mother, he had an affinity for the emotional side of human behavior. Shaan was now using emotional intelligence as a critical skill-building tool just as he did with math and science. He was constructing his identity all the while expanding his knowledge.

Six months ago, Rahul and I sat down to discuss what we should do when today rolled around and my sabbatical ended. Rahul had just been promoted, blessing us with a whole new option: I didn't *need* to return to work. Living on Rahul's income alone, we could continue building the life we wanted for our family. But for me, the decision felt more nuanced. Much of my decision-making thus far has been rooted in necessity, and the power of choice left me paralyzed. Without some brute force to power up my motivation, what was left? What was I intrinsically motivated to commit my time to?

The hard pill I finally had to swallow was that I didn't know yet. This past year has changed me to my core. Not long ago, being a detective was my personal jackpot. But as I began molding my son into the man he was destined to be, something inside me awakened. A new lifestyle sprouted, one I had deprioritized for far too long. Day after day, watching Shaan grow while experiencing the dividends of a happy marriage, I began to re-establish my self-worth. My cup was full to the brim with joy and fulfillment, and nothing else compared. My worth no longer depended on the bullet points on my résumé or the promotions I could earn because of them. I felt rediscovered as I poured back into my nuclear family. I became the seed, the soil, and the water. I was mighty and expansive, a creator and a nurturer; a mother and a wife.

"Mom and Dad, can you come here?" Shaan's voice floated in from the living room.

I nodded at Rahul, signaling I was ready to break the news to Shaan. Together, we walked to the couch, hand in hand.

We were momentarily stunned. In front of us stood a four-foot-tall boy dressed in a tuxedo that Rahul's parents had gifted him, with a PowerPoint projected on the television. Last month, we had begun our Business 101 course—a curriculum Rahul and I designed and taught on weekends. Learning to make pre-sentations was an exercise Shaan loved, and its effects were ap-parent.

"Mom and Dad," he declared as though giving a speech to a full auditorium. My heart melted at the sight of the wonderful little human we called our own.

"I would like to begin with *gra—ee-tude*. Thank you for being my mom and dad. Thank you for being honest with me about who my biological dad is. Honesty is the best policy! Dad, you are my dad no matter what biology says. I get to choose, and I choose you. You are the best dad in the world!"

I felt Rahul's hand tighten around my wrist and watched tears well in his eyes.

"And Mama, you are my superhero. Thank you for being my mom, teacher, and my principal —*ha!*"

His chuckle was electrifying.

"I know you also fight bad guys, and you have to go back to work, but you are the best teacher I ever had! I feel a thousand times smarter!"

He clicked to the next slide before I could break the news to him.

A mosaic of photos appeared, all taken from our family albums. In each picture, there was at least myself or Rahul: some of us caring for infant Shaan; others of Rahul embracing me; splattered with colorful memories of arts and crafts and outings as Shaan grew. As I watched our memories displayed beautifully by our son's creative mind, I snapped a photo of Shaan in his tuxedo, adding it to the collection.

Shaan raised his hands and twirled. "Thank you, Mom and Dad, for an awesome life! But wait—" He suddenly grew serious and straightened his posture. "There's more."

He clicked forward to showcase a directory of dogs at the Central Vermont Humane Society. He'd even added a transition (not yet taught), so we could flip from one puppy-dog eye to another until it stopped on a specific one.

"This is Honey. She is, uhh—" He glanced at the slide and read, "a German Shepherd." He clicked again to reveal a chart (also not yet taught) of pros and cons of having a German Shepherd, with the largest "Pro" being *Big and Cuddly*.

I've never been enthused about dogs. Mom always said a pet is like having a perpetual three-year-old; if it were up to me, I'd never wish three-year-old Shaan on even my worst enemy.

I couldn't help but shake my head.

"Please, Mom! Just listen!" he wailed.

"Yes, I'm sorry, pumpkin. Please continue."

He shook off the residual angst that had momentarily coated him.

"I know having a dog is a *huuuge* responsibility." He stretched his arms as wide as he could. "And for that reason, I'm going to make you a deal."

He narrowed his eyes at me, waiting for my signal.

Rahul—whose best friend Cashew was his childhood golden retriever—leaned back on the couch, already on board.

"I'm listening," I said.

He drummed his fingers on his lapel, took a deep, shaky breath, and clicked to the next slide.

Dog Contract flashed in bold, animated letters above a blown-up photo of Honey.

"I promise to take care of Honey. She is my responsibility," he proclaimed. "And to prove I'm serious, I will write up a contract."

Rahul leaned forward, perplexed. "Where in the world did you learn about contracts?"

"Suits," Shaan replied proudly — a skill he'd picked up from those late nights when I'd find him downstairs, curled in his father's arms, half-watching Suits past bedtime.

We both laughed.

"I promise to pick up her poop. I promise to feed her. I promise to schedule her grooming, and I promise to save a portion of my allowance every week for Honey."

He sighed, bracing himself.

"But I will need help. I will need help with buying her toys, bed, and leashes. I will need help walking her, because I'm not allowed to walk by myself. I will need help driving her to the vet or to the groomer. I will also need help if I am sick and cannot perform my *duties*."

He delivered the last word with calm precision, a page torn right from Harvey Specter's playbook.

"Last but not least," he said, stepping between us, "with Mom going back to work, I will need a companion. I don't have friends at my new school, and I will be lonely when you're both busy."

Rahul was now looking at me with the same puppy-dog eyes as Honey.

As I watched my two favorite people plead for a furry family member, I was overcome with gratitude. That *this* was my biggest conundrum of the day felt like a true blessing. Now that I was taking on homeschooling full-time—the news we planned to share with Shaan today—I'd also have the bandwidth to help him with a dog. Who knows? Maybe I'd even grow to love Honey.

"Write up the contract," I said seriously, then let a smile creep from the corner of my lips.

He jumped up and down as Rahul caught him mid-air and swung him around.

I slowed time in my mind, revering every sweet second of their father-son swing.

He ran upstairs when I called after him. He turned around and ran back to me. I took him in my arms and held him, still able to smell the baby powder on his neck. My decision to leave the workforce never felt so certain as it did when he hugged me back, resting his head on my chest.

When Shaan rushed back upstairs, Rahul said, "Let's wait to break the news about quitting your job to homeschool him until after we sign the contract—so it doesn't feel like a condition for getting the dog."

"I think that's a great idea."

"I'll call the shelter and ask to visit Honey," he beamed, already shuffling for his phone.

I smiled as he hummed. Behind him, the sun hovered near the mountain horizon, its fierce rays casting a mystic glow around Rahul.

"I'll go grab the mail," I said, mesmerized by the outdoors.

I was drawn to the sun like a moth to flame. As I stepped outside, a nip in the air sent goosebumps up my arms, but I shook it off and strolled down the driveway, soaking in the golden light.

Our scarlet mailbox had stood unhindered for almost half a century, ever since this home was built. Faded Rugrats stickers—remnants of Shaan's summer obsession years ago—clung stubbornly to its surface. As usual, the mail was mostly advertisements: insurance promotions, contractor offers, sponsorship letters. But then my eyes caught a single handwritten envelope addressed to me, and I paused.

Detective Gupta.

Intrigued, I placed it on top of the heaping pile of junk and closed the mailbox. I took one last breath soaking in the warmth from my favorite star and walked back inside.

Rahul was still on the phone with a shelter representative, asking questions about the adoption process, when I slipped past the living room and into my office, his voice fading in the background. The last thing I heard was him reacting with an *"Aww! That's terrible,"* just before I closed the door.

I paused in the middle of the room and looked outside. Birds were making their rounds to Shaan's homemade green bird feeder—a woodworking project Dad had taught him during one of their afternoon classes. We had hung the feeder from our old olive tree, and with Shaan's devotion to adding bird feed every morning, we were now graced by a colorful array of birds in all shapes and sizes.

I watched as a blue jay made a rare appearance, swiftly scooping food before vanishing out of sight. I looked down at the mail and pressed my nail under the adhesive, prying the envelope open.

It was a handwritten letter.

Dear Detective Gupta,

I can't believe it's been a year since Aaron's death. I promised myself I would write to you after one year, if I hadn't already been caught. Now, as I put pen to paper, I find it far harder than I anticipated.

When I killed Aaron, I had nothing to lose. But now, my life has changed drastically. I could have gotten away with murder. But fortunately for me, I now have too much to risk by staying silent. Most importantly, I no longer want to live the rest of my life with Aaron's death weighing on my conscience, destroying every good thing I've built. If I did, then what was the point?

Aaron killed my best friend.

A year and a half ago, she decided to transfer to Vermont for a summer rotation at Bear Lake Memorial Hospital. That's when she met Aaron. He had gotten into a fender bender and was brought into the ER. There, as she nursed him back to health, she also fell in love with him. I had heard about her "summer dream boy" but never met him. All I knew was what she shared: a story fit for a fairytale, and a man fit to be Prince Charming.

She told me how her days were filled with laughter and love, how his home had become hers, how she would cuddle with him during cooler eve-

nings by the exquisite furnace he owned when his guest house was empty. And when it wasn't, how the StayHere visitors would quickly become friends. She felt whole—finally in a place she had always dreamed of being.

I was over the moon for her. She deserved the best life had to offer. But little did I know, she was dancing with the devil.

When she moved back, her entire demeanor changed. At first, I thought it was because she missed Aaron, but something didn't seem right. Heartbreak manifests differently than what she showed. She became a shell of herself, terrified by the mundane and unfazed by the wonderful. She wasn't just depressed; she was broken.

As ego would have it, I eventually got offended that she wouldn't confide in me. She pushed me away, and I let her. I tried to breach her icy walls but only managed to retrieve speckles of who she used to be. Nothing under the sun was working. I even went so far as to ambush her with therapy. But her soul was paralyzed, leaving her body to fend for itself.

I chose to give her space. Maybe all she needed was space.

People say decisions create ripple effects, and we humans make thousands upon thousands of decisions every day. You'd think that as a grown adult, practice would make perfect. Unfortunately, here I am, having made the worst decision.

After two days of silence, I went to check on her. I found her, white as snow, on her living room floor, with dried foam crusted on the side of her mouth. A bottle labeled Tranquility Hour sat next to her, along with a diary bearing a pink Post-it note stuck to the front, addressed to me.

I heaved through unbearable pain and read her diary. She had accounted for everything in detail, from her summer days in Vermont to her downfall afterward.

In short, Aaron raped her, got her pregnant, and discarded her when she came forward. She transcribed how it ruined her. Every day since, she couldn't bear the violation he had done to her—physically, emotionally, spiritually. He had stripped away every ounce of her.

As different as we were, we worked. She wanted to save herself for marriage, and I wanted to bang my way through my emotions. She wanted to settle down and start a family, and I wanted to flow through the streets of Manhattan, invisible. She wanted to save me from myself, and I wanted to give her some fucking space.

She overdosed while three months pregnant.

She also made a decision that rippled into costing her life, her baby's life, and ultimately Aaron's life.

I was undone. That man didn't deserve another breath. I looked up his home on StayHere and saw it was available. I snatched her diary and the drugs, labeled Tranquility Hour, and booked the next flight to Boston.

I missed my best friend's funeral.

That wasn't intended, of course. As I drove the hours from Boston to Vermont, I finalized every detail of the night, but forgot to take into account the aftermath. I was supposed to be back in time for her funeral, but instead, I was stuck at the Montpelier Inn.

Again with these decisions! I wasn't catching a break. Instead of mourning my best friend properly, I was obliged to attend Aaron's funeral. What a cosmic punch in the gut. I can't even begin to explain how infuriating that felt. But I had to obey the ripple—and I'm grateful I did, because lo and behold, she was with me. She stood beside me, nudging me toward Andrew. She was there, floating over us as Andrew and I connected, whispering in my ear to give him a chance. Just as she was on earth, she was in spirit: a caring and selfless friend. She helped me receive everything she wanted out of her life.

I met my now fiancé and fell in love. We settled down near my father and grandmother, surrounded by the riches of a loving community. I've lived this past year in constant awe of Aubree's dream come true.

I told Andrew everything before he moved down to Long Island with me. Every sordid detail. How lucky am I to have a man who still wanted to be with me—even after I confessed to murder, and one of his childhood best friends, at that.

But as my decisions rippled the way they did, so did Aaron's.

He was dead, left unmourned, because of how deeply he hurt the people around him. I'm not saying I have a newfound love for killing bad guys, but I do not regret it.

I was a nervous wreck when I first pulled into Aaron's driveway. Upon seeing him, I wanted to jump on his shoulders, strangle him, and get it over with. Aubree's diary, still warm with her touch, lay in my bag. She had died less than 24 hours earlier. But to do it right, I had to play my part. I became his kryptonite, a woman infatuated by him. He showered me with charm as we spent dinner together. I forced myself to have sex with him, holding back agony. I had to make him vulnerable and fully susceptible to me.

What followed should have been simple. I emptied the powdered drug— careful not to touch it—I'd taken from Aubree, into Aaron's wine while he wasn't looking. Then I planned to lay him in bed, wish him an eternity in hell, and be done.

But I can't remember doing it. Altitude, grief, and exhaustion caught me off guard, leaving gaps in my memory. I woke up in his jacket, with no recollection of what happened after I drugged him. I had to go back and check, just to be sure. I knew I'd spiked his drink because I found the empty bottle in my bag the next morning. I tucked it deeper into my belongings, then later tossed it in a trash can on the street near the Montpelier Inn.

I expected to find Aaron dead in his sleep. The autopsy would confirm an overdose, and the case would be closed.

I hadn't expected him to come stumbling down the stairs—half-dead—and crack his skull on the edge of the counter. It's harder to cleanly close a case when the guy's head is split open on the kitchen floor. It was horrifying.

On the plus side, it made my statement to the police more believable.

I write this letter to you as my full confession for the murder of Aaron Moore. In providing justice for my best friend, I broke a cardinal rule, and for that, justice must be served upon me.

Detective Gupta, I ask you: Would you rather have lived a year with the love of your life or lived a lifetime without knowing he existed?

This past year transformed me. I experienced a love so pure it defied time. The memories I formed with Andrew are imprinted on my heart forever, and nothing can change that—not even life in prison.

And as for Aubree, she will always be a voicemail away.

You know where to find me.

Eva Armstrong.

I read her letter twice before allowing myself to react. I stood in the middle of the room, frozen in place. Eva Armstrong murdered Aaron. She killed him to avenge her best friend. I watched as drops of tears landed on the letter, diluting some of the black ink.

As a detective, I had a responsibility to report this letter and arrest Eva. But… on the other hand, the case was closed, and I was resigning from law enforcement. Most importantly, Aaron was an evil man. He hurt and hurt without looking back. He cost someone their life and brought years of misery to countless others.

He also fucked with me. He rejected me and hit me when I was pregnant with his child. He shattered the foundation of my love in a single blow. He manipulated me, as he did to Aubree, into believing he was a quality man, until we were trapped with a conniving psychopath. Aaron was a repeated offender, depleting us to the point we believed we had nothing else to lose once we lost him. Death didn't seem inconceivable, it felt like the one true solution to our devastated souls. I could have easily taken my life after he punched my lip when I told him I was carrying his baby. I remember feeling the lowest I'd ever felt. There was no good in me being here. No good in me being a mother. And definitely no good in me being a wife to Rahul.

I owe it entirely to luck that I made the desperate decision to tell my mom—to have someone else plan an exit strategy in lieu of death. But as lucky as I was, Aubree didn't have it in her to confide in Eva. Our lips were stitched shut the moment Aaron discarded us. *No one will understand my pain. I cannot begin to explain how I feel. I'm too weak to even attempt to heal.* The devil muted us so we could find no escape from our misery. I happened to be lucky enough to break a stitch or two and gasp for help, but the odds of being rescued were stacked against me, as they were stacked against Aubree. I understood her. I emulated her. I was her.

"Mom!" Shaan's voice echoed from the living room. "I wrote up Honey's contract. It's ready for you!"

I wiped my face and shook my head. I looked at the letter again, taking in Eva's words like a music sheet. I inhaled a quick breath, my mind made up. I turned on the shredder and fed her letter through the slit. I watched as her confession was torn into a thousand tiny pieces.

"Where do I sign!?" I roared, as I made my way out of the office.

About the Author

Photography by Allye Brillante

Anvika J. Blackburn is a psychological thriller author with a background in emotional intelligence. She writes twisty, character-driven stories that blend page-turning suspense with emotional depth. When she's not writing, Anvika enjoys discovering local eateries with her husband and two dogs or curling up with her cat and a good book. A Scarlet Mountain is her debut novel.

www.ingramcontent.com/pod-product-compliance
Lightning Source LLC
Chambersburg PA
CBHW050018120726
47903CB00006B/1823